TIMELESS TREASURES

PATCHWORK MYSTERIES

TIMELESS TREASURES

CARA PUTMAN

Guideposts
New York, New York

www.guideposts.com
(800) 932-2145
Guideposts Books & Inspirational Media

Cover design by Wendy Bass
Cover illustration by Joyce Patti
Interior design by Lorie Pagnozzi
Typeset by Aptara

Printed and bound in the United States of America
10 9 8 7 6 5 4 3 2 1

DEDICATION

Dedicated to my mom Jolene Catlett and my mother-in-love Virgene Putman. These women have supported me in tangible ways so that I could chase my dreams while having a young family I love. Thank you for always praying for and supporting me. And for being the world's best grandmas to three, soon to be four, pretty amazing kids.

Many thanks to Sabrina Butcher and Stephanie Wetli for reading and commenting on this book as I wrote it. I appreciate you gals!

Two years ago I met Beth Adams, my fabulous editor, at the ACFW conference. I was thrilled to get the opportunity to work with her on this book. Thanks for taking a chance on me. And thank you, Beth and Andy Meisenheimer, for pushing, prodding, and helping me turn this from a germ of an idea into a gem of a book. It has been an incredibly fun process to work on this series.

Finally, a big thank you to my agent Karen Solem for letting me know this opportunity existed and encouraging me to toss my ideas in for consideration.

Family Patterns
Time to Share
Muslin Mystery
Timeless Treasures

TIMELESS
TREASURES

 CHAPTER ONE

S arah hurried out onto her front porch, pulling her collar tight against the bite of the November wind. Her daughter-in-law Maggie stopped in her tracks on the sidewalk. "Eager to leave?" Maggie asked.

"I was hoping to keep you in the warmth of your truck," Sarah said, as she hurried down the steps. A sliver of wind trickled down her neck, and Sarah shivered. Maybe today wasn't the best day to head to an estate auction after all. A couple of days ago when Maggie had shown her the newspaper ad for the sale at the old Haber farm, the sun had been shining for five or six days straight and it seemed like a great idea. Now she hoped she had enough layers on, or there would be enough people around her, to block the wind. "Let me grab my bag from the trunk."

Maggie must have been excited about the auction, because she could barely stand still as Sarah walked toward her own car.

"Ready?"

"Be right there, Maggie."

Her daughter-in-law bounced on her toes beside her red SUV. Clearly she wanted to be on the road. Sarah pulled her bag out of her car, slammed the trunk, and hurried to the SUV. Maggie's cargo area could hold lots of great finds.

As she pulled her seat belt on, she turned to Maggie. "Think you'll find anything special for the store today?"

"Hope so." Maggie shifted into drive and eased from the curb.

Sarah pasted a smile on her face as Maggie accelerated faster than necessary. "I'm sure we'll arrive with plenty of time to scan the collection before bidding starts." In fact, if they got there too early, they'd have to stand around awhile, and the cold November air could make that a bitter experience. But the weathercaster had suggested the wind would die late in the morning, leaving a perfect fall day in its wake. With Maggie's twins at school and her husband Jason at his office, Sarah and Maggie could enjoy the sale.

Maggie eased to a stop at a light, and rubbed her hands together, already anticipating all the finds waiting for her. Sarah smiled. Days like this gave her the perfect opportunity to spend time with Maggie and get to know her better. Sarah loved this town, its people, and the pace of life, but when her son Jason and his family moved from Los Angeles earlier in the year, Maple Hill had evolved into something even more perfect for Sarah. Times like this morning, shared with her family, had transformed her life, adding a rich layer she hadn't even realized was missing.

Maggie hummed a tune and tapped the steering wheel in time as she guided the vehicle down Maple Hill's main street.

"Any special items you have your eye on?"

Maggie glanced at Sarah, before turning back to the road. "Why? You plan to outbid me?"

Sarah laughed. "My home is full enough. I just wondered if you had inside information."

Maggie shook her head. "Nothing that wasn't listed in the newspaper ad. Call it woman's intuition. This will be a good sale."

"Call it your finely honed skills." Maggie was an insatiable investigator when it came to antiques. The early success of Magpie's Antiques indicated others had noticed her ability to find treasures where some only saw trash.

"Maybe." The corners of Maggie's mouth tipped up in a small smile. "But if that's the case, anyone could develop a good eye."

Sarah studied her daughter-in-law's profile. Maggie had the glow you'd expect from someone who'd lived in Southern California for years. The faintest of crow's feet appeared at the corners of her green eyes when she laughed.

"You knew Mr. Haber," she said. "Did he have anything worth snagging?"

Sarah shook her head. "Once Gerry died, I only saw Mr. Haber around town or at church. He seemed to live a confirmed bachelor's life. What I remember on the farm from before Gerry's death was pretty old and dated. Mr. Haber was closer to my dad's age than mine and maintained Depression-era sensibilities." Sarah couldn't imagine he had too much of value. Either way, she'd enjoy the sale. "Do the girls have anything happening at school before Thanksgiving?"

"It's a quiet week for them." Maggie shrugged. "But I can't tell you how often I'll find out about something at the last minute. Those book bags morph into black holes when it's time to give me a note. You'd think one out of two would remember."

"Guess that's what happens with twelve-year-olds." Her granddaughters were a special delight now that they lived down the street from her. Sarah couldn't imagine life without them popping in and out of her days.

Maggie took the final turn listed in the directions. "We must be close. Look at all those cars."

Dented pickup trucks, minivans, SUVs, and luxury cars lined the country road. Sarah saw Martha Maplethorpe's minivan fifth in line. Her best friend hadn't told her she was going to the auction, and Sarah wondered why she hadn't. It didn't seem like Martha to forget. But now she could share the event with one of her favorite people while Maggie acquired inventory for her store.

"Come on, Sarah." Maggie threw her blue paisley Vera Bradley bag over her shoulder and hustled from the vehicle. As Sarah undid her seat belt, she mused that Maggie had more energy than any woman should. But of course she needed it, managing an active household and a growing business.

Sarah opened her door and hopped from the vehicle. She took a moment to absorb the atmosphere.

Tables were set up in the open space around the small farmhouse. Barn trestles and tabletops stretched in rows, back and forth across the area, covered with piles of mismatched goods, everything from table linens to stacks of ancient magazines. Behind the tables, furniture seemed haphazardly arranged, at least from what Sarah had come to expect at sales like this. It appeared the family and auctioneer had given little thought to the presentation of the items. The prices would probably suffer as a result—a good thing for Maggie. But Sarah had really expected more when she saw Bob Spencer listed as the auctioneer. He was a professional who ran estate auctions all over Massachusetts.

People milled between the tables. Sarah spotted several people she knew, but the area overflowed with strangers. There must have been about a hundred wandering around the farmyard. Some picked through the piles, while others opened and shut drawers in the furniture as if testing the runners.

Maggie dashed ahead of Sarah, headed for the back tables and furniture. Sarah lagged behind to see what she could find on the first few tables, which were littered with boxes of miscellaneous items. She stopped at a table and rummaged through the first box: nothing but stained kitchen towels.

Sarah pulled one out of the box and smiled at the dishwashing kitten embroidered on it.

"My mother used to have a towel like that in her kitchen."

Sarah startled at the rich baritone voice. Looking up, she saw an older gentleman who nodded at her and kept moving. He was dressed in pressed khakis and a tweed suit coat with a turtleneck beneath, looking out of place in a venue crowded with people in jeans and flannel shirts. He looked vaguely familiar, but she couldn't place him. Her gaze followed him for a second before she shook her head and turned to the next box.

If this sale had anything for her, it would likely come in a stack of muslin and cotton. At the moment Sarah didn't have a quilt to restore for a client—that meant she could work on a project of her own, but she didn't have anything waiting at home. Since these sales usually had stacks of antique family linens with at least a little more quality than the towels and rags she'd already found, maybe, just maybe, she'd find something that would catch her fancy.

She hoped so because her fingers itched to pick up a needle.

As she continued to pick through boxes, Sarah kept her eyes open for Martha but couldn't see her. After examining a box that contained nothing more than a random assortment of silverware, Sarah strolled between the tables, getting a feel for how the sale was set up, but the best term she could think of was mishmash. The display lacked any organization. A stack of old records sat next to a box overflowing with old butter containers. Every table was like this.

"Sarah Hart. What are you doing here?" Irene Stuart of the Maple Hill Historical Society approached Sarah, her purse tucked close to her side. Irene's fingers played with the charms on her bracelet as a smile curved her lips.

"Picking through the piles."

"Isn't the search the fun part?" Irene surveyed the assembled people and tables calmly, as if she saw things others didn't. "I haven't found much, not even a pile of old letters or family records for the society. But there's a stack of old quilts waiting for you."

"Where?"

"Over there by Martha." Irene pointed to the far corner of the tables. "In fact, she's doing a good job telling everyone how terrible the quilts are."

Sarah laughed. Martha was her dearest friend, but the woman had no sense for what made a good quilt. She knew enough to save them for Sarah's discerning eye though. Maybe Sarah should get over there and make sure the quilts were items she wanted to purchase. She'd hate for them not to sell because of Martha's overzealous defense.

"Well, I'm heading home. Keep my pocketbook happy. I'll see you the next time you have a puzzle to solve." Irene wandered off, leaving Sarah staring after her. Sure, Sarah had recently found her way into a few mysteries. But each time she'd accomplished good in the lives of people she cared about. She'd helped several friends and made new ones along the way. And when the puzzles involved quilts, she couldn't walk away from them, now, could she?

"Yoo-hoo! Sarah!"

She looked up to find Martha waving at her furiously. As Sarah approached, she overheard Martha shoo someone else away from the quilts.

"You really don't want anything to do with these. Have you seen the stains? Why, they're practically rags. I'm sure you can find something nicer and more usable somewhere else."

"Martha Maplethorpe, what are you up to?" Sarah crossed her arms across her chest and pretended to huff at her friend.

"Just keeping these jewels safe until you arrived."

Sarah shook her head, then stepped forward to hug Martha. "You're a good friend." She gave Martha a final squeeze and stepped toward the boxes. "Let me see what we've got here."

Martha stepped back from a large box. Sarah ran a hand down the side and saw five quilts stacked in it. "Hmm, I wonder what stories these quilts could tell."

Martha peeked into the box over Sarah's shoulder. "Any good?"

"Maybe." One quilt in particular caught her eye. It seemed to be in good condition, only needing some seams reinforced, but it was a complete mismatch and hodgepodge of squares—a sampler quilt. "What's your story?"

Sarah looked up to find the distinguished older gentle-man from earlier watching her again. His brows arched, and he nodded slightly. Who was he? She still couldn't place him.

Martha interrupted Sarah's thoughts. "That man seems fascinated by you."

Sarah blushed and shook her head. "You read too many novels."

"We'll see about that." Martha's grin got even bigger as the man stepped closer.

"Good day, ma'am." He tipped a slightly battered bowler-style hat toward her and then toward Martha. "I'm Chester Winslow, with *Country Cottage*, and you are ..."

Sarah studied him, uncertain why his attention brought a flutter to her heart. "I'm Sarah Hart and this is my dear friend Martha Maplethorpe."

"It is a pleasure to meet you." He looked from her to the box of quilts. "Are you a quilt expert?"

"She certainly is." Martha strutted toward him, chest thrust out like a bantam hen's. "She's earned quite a repu-tation."

"Martha." Sarah felt heat flush her neck and cheeks. "She's a good friend."

"Enthusiastic." Chester smiled, a benevolent tilt to his lips.

"Have we met before?" Sarah studied him, bothered by a familiarity that she couldn't explain.

"I can't imagine we have. Well, I'll let you ladies con-tinue with your shopping." He tipped his hat toward them and disappeared into a crowd of people pushing toward the stacks of chipped kitchenware.

"He seems taken with you." Martha stood on tiptoe watching Mr. Winslow leave.

"And you, my friend, see romance behind every bush."

"I just want you to find what I have with Ernie." A contented smile crossed Martha's lips. "You know Gerry wouldn't want you to be alone for the rest of your life."

Sarah sighed. "I'm quite content with my life."

Martha's smile had a knowing edge, the hazard of a friend who knew you inside and out. "Well, now that I've seen the quilts, I think I'll keep looking. Maybe find something else others have overlooked."

"I have no doubt you will." Martha cocked her eyebrows in the way that said she'd return to the conversation later. "Well, I didn't see anything. Good luck sifting through the piles of junk." Martha squeezed Sarah in a quick hug and then hurried toward her car.

Sarah returned to wandering among the tables. She dug through a box here and sorted through a pile there, and had to agree with Martha's assessment. There wasn't much of value to be found in the sea of stuff. Maybe Willard Haber had focused on heavenly treasure instead of earthly treasures. From what she knew of the man, that seemed likely.

The pile of faded calicoes pulled her back toward the box of antique quilts. Sarah looked around. Did the family truly want to sell them? She pulled the first one from the box, but stopped when Maggie walked up.

Maggie's hands were shoved deep into the pockets of her down jacket. "Find anything interesting?"

Sarah pulled the quilt open, intrigued to confirm her suspicion that the quilt top was filled with a hodgepodge of patterns. Instead of precise rows of repeating patterns, this quilt had a random assortment, just like a sampler quilt that someone had pieced from a variety of practice patterns. "Maybe. This box contains five quilts. I can't believe the family isn't keeping them."

Maggie shrugged. "Maybe the quilts' stories have been lost."

"Maybe."

"Besides, if they hired an estate company like Bob's, the family probably didn't spend much time going through Mr. Haber's things."

"True." Though Sarah couldn't imagine not caring enough to sort through the items. "Anything catch your attention?"

Shuffling a half step closer, Maggie grinned. "There are a few promising pieces." She glanced at her watch. "Do you think they'll start on time?"

"Probably. Bob's a good auctioneer. Likes to run a tight ship." Sarah folded up the first quilt and pulled out a second. She brushed a separated seam. "This can be fixed."

Maggie shook her head. "But few people would know how."

"While it might not be perfect, it's still a beautiful quilt." *We're all like it*, Sarah mused. *Marred people that the loving touch of God patches together*. Maybe that's why she loved quilts so much. She could see the hidden beauty, just as God found in her.

Maggie nodded. "I'll stick to larger pieces. If I get them, they'll need some refinishing, but a few are ready for the store." She reached for a quilt toward the bottom of the stack. "Restore these, and I'll sell them in the store for you."

"I'll try."

A speaker squealed as Bob turned on a microphone.

Maggie nudged her, and Sarah looked up to find Bob headed toward the raised platform. "Time for me to go guard the furniture."

Maggie zipped toward the front, but Sarah hung back. She'd let Maggie wage battle for the furniture. She'd wait with the other items, staying where she could see and hear but be out of the way. No need to give Bob a reason to tease her into a bid for something she didn't want.

It didn't take long for Bob to get the crowd warmed up on a couple of small pieces. Then he turned to the first piece that Maggie was interested in. It was a painted wooden Hoosier, one of those pieces that people used in the kitchen to store flour, sugar, and other essentials. Today, Sarah could envision someone using it to store craft items.

Bob got the bidding started, but a few minutes later pulled the microphone away from his mouth and shook his head. "Three hundred dollars? Come on, folks. That is entirely too low for a piece of this quality." The speakers screeched at the end of Bob's auctioneer prattle.

"Is there a reserve on it?" Maggie's voice cut across the distance, and Sarah tuned into the action to see if she'd get the piece.

"All right. Going once, going twice, sold to number forty-two. You've got yourself a steal of a deal, little lady."

Sarah caught a glimpse of Maggie's smile, the one that communicated how much she knew it.

Over the next fifteen minutes or so, the bidding heated up as Bob moved to other items, and Maggie focused on Bob Spencer. The auctioneer had pushed up his barn jacket sleeves and tipped his ball cap back at an angle. He'd homed in on Maggie, cajoling others to bid against her.

"Come on, folks. You can't let this sweet gal from Southern California take all of the good pieces from this sale. I tell you, she has an eye."

Maggie waved him off. "No, I don't."

He snorted. "Next item is an antique wardrobe—looks like it could be the doorway to Narnia, doesn't it? Now, I expect some lively bidding for a piece of this quality. It would grace any of your homes. Don't let it go to a store. Of all things …

"One hundred dollars is the opening bid." Bob glanced at Maggie. "You gonna let it go for that?"

Maggie smiled. "Of course."

Bob cajoled a few more bids, but the price trickled up in twenty-five-dollar dribs and drabs.

"All right. Going …"

Maggie raised her hand. "Three hundred dollars."

And with that simple gesture the bidding on the item went crazy, and Maggie dropped out when it reached six hundred.

Maggie shook her head, and her shoulders drooped. Sarah wished she could reach her and give her a quick hug.

The next couple of items were old sofas, the kind from the sixties and seventies that wouldn't be a fit in Maggie's shop. She didn't bid, and the prices stayed low on the battered couches.

The auctioneer moved to his left and pointed at a bed frame. "All right. This fine piece was made in this area in the eighteen hundreds. Quality craftsmanship all the way."

It was a gorgeous frame decorated with intricate carvings of birds and ribbons. Sarah imagined it would be a beautiful piece in a bed-and-breakfast suite or the centerpiece of a master bedroom in a meticulously restored Victorian.

"Anyone ready to start the bidding at fifty dollars?"

Maggie nodded. In moments others jumped in and the price quickly climbed. Maggie finally grabbed the piece for seven hundred dollars.

When Bob finally worked his way to the box of quilts, most attendees had lost interest, and Sarah walked away with the box at a low price. She hefted the box, and Maggie came to stand with her in the payment line.

Maggie shook her head. "The one item you want, nobody buys out from under you."

With a shrug, Sarah shifted the box. "Guess Bob didn't recognize me from his post."

"You must have bribed him. Slipped him some coffee cake on the way in." Sarah sensed her disappointment even though Maggie was teasing.

"Not this time. But I'll file the idea away for next time."

The sound of a belabored automobile engine caught Sarah's attention. She looked around until she saw a rusted compact car pull into the parking area. The driver seemed to give no thought to others as he pulled behind two cars, parked, and jumped out. A slim woman stepped from the passenger side and followed closely behind.

"Who's that?"

Sarah shook her head. "I don't think I've seen them before. But they're late if they want to buy much."

The man strode toward Bob, who continued to cajole bids out of folks from his position among the tables. The stranger waved his arms as he approached. "Sir, you need to stop this auction."

Bob looked at him, a frown creasing his face. "Excuse me?"

"I'm Willard Haber's next of kin, and I never gave my permission for this auction. I want it stopped now."

As the man's words bellowed across the area, everyone in the line around Sarah and Maggie shifted. A murmur rose as people talked to each other.

"Can he really do that?" A woman asked the man behind her.

He shrugged. "I don't know. Wonder if we'll still get to buy our items."

Sarah watched Bob, wondering what he would do in the face of the charge. What could he do? Stop an auction when many of the items had already been sold and some paid for? What else could he do?

CHAPTER TWO

"Wait here for me." Sarah picked up her box and headed toward Bob.

Bob took a deep breath and then motioned the stranger closer. "If you'll pardon me a minute, folks, I'll be right back to finish selling these fine items." He flipped a switch on the lavaliere microphone he wore and pushed the tiny microphone away from his mouth. As soon as he turned toward the stranger, an intense look colored his face. "What's going on?"

"I'm Curtis Haber, Willard's heir." He shoved a strand of salt and pepper hair out of his eyes. "All these things you're selling belong to me."

Bob looked at the man with the deep tan. "I think you've spent too much time stranded on a beach somewhere."

"Florida. It took awhile to learn Uncle Willard had died. But I'm here now, and I don't authorize the selling of any of his things."

Bob pulled his ball cap off and ran a hand through his hair. "You see, that's a problem. The moment my gavel comes down, there's a contract between the seller and the buyer. The personal representative of the estate entered into a contract with me, authorizing me to sell these items. Said they had authorization from the heirs."

Curtis's shoulders bunched as he stood tall. "That's not possible. He didn't talk to me."

"*She* says she did." Bob planted both hands on his hips and stared Curtis down.

The two men bent their heads together and gestured wildly. Sarah glanced around and noticed the woman who had arrived with Curtis. She approached her and extended her hand. "Hello. I'm Sarah Hart."

"Louise Haber." Her words had a soft Southern flavor to them, yet her pale green eyes remained dark as she watched the two men confer.

"Are you related to Willard?"

"No. My husband was related." Louise shrugged, her thin shoulders poking against her fleecy jacket.

Willard had died several weeks earlier. Why hadn't these relatives shown up before? If they were next of kin, they should have gotten a call immediately after Willard's death. Sarah wanted to ask, but didn't think she should pose such a probing question to a stranger. "I see you have a trailer behind your car."

Louise made a face. "Curtis thinks we should stay awhile. Even talks about making it permanent." She shivered and rubbed her arms. "Is it always this cold here?"

"This is actually a great day for mid-November. It'll get much worse when winter really arrives." Sarah glanced over when she heard a restless murmur work its way through those left at the auction. Bob and Curtis still had their heads together, Curtis making big, pointing movements. While they talked, Bob's employees stopped processing bids. One woman she recognized from church rocked back and forth looking from her watch to the front tables. Sarah pulled her attention back to Louise. "Where do you plan to stay?"

"Here." The woman said it as if it was the obvious answer.

"I hope you brought lots of furniture with you. Most of this has been sold. I have no idea what might be left in the house, if anything."

Louise paled, a challenge considering her tanned skin. "That's not possible."

"I'm afraid they started with the big items and worked their way down through the knick-knacks and household items. For a bachelor, Willard had a lot of them." Made Sarah wonder if he'd held onto everything other family members had left behind.

Louise looked around, her gaze darting from place to place until Sarah wondered how she didn't get dizzy. "Curtis won't like that."

"There wasn't much of value that I could tell. A few nice pieces, but most were well used. Besides you'll have fun shopping for new things."

A desperate look entered Louise's eyes. "Curtis wanted to sort through everything."

Sarah felt bad for the woman. She tried to be positive. "Look at it this way. The hard work's already done. Now you can move in and start with a clean palette," she said. "It's strange that you didn't know about the sale. It's been planned since shortly after Willard's death."

"Curtis thought nothing could be done without him." Strain lines appeared around the woman's pale green eyes.

Sarah watched Louise, concerned for the woman. "I'm afraid some people have already left with their items. I was ready to do the same."

"Really?" Louise closed her eyes and took a deep breath. "I'm sorry. What did you plan to buy?"

"A box of old quilts. I guess I'll leave it now." Sarah toed the box, already missing the opportunity to work on the quilts.

The microphone squealed as Bob hurried back to the crowd. "Sorry for the delay, folks. I regret we have to close the auction down. Please pay for anything you won by bid. But everything that hasn't been sold yet is on hold for a future day."

Neither man looked pleased with the plan. Curtis's face turned down in a scowl as he strode toward Louise. Bob watched him leave, caught Sarah's gaze, and shook his head. He turned and stomped toward the barn leaving his employees to fend for themselves with the rush of buyers.

Louise smiled at Curtis as he approached, then slipped her arm around his waist. "We made it, honey."

"But not soon enough."

Louise cleared her throat, and Curtis looked up at Sarah. "Who are you?"

"Sarah Hart. I bought this box of quilts."

He bent down and fingered the edge of the blankets. Then he pulled the top one out. Sarah watched, her mouth open, as he tugged at seams and twisted the quilt in sections. He laid it on the ground and examined every inch of the fabric.

"What are you doing?" Sarah didn't want to think about the grass and dirt stains his actions might grind into the underside of the quilt.

"Making sure there's nothing we need here." Seemingly satisfied but disappointed, Curtis folded the quilt and pulled out the next one.

Quilt after quilt, he poked and prodded until all five had been manipulated. Finally, he tossed the quilts in the box. "There's nothing there."

Sarah looked from him to the haphazard tumble of calico. "If you really want them, I suppose ..."

"No." Louise shook her head and tugged Curtis a step back. The man already seemed to have forgotten Sarah. "Go ahead and take them."

They hurried to the first person in the payment line and performed a similar process on her box of battered paperbacks. Curtis methodically took each volume out, held it up, flipped through the pages, and then handed it to Louise, who repeated the process before slipping the book back into the box. Somehow, they seemed to have a system for knowing which books they'd already looked at and which ones still needed to be examined.

The farmyard bustled with activity again. Few people seemed to pay any attention to Curtis's and Louise's erratic actions. Instead, they wandered through the tables on their way to pay or return to their cars. Curtis paused to watch. Louise cleared her throat, then tugged on his arm. He looked at her with an impatient air. "What?"

"I think we've seen about all the junk I can handle for one day. Why don't we go see about the house? It'll be dark soon." She shivered and tugged her jacket's zipper higher. "I'd like to get all the stuff in and the heat turned up. We aren't in Florida anymore." She pulled on his arm and started toward the house. She paused and turned back. "Nice to meet you."

"You too." Sarah watched as Curtis begrudgingly followed Louise, his gaze shifting among the items sprawled across the yard.

Maggie approached. "That was interesting."

"Yes." A tug of emotions warred inside her. On one hand she felt bad for them. What must it be like to have made that long drive from Florida and arrive to find a stranger selling everything? But on the other hand, if they didn't want the sale, why hadn't they stopped it before it started? Surely, it couldn't have proceeded without their consent. Maybe Curtis had been too vague when talking to the executor of the estate.

Sarah and Maggie worked their way through the payment line. Sarah kept her mouth closed when she saw the amount of Maggie's bill. Either Magpie's was doing well or the girl had a great line of credit. Maggie was oblivious to Sarah's thoughts as she grabbed a couple of men to help them load the Tahoe and the small trailer. As they wrestled the bed frame onto the trailer, Sarah was glad Maggie had brought it along. By the time the men shoved in the last piece Maggie had purchased, Sarah thought she'd have to carry her box in her lap.

"Here, ma'am. I'll find a spot for it." One of the men reached over and relieved her of the box. Somehow he found the perfect pocket of space and slid it between a small chest of drawers and an odd wooden box.

"What is that?"

"An old letter box." Maggie stroked the surface as if shining it. "A bit of polishing, and it will make a beautiful piece. Perfect for someone who likes old, practical items. Come by the store in a week. You'll be amazed." As they climbed into the car, Maggie waxed on about her finds, showing no signs of fatigue after the hours on her feet on the cold November day.

Sarah enjoyed her enthusiasm. "I can't wait to see how you transform your finds."

"It'll take time, but wait till I sell them." She smiled in the way that lit her face from the inside. "Jason will be so pleased."

"I bet he will." The two laughed, Maggie's soprano mixing with Sarah's in a way that warmed Sarah's heart. She looked forward to more days like this in their future.

Maggie worried her lower lip between her teeth.

"Concerned about something?"

"It's silly. Thinking about the pieces I didn't get."

"Bob really laid it on thick today." Sarah put a hand on Maggie's shoulder.

"If he doesn't stop, I might have to avoid his auctions in the future, even if it's bad for business." Maggie's words whistled quietly from the corner of her mouth. "Why does he have to be the best auctioneer in the area?"

"Maybe you need a new strategy. Like letting others start the bidding."

"Then I'm playing catch up." The competition in her voice didn't surprise Sarah.

"But you still don't have to go higher than you planned."

Maggie shrugged. "Bob isn't doing me any favors."

Sarah laughed. "Face it, Maggie. You're a local phenomenon now. People notice the items you bid on. In fact, I think they piggyback on the items you like. Once they know you approve, the bidding takes off."

"I suppose I should be flattered."

"I would."

The drive back to Maple Hill passed quickly, the rolling hills and mountains of the Berkshires giving a deep sense of peace to Sarah. She could never study them without being amazed by the God who had created them, that he had gone to such trouble for the sake of beauty.

They reached town, and the light on Main Street turned red as they approached Jason's law office on the green.

"I hope his meetings went well," Maggie said.

"I'm sure they did. Jason's always been well liked around here."

"I don't know, Sarah. He's had a hard time getting traction. It's one thing when the girls talk about their old school and friends...but to hear him talk about the old firm like those were glory days. It's unsettling." She sighed, the sound coming from deep inside her. "It's hard when my business is going so much better than we'd expected, and his... isn't."

Sarah considered Maggie's words. "It takes time to build a law practice."

Maggie nodded as she turned onto Hillside Avenue and pulled alongside the curb at Sarah's house. "Thanks for going with me. It has to have been the oddest auction I've ever attended."

Sarah nodded. "I've never seen anything like it either. But even with all the added excitement I enjoyed it." Sarah slipped from the seat and then tugged the box of quilts from its spot. She leaned back in. "I wouldn't have found these beauties otherwise."

"Only you can see the potential in that pile. Just bring the restored ones to me first."

"Tell Jason and the girls 'Hi.'"

"Yes, ma'am." Maggie waved as Sarah shut the door. In no time, Maggie had disappeared down the road.

CHAPTER THREE

Sarah hefted the box and carried it up her front steps. As she set it down and dug the house key from her purse, her thoughts kept turning to the auction and its interrupters. After unlocking the door, she tugged the box over the threshold, then arched her back.

"Belle?" The house was quiet. Maybe the girl was still at work. Belle Silver, Sarah's current boarder, worked hard, and when she wasn't working she'd take off hiking and spelunking, her camera strap thrown over her shoulder.

Leaving the box by the door, Sarah kicked off her shoes and padded down the hallway to the kitchen. Dusk had started to fall, so she closed the blinds and flipped on the light switch. After she stepped into the cranberry colored room and set her purse on the island, she decided to make a quick bite to eat before evaluating the quilts.

Curtis's prodding every square inch of the quilts left her wondering what he was looking for. If he'd missed something, she would find it. If nothing else, she needed to satisfy her curiosity over his odd behavior. In the light of her sewing room, she was sure she'd see things about each quilt Curtis had missed. She made a quick grilled cheese and tomato sandwich, brewing a cup of tea while she ate. She carried the cup into the sewing room, set it down on the desk, and then hurried down the hall to pull the box down the hallway.

Her mind spun as she picked through the quilts and imagined what they would be like after they were lovingly restored. The top quilt still intrigued her—the crazy conglomeration of squares didn't mean anything to her yet, but it would. Because it called to her, she set it aside for the moment and forced herself to work on the others first.

Beneath the sampler, a more traditional log cabin quilt rested. She tugged it free and spread it on top of the quilting frame. Its fabric contained shadows of once brilliant blues and reds that had now faded. She could see it hanging in Magpie's. It would make a nice addition to someone's home after she restored it. She leaned over the quilt, and pulled out her magnifying tool as she examined each seam. When she had finished that, she ran her fingers over the surface, feeling for...? What had Curtis hoped to find?

The longer she spent looking for something she wasn't sure she'd know when she found it, the sillier Sarah felt.

At the same time, she couldn't stop until she'd flipped the quilt over and repeated the examination. She heard no tell-tale crinkling that would suggest paper between the layers. There were no odd lumps that indicated anything had been inserted. On the whole, the quilt was exactly what it was supposed to be. Two pieces of fabric with batting in between.

She carefully folded the quilt back into a neat square, and turned to the next quilt. This one had a more utilitarian feel, being made of simple flannel squares, tied off with yarn rather than quilted. After a careful examination, she saw nothing but a battered coverlet that would be useful only as batting for another quilt.

A key slid into the front door lock, and Sarah looked up. "Is that you, Belle?"

"Yes, ma'am." Belle hung her jacket on the coat tree, shaking her hair free of her hat. "I didn't keep you up, did I?"

"Goodness," Sarah glanced at the kitchen clock, surprised to find it was after nine o'clock. "Lost track of time while examining some new quilts I got today."

Belle leaned against the door frame, a nearly empty water bottle in her hand. "Anything I can do to help?"

"Absolutely." Sarah straightened her back and grinned at Belle.

"Why do I think I'm going to regret my offer?"

"No reason. No reason at all. You just get to help me examine these last three quilts."

Belle entered the room, a game expression on her face. "What are we looking for?"

"I hope we'll know it when we see it."

"That's not very detailed."

"No, but it's all I can offer. A man came to the auction I was at and had it stopped. After that he took each quilt out of the box and examined it."

"Did he find anything?"

"No. But I want to make sure there isn't something he overlooked."

The two stretched the third quilt across the frame. Belle took up the magnifying tool while Sarah ran her fingers over the seams and squares. This was another quilt made of flannel squares, tied off rather than quilted. It was in bad shape even for what Sarah was used to. She frowned when she saw the fabric had frayed along the fold lines, and wrinkled her nose against the strong musty odors that clung to it. Would it fall apart if she washed it? This coverlet would require the most work—and there was no guarantee she'd be able to make it usable again.

Belle refolded the quilt while Sarah pulled out the next quilt. They reversed their roles as they examined this one. Its faded calicoes formed log cabin squares. Smaller than the others, it looked like it might have been made for a twin bed or trundle. It barely crossed the frame, and Sarah and Belle needed only a few minutes to examine, flip, and examine it again.

Sarah put her hands on her hips as Belle refolded the quilt. "What was he looking for?"

It didn't make any sense to her. None of the quilts looked like they'd been altered since they'd been crafted. The first four were well worn, leading her to believe that if there had been anything to find in them, it would have been uncovered long before the auction.

"Maybe he just wanted to be dramatic. Some people are like that, you know." Belle's quiet words settled over Sarah.

"I don't know." As she remembered his actions, it didn't fit that Curtis had only meant to make a scene. Instead, he'd seemed to be earnestly looking for something. But what? And he hadn't seemed as focused on the other items he'd examined, though Louise had led him off before he'd had a chance to finish his odd search.

As Belle placed the new quilts on a shelf in the sewing room closet, Sarah unfolded the last quilt, the quilt made of mismatched blocks that had first caught her attention at the sale. She spread it across the quilting frame and stepped as far back as the crowded room allowed.

This quilt was made up of what appeared to be a truly random assortment of patterns. Had each block been created at a different time or by a different individual? A sampler quilt could contain blocks sewn by different members of a class, a quilting circle, or a group of friends. Or one person could make it, trying different patterns or using up scraps of fabric.

There was one way to get a better sense. As she examined the stitches carefully, looking for whatever Curtis had been searching for, Sarah was also trying to determine whether they indicated one or multiple creators. They were uniform, suggesting one person had stitched each square. The quilt top was in good shape, with only an occasional seam that would require reinforcement.

With Belle's help, she examined the surface before turning the quilt over and repeating the process.

"I don't think there's anything on this one either." Belle looked at the quilt with eyes and mouth drawn down.

"I'm afraid you're right." Sarah sank onto the chair next to her desk. Of the five quilts this was the one she wanted to work on. It had drawn her at the auction, and it still called to her now.

"Based on the stitches, I think one person made it, and tried an assortment of quilt patterns." Sarah scooted her chair closer and eyed the surface. If one person had created the quilt then there might be a story behind it. "But it's an odd quilt."

"Why?" Belle ran a hand over the top. "I think it's artistic. Look at the variety of colors and styles of patterns."

"That's exactly why it's odd. Normally, a quilter will stick to a uniform palette of colors or to a group of patterns that have similarities. This..." Sarah gestured at the quilt, "is a hodgepodge. Colors clash. Patterns with circles, next to those made of diamonds or triangles." She shook her head. "It's unusual."

She stood and stretched. "Guess I'll start by making notes in my notebook."

She'd need a good record of the blocks before she set to work. After grabbing her notebook and a pen from the bookshelf, Sarah adjusted the quilt across the top of the quilt frame. Belle helped her shift the quilt until it was squared. She'd stretch it later, but right now she needed a good look at it. One of the blocks wasn't a square. The right-hand edge was actually one long rectangle. Opening her notebook, Sarah sketched a rough outline of the quilt.

"Why take all those notes?" Belle looked over Sarah's shoulder and then her stomach growled. "Sorry. Long day, haven't eaten much."

"I can make you a grilled cheese sandwich."

"No, thanks. I'll grab something from the fridge. Good luck with that."

"Can I ask you a question before you leave?"

Belle paused in the hallway, "I guess."

"You're always on the run. Why?"

"I like staying busy." She shrugged, "Maybe I live with a sense of urgency. I don't know how much time I have here, but I know everything I want to accomplish. Guess it motivates me."

Sarah pondered her words a moment. Did Maggie feel the same way? Motivated by a sense there was much to do in an uncertain time frame.

"Why?" Belle asked.

"No reason really. Just noticing that many of my young friends like to stay far busier than I do. Must be generational."

Belle laughed and headed down the hallway. "Anything's better than spending life in front of the TV." A minute later her steps clumped up the stairs, and Sarah could hear her settling in upstairs.

Sarah turned back to the quilt. It was small, five squares by four. It would cover the foot of a bed or the back of a couch, but it wouldn't fully cover a twin-size bed. The right-hand side of the quilt featured a Split Rail pattern. Green, brown, and cream calicoes were sewn together in a modified zigzag pattern that sliced down the side of the quilt. The green flowered fabrics were the color of shaded moss, and there was a hint of yellow in the flowers' centers. The browns were a rich shade that hinted at mahogany and contrasted sharply with the faded floral pattern of the cream fabric.

The rest of the rows formed a more traditional sampler, each square separate and distinct with no apparent thought given to the colors of the fabrics that made up the squares. It was as if the creator had grabbed every flour sack and feed bag she'd accumulated over a lifetime and used the scraps to piece the quilt. Sarah studied the fabric, enjoying the riot of colors and patterns. A dogwood print in a pretty lavender and teal caught her eye where it formed part of a Fox and Geese pattern. Then there was a smart red that had been used for the leaves on a tree pattern. While there didn't seem to be an overall design, the colors had a pleasing effect.

Sarah stepped back and tried to get a general impression of the quilt. Had the quilter merely tried her hand at seventeen different patterns, some simple and others incredibly complex? Or did she have a reason for choosing each square and placing it where she had?

No matter how long she studied the quilt top, it wouldn't tell her. But she strongly suspected one thing: there was a Haber family story this quilt could tell, if only she knew how to decipher it.

Sarah glanced at the clock and then back at the quilt. It was getting late, and while the quilt had secrets to share with her, it would have to wait to reveal them.

CHAPTER FOUR

The next morning, Sarah threw her quilt to the side and climbed from the bed. Her sleep had been troubled, filled with scenes from the auction. Had the Habers found a place to lay their heads last night? There was one way to find out how they were. She'd jump on the welcome wagon and take them a gift. If they needed help, she could give some of her time too. If she hustled, she could make a batch of homemade blueberry muffins and still reach their home by ten. Early enough to take them a treat, but not so early they'd still be in bed.

Sarah whipped up some batter and ate a breakfast of oatmeal and yogurt as the muffins baked. As soon as she pulled the muffins from the oven, she tucked them in a basket topped with a pretty napkin. The sweet blueberry aroma filled her car on the drive over.

As she pulled up to the farm, Sarah noticed the windmill spinning lazily in the breeze. Its tail eased from side to side in a slow dance against the blue sky. Willard had cared for the place through the spring, but the grounds had begun to show signs of neglect beyond the trampling they'd received during the sale. One section of the split rail fence bordering the yard looked about ready to collapse, as if someone had pushed against it or put too much weight on it during the auction. The next big storm might make that portion give. Tables lined one area of the yard as if they'd been forgotten in the prior day's mayhem.

Louise and Curtis's U-Haul sat in the yard, still attached to their rusty sedan. Sarah pulled her car next to the sedan and parked. She climbed from the car and noticed that one door at the back of the trailer hung open. When Sarah peeked inside, she saw that the Habers had already emptied it.

She turned her attention toward the house. Several trees ran alongside it, each surrounded by a raised bed that probably held flowers at other times of the year. Right now, with their dead stems and dried flowers, the beds looked like nobody had cared for them in years.

The door opened, and the wind caught the screen door, slapping it against the house and causing Sarah to jump. Sarah turned and saw Louise Haber standing in the doorway, watching her.

"Good morning." Sarah reached back into her car, grabbed the basket of muffins, and then closed the door. "I brought you some fresh muffins. A little something to welcome you to town."

Louise squinted at her, as if unsure what to make of the offering.

"Can I come up?"

Louise stiffened, then nodded. She stepped out of the doorway. "Please. Come in. I warn you, it's a mess."

"It always is for a while after moving. Nothing a little time won't cure." Sarah stepped through the doorway and stopped. *Chaos.* That described the living room area. Boxes lined a wall and others looked like they'd been dropped as soon as they'd been carried inside. Random pieces of furniture sat at awkward angles, even a few couches that looked like they'd come straight from the set of *Happy Days.*

"No one helped you unpack yesterday?"

"Did you?"

Louise's words stung Sarah. "I'm sorry. Usually, Maple Hill does a better job of welcoming people. Your arrival was unexpected." Sarah set the basket on top of a stack of boxes and pulled off her gloves. She stuck the gloves in her jacket pocket and then looked at Louise. "Where can I start?"

The woman's shoulders relaxed, then tensed as if she wasn't sure whether to accept the help or chase Sarah off. She played with her long-sleeved polo's collar. "If you're sure?"

"I'm yours for the morning."

Louise gave a small smile. "Let me see if I can find some coffee to go with whatever wonderful-smelling goodie you've brought."

Sarah watched her go to the kitchen, uncertain whether she should follow or stay put. She certainly didn't want to rummage through their things. The best thing was probably to wait for Louise, so Sarah eased onto the edge of a couch. Covered in a worn pumpkin-colored velvet, its springs poked into her no matter how she shifted.

Just when she was ready to abandon the couch, Louise returned from the kitchen carrying a tray filled with a coffeepot, cups, and other items. "You found the comfortable spot."

Sarah studied the woman, hoping she was joking.

"I don't have any cream, but I did find a few packets of sugar." Louise set the tray on a box and then grabbed the basket, setting it next to the tray. "Guess this will do."

Sarah poured a cup of coffee for each of them, then sniffed hers cautiously. It looked dark, but smelled like it had a hint of vanilla in it. "Tell me more about how you got here."

"Interstate ninety-five all the way. Basically start to finish. I didn't think we'd ever leave that road."

Sarah smiled, though she'd expected more of Louise's life story. "The trip must have taken days."

"Felt like weeks. I thought I'd molded to the seat." Louise picked up a sugar packet and poured its contents into her cup. She stirred the sugar in and then took a cautious sip. "Not bad. I have no idea how long things have been in those cupboards."

Sarah eyed her mug, unsure whether to risk drinking it. "I'm surprised you didn't know about the auction."

Louise shrugged and lowered her voice. "Curtis doesn't stay in touch with the relatives around here. A falling out of some sort or another."

"That's too bad."

"I know. I'm just relieved we got here when we did." She sighed and stirred her coffee, without seeming to notice. "Curtis is desperate to find a family heirloom. He's afraid it's gone."

"What is it?"

"That's the thing." Louise looked at Sarah, intensity radiating from her eyes. "I know this sounds crazy..."

"You don't have to tell me."

"I'm surprised you've never heard about..." Louise looked toward the other side of the house and cocked her head as if listening for something. "I don't think he wants anyone to know yet."

"Then don't tell me. If your husband wants to keep the information between you two, you should honor that." That was one thing Gerry had stressed to her throughout their marriage. Any time she'd slipped and mentioned something he thought was just between them, he'd bristled at the breach of trust. She'd never forget the time she mentioned something in innocence at one of his company Christmas parties. It had taken him weeks to explain why he'd felt so violated, but she'd come to realize those breaches of trust pained him deeply. She wouldn't encourage Louise to do the same to Curtis. Just because she thought it was fine to share something with others, didn't mean he agreed. And if Curtis clearly didn't want something shared, Louise should accept his decision. After all, Sarah had been surprised more than once by how right Gerry had been to take the cautious approach.

Sarah finished her muffin and wiped her hands along her pants. "So how can I help?"

Louise looked around the room, lines forming across her nose as she frowned. "Well, I don't know. Curtis hasn't said we're staying. I might leave everything in the boxes."

"Live with this?" Sarah straightened and looked around the room again. "Please let me help. Together we can get at least this room organized. You need a corner to relax in."

"Maybe." Footsteps sounded from somewhere in the house, and Louise jerked. "I really should talk to Curtis first. And after yesterday, today's not the time to run to him with questions."

"I imagine he's exhausted."

Louise launched to her feet, knocking the box in the process and causing the tray and its items to rock. Sarah reached out to steady it.

"The muffins were wonderful. Maybe you can come out another day." Louise's words rushed out on top of each other. Sarah's welcome had clearly expired. "I'm sure I'll see you around town."

"I'm sorry if I did something . . ." Sarah really didn't know what to apologize for. Usually people appreciated when she showed up ready to get to work.

"Maybe another day." Louise moved toward the door.

Sarah looked from Louise to the kitchen and then stood. "All right." She pulled a piece of paper from her purse and scribbled her name and number on it. "If you need anything, please call. I've heard it can be hard moving to a new town. But then I've always lived here." She slipped her purse's strap over her shoulder. She stopped when she reached Louise and gave the woman a quick hug. The small gesture caused the woman to stiffen, but tears filled her eyes. "Enjoy the rest of the muffins, Louise." Sarah slipped through the doorway and onto the porch. She paused, wondering if Louise would say anything or follow her. Instead, the door closed.

She stood rooted in place, suddenly unsure what to do next.

She could go home and resume working on the quilt. Or maybe stop at Liam's and pick up tea and a muffin to share with Maggie, though she would either be busy with her new purchases or home with Jason and the girls.

Time to go home she supposed.

"Who was that?" The voice carried through the door.

Sarah knew she should move, but if Curtis was angry at Louise, she couldn't leave the woman alone with him. Especially if his anger stemmed from Sarah's visit.

"Just one of the townspeople stopping by. You should try a muffin."

"Why? What did you tell her?"

"Why would I tell her anything?" Louise's voice pitched higher. "She thinks what everyone else does. We inherited your uncle's estate."

Sarah shook her head. Standing here she was nothing more than an eavesdropper. She moved down the stairs and to her car. Slipping behind the wheel, she started the car and pulled to the road.

As she drove through Maple Hill, she replayed the morning in her mind. Louise seemed hesitant to have Sarah there. But that wasn't what nagged at her. No, her mind recycled the short conversation between Curtis and Louise.

Was there something funny in the way Louise had emphasized the word "uncle"?

CHAPTER FIVE

The doors to the Bridge Street Church pushed outward, revealing a crisp fall sky. Sarah paused in a patch of sunlight, shoulders slumping at the realization she couldn't tell anyone much about Pastor John's sermon, because her thoughts had strayed to the sampler quilt she had bought at the Haber estate sale.

"Grandma!" Audrey barreled into her side.

Sarah squeezed the girl and then pulled Amy into a hug. "Still coming for lunch?"

Audrey looked at her, sandy blond hair pulling free of the paisley headband she wore. "I hope so, Grandma."

"I don't think Mom started anything at home." Amy slipped an arm around Sarah's waist.

"You know she loves any excuse not to cook."

"Then it's settled." A quiet meal, with the promise of the Patriots football game in the background after the meal, sounded like the perfect Sunday afternoon. "Would you like to ride with me?" Both girls nodded until their heads bobbed like bobble-heads. "Here." Sarah handed her keys to Audrey. "Go ahead and climb in my car. I'll tell your folks."

Jason and Maggie stepped out of the church holding hands as they walked down the stairs. Sarah's heart flip-flopped at the sight. It had been so long since Gerry had held her hand like that. Hers suddenly felt cold and empty without his strong hands to hold them and tuck one in his jacket pocket on a day like this.

"You okay, Mom?" Jason studied her.

She opened her mouth, then cleared her throat. "Watching you made me miss your father." She didn't mind living alone, not really. She pasted on a smile. "The girls wanted to ride with me. We'll have the food ready when you get there."

"Sounds good, Mom. Thanks." Jason grinned. "Nothing like a meal at Chez Mom."

"I'd love the day off." Maggie's smile fell a little short.

Sarah cocked her head and studied her, glad to have someone else to focus on. "Working hard on your auction finds?"

"Always." Maggie's smile this time was genuine and almost chased the shadows from beneath her eyes.

"We'll get her more sleep one of these days." Jason rubbed his hands along her shoulders.

"It's worth it. Wait till you see how the dresser looks."

Maggie beamed as Jason led her toward the SUV. A horn honked, and Sarah startled. Audrey waved at her and mimed hitting the horn again. Sarah shook her finger at Audrey with a mock frown, then hurried to the car. She climbed in, made sure the twins had buckled up, and then headed for home.

The quiet streets of Maple Hill passed with Sarah soaking in the fireworks of color that exploded from the trees. The last leaves had turned and soon the trees would look like barren scarecrows. Until then, she'd enjoy the visual display.

She pulled into her empty driveway and back toward the garage—Belle's car was missing, so she probably was out for the day—and parked. The girls bounded from the car before she opened her door. "Go ahead and get the plates on the table, girls."

Their good-natured groans met her as they danced on the back porch rubbing their arms while they waited for her to catch up. She snagged a couple of gold mums from the walkway as she hurried to the door, then slid one behind each girl's ear. "Now you look festive."

Amy rolled her eyes as she blushed, but she didn't tug the flower loose.

After unlocking the door, Sarah stepped into the kitchen, the warm, hearty scent of roast and potatoes leading her. Pulling an apron from a drawer, she slipped the loop over her head and tied it in back. She hurried to the Crock-Pot and lifted the lid. She jabbed the meat with a fork, watching it fall apart. "Perfect. Amy, can you unlock the front door for your parents?"

"Sure." The sound of her footsteps clattered on the wood floor.

"Grandma?" Audrey leaned against the doorway. "Do you have any fall place mats we can use today?"

"Check the middle drawer of the china cabinet."

"I didn't see them."

"I'll look." Sarah replaced the lid on the Crock-Pot and entered the dining room. It took only a moment to find them under the red and gold Christmas mats. Sarah handed them to Audrey while she watched Amy pull out a stack of china plates. "Here you go, Audrey. Now get the silverware out. No leaving all the work to Amy."

"Yes, ma'am."

Sarah tweaked her cheek affectionately. "What would I do without you?"

She hummed a hymn as she returned to preparing the meal. By the time Jason and Maggie arrived a few minutes later, she was pulling a pan of golden crescent rolls from the oven.

"Perfect timing. The girls have the table set and the green beans are about ready. Jason, carry the platter of meat to the table, and we'll sit down."

They settled into their chairs around the antique pine table, and Sarah felt her heart lift at the sight of a full table.

"Jason, will you bless the food?"

He nodded, and everyone grabbed the hand of the person next to them until they formed a united chain. "Father, thank you for this food and for the opportunity to spend time together. Thank you for protecting us and for your many blessings. Amen."

The girls chattered about their week at school while the serving dishes circled the table. Sarah took a crescent roll and passed the plate to Audrey. When all the plates were loaded with food, Maggie leaned on the table, looking like a slightly older version of her girls.

"Next weekend will be a busy one for me. Did you meet Chester Winslow at the auction?"

Sarah wrinkled her forehead, trying to figure out how those two thoughts went together. The name sounded vaguely familiar. "I think so."

"I saw you talking to him for a moment." Maggie smiled as she waved a fork in the air. "He's agreed to come to the store Saturday to do appraisals."

Sarah looked at Jason, who shrugged.

"Come on, you two. He's the antiques expert for *Country Cottage* magazine. We chatted briefly at the auction, and he mentioned he'd like to see my store. I thought, let's go one better and make it an event. Kind of like *Antiques Roadshow*. He'll examine peoples' treasures and give an appraisal."

"On Saturday?" Sarah looked from Jason to Maggie.

"I told her that's fast." Jason speared a potato and dragged it through the gravy.

"I'll manage." Maggie wrinkled her nose at Jason. "It's almost a week."

"Let me know how I can help." Sarah imagined a long to-do list if Maggie hoped to spread the word in such a short time frame.

"Oh, thank you, Sarah. It'll be a great way to get publicity. Imagine all the people who've never set foot in Magpie's Antiques, but will to have Great-Aunt Betty's jewels or painting appraised."

Jason leaned back and put an arm around his wife's chair, a grin stretching across his face. "If only I had that kind of marketing genius."

"I could teach you. I need help spreading the word." Maggie said playfully.

"What's in it for me?"

"Kill two birds with one stone. Take a flier around about this event and distribute your business card too."

He pulled his arm back to his side, forehead scrunched as he considered. After a minute, he nodded. "All right. I could do that."

"Really?" Maggie's eyes lit, and she leaned her shoulder into his. "Thank you."

She kissed him until the girls groaned.

Suddenly Amy pulled her mouth down in a horrified expression. "Who came up with that terrible saying?"

"What?"

"Killing two birds with one stone."

"Gross!" The girls squealed in unison, eliciting a laugh from the adults.

Sarah placed her napkin on the table and stood. "Ready for pie?"

"Apple?" Jason asked.

"Of course. What else would I make this time of year?" Sarah grabbed her plate. "I'll get it sliced. Come on, girls. You can clear the table while I get dessert ready."

Sarah positioned the pie plate on the kitchen table so she could watch Jason and Maggie through the doorway. The two had their heads together, lost in conversation. She loved watching them work through their challenges together. She couldn't imagine trying to run two businesses and keep up with two active preteens. Life had changed so much since Jason and Jenna had been kids. A sigh escaped at the thought of how long it had been since she'd seen her girl. It was nice having one of her kids and his family in town, but it didn't alter the way she missed Jenna.

The clatter of the girls bringing the first load of dishes into the kitchen pulled her from her thoughts.

"Mom said you got a bunch of quilts at the auction," Amy said, scraping the dinner plates into the sink.

"That's right." Sarah said. "Would you like to see them?"

"What about pie?" Audrey grinned.

"It'll stay warm." Amy patted her stomach. "We need a minute to digest."

The girls each grabbed one of her hands and pulled her from the kitchen into the sewing room. Four of the quilts sat on the shelf in the closet, but the sampler lay where she'd left it across the frame. Sarah pulled the quilts from the closet, kicking the box under the frame at the same time.

Amy let go of her and ran a hand over the top quilt in the stack. "These don't look like much."

"Oh, but they will. Here." Sarah dug through the pile until she reached the patriotic quilt. "Look at this one. See the fabrics and colors the quilter chose. They work together in each square to make a beautiful design. Now look at the full picture in the entire quilt. The individual squares form a larger whole that is even prettier."

Amy cocked her head. "I don't see it."

"I understand it's hard to see the patterns. I'll wash and mend this quilt along with the others. When I'm done you'll get a better glimpse of their beauty." Sarah patted the top quilt, then looked at the girls.

Audrey knocked the box with her toe as she stroked the sampler quilt. Was that a small clank? Sarah started to bend down to check when Audrey pulled on her arm. "What's this one on the frame?"

"I'm calling this a sampler quilt. See how it's made up of lots of different patterns?"

The girls nodded.

"Looks like this was a hard one to make." Amy's eyes crinkled with worry lines as she folded her arms across her chest.

"Some of the squares probably were. I think whoever made this one wanted to play with lots of fabrics and patterns. See all the different ones she used?"

Audrey shrugged her thin shoulders. "It's a mess if you ask me."

Sarah tweaked her nose. "Guess it's a good thing she didn't ask you before she made it." Sarah stepped back and considered the quilt again. "It's different, but I think that's why I like it the most of the quilts I got at Friday's sale."

"Well, I'm glad Mom got furniture. It's a little more useful than a small quilt."

"I guess." Amy hurried out of the room, with Audrey on her heels.

"Mom, did you see those ugly quilts Grandma bought?" Audrey's voice carried back to Sarah.

Sarah covered her mouth hoping the girls couldn't hear her laughter. Leave it to the girls to call the quilts what they were. Ugly.

"They weren't that bad. And you don't want to hurt Grandma's feelings." Maggie's words trailed off.

Sarah shook her head and headed toward the living room where the others had gathered around the television. It would take more than a little honesty from her girls to hurt her feelings. Jason had zeroed in on the football game, so much like his father used to on long-ago Sunday afternoons. The only thing missing was Gerry's tattered sweatshirt. He'd worn that like it was a good luck charm. Sarah used to sit on the couch next to him, working on piecing quilt squares while he watched, so she could be close to him. It looked like Maggie was doing the same thing, though she'd pulled out a notebook and was scribbling notes.

"Who's ahead?" Sarah sat in her rocking chair, listening to the leather creak as she shifted.

"The Colts." Jason grunted.

Maggie looked up and grimaced. "And you know how happy that makes us." She sighed and rubbed her hands over her face. "Maybe I was crazy to tackle an event like this on such short notice. This was the first date Mr. Winslow mentioned he could come. I couldn't let it pass."

"Can I help?"

"Would you post a hundred fliers around town and under doors?"

"I've got that covered, Mags." Jason rubbed her shoulder, never taking his eyes off the TV. "I'm sure people will come. Remember, you're using this to attract people. This one might be small, but it'll build with each stellar event you host."

"But what if it wastes Mr. Winslow's time, and he won't come back?" Maggie twisted the pen between her fingers.

"Each day has enough trouble of its own. Let's get you through Saturday's event without worrying about the next one." Sarah caught Maggie's gaze and shrugged. "Maybe Chester will be terrible, and you'll decide not to have a second after all."

Maggie leaned into Jason. "You're right." She jotted another note, then nudged Jason. "If you'll take those fliers around tomorrow then your mom can help at the actual event."

"Sure, hon." Jason nodded but didn't pull his attention from the screen. "Woohoo." He jumped to his feet and pumped his fist. "That's the way it's done."

Amy and Audrey high-fived him. This was exactly what Sarah's quiet home had missed all the years they'd lived in California. Noting the furrows that continued to work across Maggie's face, Sarah tried again. "Need me before Saturday?"

"I'll be fine." Maggie looked up, a tired smile creasing her lips. "It'll be a great event."

Sarah had no doubt it would be, even if it meant Maggie didn't get a wink of sleep between now and then.

 CHAPTER SIX

The house felt strangely still. Jason, Maggie, and the girls had left at the end of the game, and Sarah felt the quiet like a weight. She grabbed a dishrag and swiped the counters. When Belle came in, she stayed downstairs only long enough to get a glass of water and a snack from her shelf in the fridge before heading upstairs to her room.

"Enough feeling sorry for yourself." Sarah threw the dishrag in the sink and marched to her sewing room. Pulling a quilt block book from the bookshelf, she flipped it open. Unless a pattern was truly unique, she should recognize them quickly.

She opened her notebook and went to work. There were ten squares left to sketch and identify.

She quickly drew the outlines of the patterns, pausing to take time on the middle column that featured an intricate, interlocking pattern. The top square was filled with diamonds lying side to side, the purple and lavender calicoes creating a swirl of violet. The piecing had been done with great care so that the diamonds filled the square precisely and didn't bleed off the sides. Overall, it looked like some kind of 3-D box pattern, but Sarah wasn't sure. She made a note next to it, to find the title.

Triangles in alternating yellow and orange fabrics composed the second block in the column. The orange had faded to a soft pumpkin, and red flowers outlined in white crisscrossed the fabric. Sarah's initial guess was that the triangles created an arrow pattern, Cupid's Dart, and she marked it in the notebook.

Beneath the triangle block lay a square Sarah identified as Star and Cross. It contained three fabrics instead of the two usually found in this pattern. The quilter must have had a third fabric she wanted to use and had added it to make the pleasing blend of pink, cornflower blue, and faded lemon prints.

Finally, the last block in the column had a circular pattern. Sarah flipped through her quilt block book trying to decide if it was Bird's Eye View or a modified fan design. A black print alternated with a red to form the central circle. A muted gray fabric filled the rest of the square. If it was a fan design, the quilter had compressed what would normally have been four squares onto one. Sarah cocked her head, trying to imagine why the quilter had selected the gray fabric. The drab color did nothing but look dirty.

She felt a headache coming on, so Sarah sat back and forced herself to relax. Where a moment before she'd been looking at individual squares, now she was drawn to the collective image the quilt presented. The quilt maker had mixed the fabrics, colors, and patterns together in a creative way. There didn't seem to be any rhyme or reason to the placement of the patterns. Was she missing something or was it simply intended to be an unusual mix?

As Sarah studied the quilt top, her instinct that the blocks weren't randomly positioned grew into a certainty. She just knew they'd been placed to tell a story. The question was what and why?

What story in the Haber family history did this quilt tell?

Sarah yawned and picked up her pencil again. If she hurried, she could get the blocks in the second column documented before calling it a night. The top block was easy to identify. Nothing hidden or secretive about the Weathervane block. And just below its swirling blades, sat a pattern in calm mint and baby pink that looked like Shoo Fly, with its cross and triangle pieces.

The block below Shoo Fly was another intricately pieced square. The center was a square of rich green fabric, filled with bold orange and gold flowers. This was surrounded by a carefully pieced border made up of triangles. A border of a solid orange fabric came next, followed by a border of a solid gold fabric. The final, outside border was another intricately pieced border of triangles. Sarah flipped through the book, landing on a similar pattern called Massachusetts.

Questions filled her mind. She had to be honest—sampler quilts' stories were rarely told in the quilt itself.

Patterns were tested and tried and sewn together without a plan. Selecting a pattern simply because you liked it had worked well for her as she quilted. It wouldn't be unusual for a woman to do that and nothing more. Maybe she should go to bed before she read too much into the eclectic collection of patterns.

The final pattern in that second to last column was a pretty combination of yellows, a white floral, a tiny Swiss dot in palest blue, and a red and white stripe. It looked like a variation on Shoo Fly, although it certainly had more colors than the ones she'd seen before. She yawned and closed her notebook. Time for bed.

As she stood, she kicked the box the quilts had been stored in. She should put that in the garage with the rest of the things to be recycled with the trash. She set the box on the counter by the backdoor. The glint of something metallic caught her eye. She searched the bottom and pulled out an old iron skeleton key. "What do we have here?"

How had Curtis missed the key? Or had he seen it and left it?

She turned the key over in her hand. It looked big enough to fit a door somewhere. Or maybe a large piece of furniture. Sarah opened the junk drawer and dropped the key inside. She'd have to see if someone could help her figure out what it went to.

Sarah made a cup of chamomile tea, then headed upstairs with the quilt book. After getting ready for bed, she slipped under her quilt and opened the book again.

Nothing caught her eye though as she glanced through the pages for something that might help unlock the randomness of the sampler quilt. Sarah let her gaze roam the patterns, soaking in the ideas and inspiration. The patterns swam in front of her. Time to close the book and clear her mind. She placed the book on the floor and sipped her tea.

On Monday morning, Sarah had just sat down to finish identifying the quilt's remaining blocks before visiting her father at the nursing home when her phone rang. She clicked on the cordless.

"Mrs. Hart, I hate to bother—" Louise Haber's voice sounded rushed and out of breath. "Could I come over for a minute this morning?"

Was the woman that lonely? Sarah gave the quilt another glance and then pushed to her feet. "That would be fine."

"I'll get there as soon as I can. I promise not to take much of your time. Thank you." The woman hung up before Sarah could say anything more.

She studied the phone a moment, wondering if it would ring again and be Louise with some type of explanation. After a moment, she set the phone down. Better get the teakettle going if company was on the way. She pulled a few cranberry scones from the freezer and defrosted them. The teakettle whistled, and she heard a knock.

After turning down the burner, Sarah hurried to the front door. When she opened the door, Louise stood on the porch, the collar of her trench coat pulled up around her ears. With her shoulders hunched, Louise looked like a turtle trying to hide from the cold.

"Come in, please."

Louise slipped past Sarah, her gaze darting from side to side as if trying to take in Sarah's furniture and artwork in a few moments.

"Can I take your coat?"

Louise shook her head and cinched the belt tighter. "It'll be months before I'm warm again."

"A cup of tea will be perfect to warm you."

"We drink our tea on ice in Florida."

Sarah laughed as Louise's face twisted into a skeptical mask. "Trust me."

"Y'all really are different here." Louise shook her head and followed Sarah down the hall.

Sarah kept the conversation going as she filled two teacups with hot water and set an assortment of tea bags in front of Louise. Eventually the woman would share what bothered her. "If you're not sure about tea, try the mint or Constant Comment. Neither is strong, and the Comment has a hint of orange you might enjoy."

Louise opened a packet of the Constant Comment and plopped the tea bag in the water. She dunked it a few times, studying the water as if her life depended on it.

Sarah propped her chin on her hand. "What's bothering you?"

"Curtis is convinced we arrived at the auction too late."

"For what?"

"To find the heirloom we drove all the way from Florida to get."

Sarah waited. The silence stretched as Louise broke off a corner of a scone. Then she took a sip of tea.

"He's convinced there's an important family heirloom that's disappeared from that mess of odds and ends." She stared into the tea as if expecting it to show her something important. "Can you imagine? Around that barren farm?"

"It *is* odd." Sarah tried to think if she'd heard anything like that about the Habers. "I'm afraid I've never heard about anything like a special family possession at the Haber farm."

"Doesn't matter to Curtis. He's raving about having to find it." Louise looked up, her sad eyes searching Sarah's. "I thought maybe you saw something at the auction. That you might have an idea where we should go next?"

So this was what Louise needed? Sarah's heart went out to Louise. She looked like she hadn't slept well in the days since her abrupt arrival. Sarah searched the woman's gaze, but found nothing that hinted her story was more or less than she said. Sarah nodded and reached out to cover Louise's hand. "I'll help if I can. Tell me what you know."

"That's the problem. All Curtis knows is there's supposed to be an heirloom."

"Does he have any idea what it looks like or whose it was?"

"No idea, but the rumor seems to have originated a couple of generations ago."

"That doesn't help much."

"Exactly."

"So what does he think it is?"

Louise puckered her lips and looked away. She shrugged, then took another sip. "Something related to World War II. That's not much, but it's all I know. I really hoped you could fill in the gaps."

"I knew Willard, but he was barely more than an acquaintance. And Mr. and Mrs. Haber would have been older than my parents."

Louise sipped her tea, then set the cup down and studied her hands. "Can you tell me about what people bought at the auction?"

Sarah stared at the woman who refused to meet her gaze. "Surely Bob gave you a list of who bought what. He would be the one to ask."

Louise looked up and locked eyes with Sarah. "Yes, but a list of person X bought one lot of kitchen towels, person Y bought a dresser isn't very helpful." She leaned forward, intensity radiating from her tight posture. "I have to find out who has that heirloom."

"But without knowing what the heirloom is, you're searching blind."

"Not if you help. Please." She reached for one of Sarah's hands. "You know everyone in this town. Surely, you'll be able to help me decipher this list." She released Sarah's hand to pull out several sheets of folded paper from her purse. "See? All these columns might as well be written in Russian for all the sense they make to me."

Sarah scanned the pages. "I know many of these people but not all. I'm surprised Irene is on the list since I know she left before the bidding. And Maggie's list looks accurate, but all I can really tell you is she filled her Tahoe and trailer with items." Sarah continued down the list, but as she skipped entries, Louise became agitated.

"You have to know what this Terry Adams bought."

Sarah sucked in a breath between her teeth. "Louise, I'm trying to help, but I won't lie to you about items or people I don't know."

Louise sat back as if Sarah's words had slapped her. She straightened and then stood. "I'm sorry, but I think I should leave. Curtis doesn't like me to be gone long. I promised to help him look through more boxes." She grabbed her papers from Sarah, shoved them in her purse and hurried down the hallway. She turned and a small smile pinched her lips. "Thanks for the tea."

Before Sarah could stand, Louise had opened the door and disappeared through the doorway. What kind of family heirloom could it be? In Maple Hill? Related to World War II? It had to be something important if they'd come all the way from Florida to find it. Yet Louise didn't seem to know much about the heirloom. Or the Habers. In fact, the little she did know didn't ring true.

And Louise's odd behavior regarding that list didn't settle right. Sarah didn't appreciate being called a liar. Especially when she was trying to help someone.

While she might not have heard of the heirloom, that didn't mean she wouldn't look into it.

In fact that sounded like something she'd enjoy. Immensely.

CHAPTER SEVEN

After Louise's abrupt departure, Sarah grabbed her quilt notebook and jotted a couple of notes. If she hurried, she could still make it to the Bradford Nursing Home to visit her dad before the residents headed to lunch. She filled a tumbler with coffee, sugar, and cream to take along while she visited her dad. While she appreciated all the nursing home staff did for her father, she'd yet to be there when a good pot of coffee waited. Mornings tended to be slower around the nursing home, so she hoped he'd be having a good morning—one where he'd remember her and spin stories of the past for her. How she treasured those times. They fed her soul as she waited through the droughts for the next visit when her dad, and not a shell, smiled at her and wrapped her in a feeble embrace.

She made the drive to the Bradford Nursing Home without much thought. The home's pastoral setting on Creek Side Road overlooked Maple Hill. The lawns that surrounded the home weren't their usual verdant green with the fall weather, but it still sat like a welcoming friend. The mountains towered in the background and there were patios where the residents could sit and take in the sweeping views.

Sarah turned off Creek Side Road onto the gravel road that led to the parking lot. She parked and then walked through the front entrance and into the large sitting room where clusters of furniture were arranged in conversation groups on each side of the walkway.

When she stopped at the nurses' station to sign in, the nurse directed her to the lounge. It must be a good day if her father wasn't spending the morning in his room. At the lounge, he sat at a long table with several other residents working on a puzzle. His tongue had slipped between his teeth as he concentrated, a gesture she'd seen since her earliest childhood. It brought a smile to her face as she strolled to his side. "Hi, Dad. Can I join you?"

"There's my little girl!"

She leaned over to kiss his cheek. "How are you feeling today?"

"Fine and dandy." He studied her a moment. "How's my girl?"

"I'm good, Dad."

The smile on his face reminded her of those he wore the times they'd gone fishing when she was a little girl. She scooted a chair beside his and watched the men work on the puzzle. The others looked up and gave her a quick grin or short acknowledgment before turning back to the sea of pieces waiting to be snapped into place. Mr. Frazier, her high school science teacher, winked at her before looking back down at the puzzle on the table. The silence was comfortable as they worked.

William's tongue slipped into one corner of his lips. He studied a piece, then laid it down and picked up another. He must have done that with a dozen puzzle pieces before finding one he snapped into another piece. Watching him reminded Sarah of the process she went through with her mysteries. Investigate a bit, then follow another trail. Back up and try again. Repeat until finally the individual pieces begin to fit together in a way that tells a story. While she didn't have the patience to repeat the process for hundreds of puzzle pieces, she loved it when she was helping a friend.

Sarah leaned forward. "So I went to an estate sale on Friday. One at Willard Haber's farm."

William nodded but didn't raise his eyes from the table. "He was a fine man."

"Yes, sir. The sale was pretty normal until the end. An ocean of items scattered around the farmyard. Furniture mixed with kitchen and other household items."

"So what made it not normal?" Mr. Frazier said, glancing up, his sharp gaze reinforcing that he'd caught what she hadn't said. The man remained as sharp as a tack.

Dad nudged the man in the side. "She'll get to it. My girl likes to spin her stories out one layer at a time, kind of like you."

The two laughed, their gazes fixed on Sarah.

"You were saying…" Mr. Frazier peered at her through his oversized glasses, curiosity making his eyes seem even bigger. William glanced down and picked up a puzzle piece, this one a mottled mix of blues and greens.

"Well, we'd gotten through the big pieces of furniture—Maggie got a lot of those for her shop—and had worked through a third of the small items when a rusty old car pulled into the farm. A man hopped out and insisted the auction stop. Said he was Willard's heir and hadn't approved the auction. Bob stopped the auction at that point, but didn't reverse any of the items already sold. Guess once the gavel comes down there's a contract or something. Curtis wasn't happy, and he started poking through everything that had been bought. He started with the box of quilts I'd won."

"Nothing strange about that, honey."

"Maybe. But the way he manhandled each quilt as if searching for something in it was. Then this morning his wife came and grilled me about who had purchased what. When I stopped by on Saturday, she seemed nice, if a little on edge. Today she seemed downright pushy. They're on the hunt for a family heirloom they know nothing about. She thinks it relates to World War II, and may have been sent home to Mr. and Mrs. Haber by one of the kids." Sarah picked up a puzzle piece and then tossed it back on the table. It made no more sense to her than the Habers' actions. "It's been an odd sequence of events."

"Sounds like it. Some folks are just that way."

Mr. Frazier looked at the other men at the table. They seemed preoccupied with their own thoughts or with the puzzle. He leaned close to Sarah. "Or it has something to do with the treasure." The last word whispered from his lips in a whistle.

"Treasure?"

"Don't pay any attention to him, Sarah." William shook his head. "There's no treasure or anything like it. Just look at that farm. It hasn't changed a lick since before the war. Adam would have invested in a new barn or two if there'd been any money or treasure lying around."

"Nonsense, William. The whole point of a treasure is hiding it."

William smiled, a twinkle in his eyes. "What kind of fool statement is that? You think there were pirates around here?"

Mr. Frazier waved his hands at William in a disgusted motion. "You always were full of bah humbugs. And what if one of the kids found it and brought it home after the war?"

"A highly unlikely scenario."

Sarah looked from man to man. "I don't know. A treasure might explain the Habers' odd behavior. If you thought there was a treasure, you'd search without letting others understand what you were really up to."

Her dad snorted. "Treasure in Maple Hill? I don't believe it for a moment."

Mr. Frazier shook his head. "William."

William shrugged, then picked up another puzzle piece.

Mr. Frazier put a puzzle piece down with an unsteady hand. "I suppose not everyone around here knew the story of a Haber boy coming back from the war with a pricey souvenir or two."

"Dad, which Haber boys served in the war?"

"Haber boys? All of them did. That's the way it was back then. One could have tried for an exemption, I suppose, but they all wanted their piece of the action." He studied the puzzle then pushed back from the table. "Walk with me in the garden?"

"Only if you have a jacket."

"This sweater will be just fine."

Sarah shook her head, but slid her arm around his shoulder. "It'll be a quick stroll then. Good bye, Mr. Frazier."

Mr. Frazier continued muttering to himself, shaking his head from side to side as he slid another puzzle piece into place.

Sarah pulled her dad's wheelchair from the table and pushed him toward the French doors. As soon as the door closed behind them, he sucked in a deep breath and smiled. "Just what these old bones needed." They walked in silence for a moment. "Now tell me what's really bugging you about the Habers."

Sarah stared at the dried and withered flower beds, itching to deadhead the plants in preparation for winter. "I don't know, but something seems a bit off. Maybe it's the way the auction ended."

"You've got good instincts. Always have. If it bothers you, keep thinking."

A breeze blew down the collar of her jacket, and Sarah shivered. "The idea of a treasure seems far-fetched. Yet what if Mr. Frazier is right and there is a treasure?"

Her dad yawned. "Sounds like you need to do some research."

Sarah nodded. "Maybe." Her mind spun with questions. "I'm just not sure which direction to go."

"You've never run from that."

"True." They walked a few more feet before she noticed that William was shivering. She wished he had one of the lap quilts she'd made for him. "If the treasure was real, why did it never move past the rumor stage?"

"Back then we were all focused on rebuilding the country and our lives." He spoke slowly and deliberately. "Treasure was made with hard work. It wasn't the stuff of stories and daydreams."

"Maybe that's all this is. A daydream."

"Possible. But it sounds like a few people believe in it."

She pushed him back to the doors where an orderly held open the door for her. A blast of warm air hit them as soon as they entered the family room. "Would you like to stay here or go back to your room now?"

William stifled another yawn. "I think I'll rest for a bit now. Can you wheel me to my room?"

"Of course." She rolled him down the hall until she reached his room. He pulled the TV remote from his pocket and hit the button. Some courtroom show flooded the screen as Sarah walked to the windowsill and made sure the plant there had enough water. Sunlight bounced off the pale green walls, and the room looked tidy and neat. She watched her father a moment, then filled a glass with water from the pitcher beside his bed. She handed it to him, then leaned down and kissed his cheek. "Would you like a blanket?"

"Sure." He never took his gaze from the show.

She pulled a small quilt from the foot of his bed and straightened it across his lap. She watched him a moment, and when it was clear he'd settled in, she headed back toward the front. Maybe it was time to check the historical society or the library to see what she could learn about the Haber boys who served in World War II.

When she reached the main room, Mr. Frazier still sat at the table picking through the puzzle pieces. She paused in the doorway and decided to take a moment to see if he had anything else he could tell her about the treasure rumors. She eased into an empty chair and flipped a few pieces right side up. She found a tiny, multicolored piece that looked like it fit the border and searched for its spot in the groupings of color.

Mr. Frazier studied the piece, then snatched it from her hand. "It goes here."

"Thank you." She watched him closely. He might be an older man now, but all she could think of when she looked at him was the middle-aged man who had tried to drill scientific minutiae into her brain.

"Spit it out, girl."

"Yes, sir. Can you tell me more about the Haber treasure?"

"There's not much to say. I heard about it when one of the three got a bit mouthy at a bar."

Sarah couldn't imagine Willard Haber at a bar, but maybe after the war, when he was still a young man, he had frequented them.

"I wouldn't waste time looking, if I were you. I don't know why you think you'll have better luck than anyone else who's looked." He picked up a piece, studied it, and tossed it on the table. Then he creaked to his feet. "Maybe your dad's right after all. It's nothing more than rumors."

"You don't really believe that."

He studied the tabletop, but she noticed the edges of his mouth twitching in a suppressed smile. "Mr. Frazier, did you look for it?"

"Some things are best left in the past." He stood and tipped an imaginary hat toward her, then moved away from the table without really answering her question. Sarah watched him shuffle off.

This behavior didn't ring true with the Mr. Frazier she remembered from high school. That man had had the curiosity of a dozen cats. Willard Haber would have been older than Mr. Frazier. Would he have shared something like that with a younger man? But if he had, why wouldn't Mr. Frazier answer questions now? It didn't make much sense to keep a secret when the holder of the secret had died.

Maybe there wasn't anything to the rumors, but she'd do some research and chase them down just in case. A kernel of truth often hid in the craziest stories.

 CHAPTER EIGHT

After Sarah left the nursing home, she pointed her car toward downtown and the historical society. A few cars were parked along Main Street, but all looked quiet except in front of The Spotted Dog. Liam waved at her as he held onto Murphy's leash. The dog sniffed each square of sidewalk as if convinced someone had violated the space since his last inspection. With a smile, Sarah waved at the familiar duo.

A few minutes later she pulled into the parking spot in front of the historical society's hitching post. She imagined reaching the historical society in a buggy with matching bay geldings pulling her. Fortunately, her car was easier to climb out of than a buggy would be.

She marched up the steps and opened one of the double doors. A fire roared in the fireplace, filling the room with soft pops and crackles. Classical music floated through the space, a perfect complement to the rustic scent of burning oak logs, and a signal Irene Stuart was working.

"Are you going to close the door or stand there all day?"

Sarah smiled at Irene. "Good afternoon, Irene. I love the fire."

"The day called for it. What a nip in the air. Time to have a load of wood delivered to the house for some fires at home." She pulled her cardigan tighter around her middle.

"I agree." Sarah imagined a fire roaring in the fireplace on Thanksgiving. It would be the perfect touch.

"What brings you to the society today, Sarah? That is, what's the new puzzle you're trying to solve?" Irene smiled.

"I need some information for a new project I'm working on. Could you help me learn about the Haber boys who served in World War II?"

Irene nodded and pursed her lips. "All three served if I remember correctly. Willard in Europe. Kevin and Eric in different parts of the Pacific theater. Willard's service was easy compared to Kevin's and Eric's, and later in the war than theirs, since he was the baby of the family."

"I know how to check the military records database, but do you think you have any information in hard copy?"

"Of course." Irene closed her eyes, as if running through the bookshelves in her mind. With enough time, Irene would spring from her chair and head to the right stack. While Tim Wexler, the high school student who helped out, was a whiz on computer databases, Irene relied on her amazing memory.

Another second passed, then Irene nodded her head. "Follow me!"

Irene pushed to her feet, then headed across the room to a row of file cabinets Sarah had never explored. "I think I might have some family papers. While I check for those, you can start here. This cabinet contains the military records of many of the boys from this county who served going back to the Spanish-American War. They should be in alphabetical order, so start near the middle. If you don't find what you want there, you might try this drawer down here." She pointed at a bottom drawer in one of the cabinets. "It contains some records on the women who participated in military service, in the Waves, for example, or in groups like the Red Cross. You should find Kay Haber's file there."

"Kay?"

"Willard's sister. She served for a while in the Red Cross."

"Thanks, Irene."

"Any files you pull out just place in the baskets on top when you're done. Tim or I will refile them. Now don't get into trouble."

"What kind of trouble could I find here?" Sarah smiled at Irene, but the woman gave her a knowing look, then moved back to her desk.

Sarah settled her bag on the top of a cabinet and pulled out the first drawer Irene had pointed out to her. It took only a moment to see that Irene's extreme efficiency had left its mark on the drawers. Every file was in precise alphabetical order. She moved down a couple drawers and flipped through the Hs. She pulled out the Haber boys' files and placed them next to her bag. Then she looked through the women's drawer and pulled out Kay's file.

After carrying the files to a nearby table, Sarah flipped to the boys' files. She glanced through each file quickly, trying to catch an overall feel for what each boy had done.

Each Haber boy had served in a different role. Kevin spent his days in the war as a swabby on a Navy destroyer in the Pacific. Eric, a Marine, had died during the Bataan death march. Sarah shuddered as she imagined the horrible deprivation and torture the young man must have experienced during that journey. And Willard had served in the European theater.

Sarah made a few notes and dug deeper into the files. Was there a way to figure out which of the boys might have brought treasure home from the war?

As Sarah scanned Kevin's file, it appeared he'd spent the entire war on the ship. There were no transfers or records of land battles he'd participated in. That seemed to narrow the possibility he'd have run into anything that could be construed as a treasure.

In Eric's file, Sarah found a faded photocopy of a letter that brought tears to her eyes. Dated April 1946, it was from a James Applewood.

> Mr. and Mrs. Haber,
> I know words aren't sufficient to express my deep gratitude for the bravery of your son Eric. You see, he served with me in the Marines. We were in the same platoon and saw a lot of combat in the Pacific. The kind of hand-to-hand combat that is exhausting and can bring out the best or worst in a man.

For Eric, the choice always seemed to be the best.

When our platoon was cut off and made prisoners, he and I, along with many others, were sent on the Bataan death march. Now we know how terrible that journey was. Then, we just wanted to put one foot in front of the other and find a way to survive until the war ended. The guards were brutal. Eric died taking a blow from a rifle intended for me.

I will never be the man Eric was, but know I will live the balance of my days striving to honor his memory and sacrifice.

Sincerely,

James Applewood

Sarah closed her eyes, feeling the pressure of tears. What must that ghastly journey have been like? And then to die in such a way. A shudder coursed through her at the thought of Eric's brutal death as he tried to help a fellow prisoner. She opened her eyes and sifted through the rest of the file. While he had served heroically, she couldn't imagine how he'd found anything of value in the jungles of the Pacific. Even if he had, how would he have sent it home before being captured and eventually killed? No, it seemed unlikely he had found the treasure—whatever it was.

Willard had enlisted the day after he graduated from high school. Underage, he'd needed his father's signature. Had it been hard for the man to give, knowing he'd already lost one son and had another floating somewhere in the Pacific. Instead of heading West like his brothers, Willard joined the Army and shipped to the European front right after D-Day. From the documentation, it looked like he'd stayed after V-E Day. By staying, had he somehow run into someone who bartered family jewels for protection, food, or other necessities in the war-torn continent?

Sarah closed Willard's file and rubbed her eyes. It was almost impossible to know what could have happened during his tour. If he hadn't said something—*if* he'd found something—it wouldn't be public knowledge.

Finally, she pulled Kay's file to the top of the pile and opened it. A quick glance showed the woman had served with the Red Cross in Europe. Maybe Willard and Kay had overlapped at some point during their service. Sarah tugged a photo of Kay in her Red Cross uniform from under a paper clip. The girl in the photo had an infectious grin revealing slightly bucked teeth and a dimple in one cheek. Her eyes glowed with excitement, and the suit showed off feminine curves. Her hair was cut in a soft shoulder-length bob that was slightly curly.

Sarah bet that to an army of war-weary soldiers Kay would have been a pleasant and welcome sight. Had Kay possibly fallen in love with a G.I. who was later killed? Or had she somehow turned the head of a European lad? One who wanted to show his gratitude to the Americans, maybe to one in particular?

Sarah tried to rein her thoughts in before they ran away from her.

Nothing in the file indicated that either scenario had occurred. And why would it? It was a record of her service. Not of her experiences. No, Sarah would need to find journals or letters home to find out whether something like a love affair might have occurred.

Sarah closed her eyes and imagined the life Kay had lived driving a Red Cross truck across the battle-torn countries of Europe. Bouncing down bombed-out roads and around debris as she drove a truck filled with entertainment for the troops—books, games, snacks, tastes of home. The troops must have greeted her enthusiastically. Could she have tired of fending them off? Anything might be possible.

After closing the file, Sarah made a few notes. Kay and Willard each had had the opportunity to run across property while in Europe. But would either have found anything worthy of being called a treasure? And if they had, how would they have brought it home from Europe? If it were something large like a painting, the treasure would have been difficult to transport. And it certainly would have been a challenge to keep something like that hidden since the war—sixty years is a long time to conceal anything of size and value.

But what did that leave?

Sarah made a few more notes in her notebook, then placed the files in the baskets Irene had indicated.

Irene glanced up as Sarah approached her desk. "Did you find what you needed?"

"I'm not sure." Sarah bit her lower lip. "Do you have any family records, things like journals or correspondence?"

"I checked while you were in the files. I can't find a thing. Doesn't surprise me. Adam Haber never stressed education with his kids." Irene shook her head as if offended by his lack of appreciation for the written word. "They were a family of farmers. I really thought I might have something from Kay.

I remember hearing she was a letter writer, but I couldn't find a thing. Couldn't even at that crazy auction."

Sarah nodded. "It was unusual. Well, thank you for all your help."

As she left, Sarah knew she'd accomplished something. At least she now knew the treasure finders couldn't be two of the Habers. That left Willard and Kay. And a host of questions.

CHAPTER NINE

Sarah's mind buzzed with images of the Haber siblings, each participating in the war, each in their own way.

She pulled her car back onto the road, but pulled over again when she reached Jason's office on the green. His second-story office was in a prime location, easy for people to find. But his practice hadn't taken off yet. The strain had been clearly visible Sunday after church. Maybe a quick visit would brighten his day. And if trouble brewed in Jason and Maggie's paradise, maybe he needed someone to talk to. She would definitely pray, but she needed to do more if she could.

She bowed her head. *Father, help me know how to help Jason and Maggie without interfering and making things more stressful for them.* She opened her eyes and looked up, peace in her heart.

A few crushed leaves cluttered the sidewalk in front of his door. Sarah swept them aside with her foot, and then opened the door to the stairs that led to the second floor office. When she arrived at the top, she opened the office door and took in his cluttered space. The man he'd bought the practice from had been notorious for his disorganized manner, and Jason seemed to have adopted that attorney's decorating style: piles everywhere. Books were piled haphazardly in several barrister shelves that lined one wall. And a stack of magazines slid across the coffee table. As usual, no one sat at the battered reception desk when she entered, but she heard Jason call from his office.

"I'll be right there."

"It's me, Jason. No need to rush."

"Oh." She thought she heard disappointment in his voice, but that made sense. He wasn't disappointed that she had stopped by, he was disappointed that she wasn't a client. "Come on back, Mom."

She hurried down the short hall to his office, but stopped in the doorway. Jason lurched toward his monitor, hitting a button on it, then pushed some papers together in a hasty pile. He lunged from his chair, and it bounced up and down behind him. "Mom."

"You told me to come back."

"Yeah, I did. Sorry." He rubbed a hand over his hair, mussing it as he smiled at her sheepishly.

She gave him the look that always made him spill the beans as a teen. "Slow day?"

"You could say that. One in a string of them." His shoulders slumped, and he sank back into his chair. His phone rang, and he looked from her to the phone.

"Go ahead. Maybe it's your next big client."

"Make that the first."

"All the more reason to grab the call."

Jason cleared his throat and then picked up the phone. "Hart Law Office." He stiffened and half turned away from Sarah with a sheepish grin. "I'm sorry, but I really can't talk now ... you could say that ... Can I call you back? Shouldn't take long ... Great." Jason hung up and turned back to Sarah, lacing his fingers behind his head as he leaned back in his chair. His attempt at nonchalance didn't lower Sarah's curiosity one bit. "So ... "

"I can leave if you need to call whoever that was back." She started to get up from her chair, but he waved her back down.

"You're the first person I've seen all day, Mom."

"So what are you doing about that?"

"What do you mean?"

"How are you working to generate business? Other than telling people you'll call them back?"

"I took those fliers around for Maggie and introduced myself. People seemed more excited about having their stuff looked at than bringing legal problems to me."

"There are many more people who own antiques than people with legal problems. It must be hard."

"Sure. It's hard when Maggie's doing a bang-up job with the store, and I can't get enough clients to pay the bills on this office."

Sarah studied her son, concerned by the lines of defeat in his posture as he slumped forward. "I'm sorry, honey. Is there anything I can do?"

"Other than pointing your friends to me when they need an attorney?" Jason shook his head. "It's something I have to do. I'm working on it. Maggie joined the Chamber of Commerce before I could. And part of me doesn't want to be known as her husband."

"What makes you think that would happen? Remember everyone in Maple Hill has known you a long time. Maggie's the newcomer."

"That's true. I guess I wanted it to be easy." Jason raised his hand, stopping the words that burbled up her throat. "I know what you'll say. Nothing worth doing is easy." He grinned ruefully. "I think I expected things to be simpler since everyone knows me. I didn't expect that I'd have to convince them I'm not in high school anymore. It's like I've entered a time warp as far as people are concerned. They see me as an eighteen-year-old rather than a successful attorney."

Sarah nodded, pausing a moment. "I suppose we get stuck in old expectations."

"And I refuse to chase ambulances." Jason leaned forward on the desk. "I never thought it would be this hard. I hate watching Maggie run herself ragged while I can't seem to get a good start." His voice held a lost quality. "I didn't think I'd miss the firm, but at least I was busy there. I had clients and was useful. Here…well, I just waste time until I can go home. Only when I get there, Maggie probably won't be there. And the girls and I will be on our own for dinner unless she remembered to put something in the Crock-Pot.

"Her energy is focused on the store." He shrugged. "The girls and I fend for ourselves a lot."

"I'm sorry, Jason. I wish I had the perfect advice or suggestion. I am praying for you." She bit her lower lip and studied him. Did he want her to offer suggestions? "Have you considered seeing if there's work you can do for your old firm from here while you build your practice?"

Jason looked over her shoulder into the hallway. "It's a thought. I need to get creative or find a silver bullet of a case that will get people talking about me as an attorney. There's lots I can still do to make this work."

"I do have a quick question for the attorney."

"All right."

"If someone discovered a treasure in Massachusetts, who would it belong to? The finder or someone else?"

"That's complicated. It depends on who the treasure belonged to originally, and if the original owner can be found. And lots of other factors. I'd need more facts to give you an answer."

"If I knew more I'd give them to you." Sarah studied him, seeing the light of curiosity in his gaze. "Never mind. It's too early to ask anyway."

Jason cocked his head as he studied her. "Are you planning to go on a treasure hunt?"

"No. Just curious." Sarah stood and leaned across the desk to kiss his cheek. "I love you. Hang in there and remember an abundance of grace and patience will go a long way."

"I know, Mom." The phone rang again, and he gave her an apologetic smile before picking it up. "Hart Law Office."

Sarah slipped from the room, praying this call led to a paying client. It was hard having a hurting adult child. How much could she say without interfering? It looked like God had given her an opportunity to pray first.

She left Jason's office, her heart unsettled within her. Why did it seem like everything had become a jumbled mess for the people she loved? Jason felt unfulfilled with his floundering practice and a busy wife. Maggie felt overwhelmed by the multiple demands on her time. And the girls struggled to make Maple Hill their home. Their complaints had become less frequent, but she knew they missed L.A., their friends, even their school. Yet there was only so much she could do without overstepping her role.

She heard echoes of the struggles she and Gerry had gone through while listening to Jason. No marriage was perfect. But she wondered if Jason remembered how hard his parents had worked to keep their marriage together. Sometimes they had argued over silly things like whose turn it was to put the kids to bed. Other times the struggles had been over finances and how to spend or save their money. Gerry had always been tight with money, while it flowed through her fingers if she wasn't careful. Through a lot of effort on Gerry's part, he'd convinced her to be more responsible and to think of the long-term costs of spontaneous purchases. And she'd helped him be a bit freer about buying things that weren't an absolute need. Today, she was grateful for all his work and savings, since they had allowed her to have the house free and clear after his death. There was still some money squirreled away in an account for emergencies or times when she didn't have a boarder.

Thanks to his efforts, she was comfortable if not wealthy. And that was one example of how the struggles had been worth it.

But that kind of experience came through living. It couldn't be conveyed through a conversation, especially if the other person wasn't quite ready to hear yet.

No, prayer looked like the best option. She'd continue to carry the kids and their marriage to the Father's throne. She could trust him to see them through the current challenges and make them stronger in the future as a result.

How she wished her dad could share some of his wisdom too. Somehow, in his presence, things looked better, more manageable. With one hug from him, she regained her outlook. She smiled at the memory of their good time that morning. What a blessing that had been. Maybe he was still having a good day.

Sarah slipped into her car and pulled her phone from her purse. She dialed the nursing home's number from memory and waited for the charge nurse to pick up.

The phone rang until she wondered if someone would pick it up. "Bradford Manor Nursing Home."

"This is Sarah Hart. Could I speak with the charge nurse please?"

"One moment."

Sarah tapped the steering wheel while she waited to be transferred.

"Grace Fletcher."

"Hi, Grace. This is Sarah Hart. I wondered if I could talk to my dad if he's still having a good day."

"Let's see, William Drayton. I'm sorry, Ms. Hart, but we've already helped your father get ready for bed. After your visit this morning, he was pretty worn out. I'd recommend waiting until the morning and call or come by then. Hopefully, a full night's rest will give him a chance to have a clear day tomorrow."

Sarah sighed, but agreed. "All right. I'll do that. Thank you."

She closed her phone and then edged out of her parking space. She was so grateful her father had had a good day earlier. But at times she really missed him.

When she reached home, Sarah checked her answering machine. There was one message from her grandson Thomas. The sound of his sweet voice warmed her.

"Hi, Granma. This is Thomas. I miss you. Will you come visit soon? Luv you. Bye."

It had been too long since she'd seen her daughter Jenna and her family. Suddenly, Sarah had a desire to talk to Jenna and maybe catch Thomas and his brother Jonathan playing in the background. She picked up the phone and dialed. The phone rang four times before switching to voice mail. "This is Grandma. Just calling to say hello and thank Thomas for his call. Sorry I wasn't home. Hugs and kisses to each of you."

Sarah held the phone a moment before placing it back on the charger. She had two choices. She could dwell on how long it had been since she'd seen her grandsons and Jenna. Or she could do something productive. Something that would distract her and keep her mind occupied.

CHAPTER TEN

The next afternoon Sarah grabbed the most recent issue of *Country Cottage* and read Chester Winslow's column. With his visit to the store in a few days, she wanted to get up to date on his columns. The man came across as having a passion for the stories behind pieces of furniture and other household objects. The older the better as far as he was concerned.

The phone rang, and she tossed the magazine to the side. She grabbed the phone from the kitchen counter and clicked it on. "Hello?"

"Mrs. Hart, this is Chester Winslow. I don't know if you remember meeting me at the estate sale last weekend."

Sarah smiled, even as she wondered why he'd called her. "Yes. Thank you for agreeing to come to Maggie's store this weekend. She's excited, and the word is circulating."

"My pleasure." He cleared his throat, a sound that was strangely awkward. "I wondered if you might be free tonight for dinner. I know it's short notice...but I'll be near town and hate to dine alone."

Sarah sat up straighter. *Had she heard the man correctly?*

"Sarah? Dinner? Tonight?"

The pause stretched while she tried to find words. Should she do it? She didn't really know the man, but the prospect of eating home...alone...didn't appeal either.

"I could meet you somewhere. What time and where?"

"How about I pick you up at five forty-five. I can get reservations at the Old Mill for six o'clock. I'd like to try Maple Hill's finest establishment with its finest quilt restorer."

Sarah bit her lower lip and nodded. "I'd like that."

"It's settled." Relief filled his voice. "I'll see you then." He clicked off, and Sarah held the phone a moment.

Had she really agreed to dinner with someone who was practically a stranger? What would she have thought if her kids had done something like that? She shook her head and then glanced at the clock. She had a little over an hour to get ready. Plenty of time to shower and change if she didn't delay.

Thirty minutes later Sarah stared at her image in the mirror. It had been a long time since she'd prepared for a dinner that had the air of a date rather than a friendly outing. Tension knotted her shoulders, and she forced them to relax.

Should she feel flattered by the out-of-the-blue invitation? And enjoy the unexpected attention?

She studied her reflection in the bathroom mirror. Add more blush? Put on eyeliner? She usually kept her makeup natural, so she didn't want to do too much. She really shouldn't get so worked up since it was just dinner.

Sarah applied mauve lipstick, the kind the company promised would stay on for hours. A glance at her watch made her hurry to her closet. No time to waste on makeup when she had five minutes to dress before Chester arrived. She topped her black slacks with a teal sweater. Then she stepped into black flats and headed to the stairs.

Belle's door stood open, and Sarah peeked in. The girl's sandy blonde hair bounced as she hopped up and down in rhythm to whatever music piped into her ears through her MP3 player. The girl smiled when she caught Sarah watching her but kept moving.

"I'm headed out."

Belle nodded, and Sarah hurried down the stairs. The phone rang, and Sarah followed the sound to the kitchen where she picked up the receiver. "Hello?"

"Grandma, can you come over?" Amy's voice vibrated with excitement.

"Oh honey, I wish I could, but I have plans tonight."

"Please...I miss you and want to see you."

Sarah bit her lower lip. So much for the newly applied lipstick.

"How about I come over tomorrow after school to see you?"

Amy's sigh reverberated to Sarah's ear. "Promise?"

In the background, Jason's voice caught Sarah's attention. He sounded frustrated.

"I have to get to the Chamber of Commerce business mixer—"

Their voices dropped off, but Sarah had heard the tension between them.

"Grandma?" Amy's voice held an impatient tone.

"Yes?"

"You promise you'll come tomorrow?"

"First thing after school."

"All right. Love you."

The doorbell rang, and she hung up the phone. Jitters surged through her, and she stifled a giggle. She must be more nervous than she'd thought. It wasn't as if she was a high school student headed out on her first date.

No, it just felt like it.

She opened the door and felt her cheeks round in a smile at the sight of Chester. Tall and thin, he'd lost some of the hair off the top of his head, but she liked the look of the man. His tweed jacket and turtleneck sweater gave him the air of a professor. Add the khakis that held a stiff crease down the middle of each leg, and he looked dashing. He held a bouquet of gerbera daisies in an assortment of scarlet, yellow, and orange.

"Sunny flowers for a delightful woman."

For a moment she wished the flowers had a scent so she could bury her face in the fall colors to hide the heat climbing her neck. She couldn't remember the last time someone other than Gerry had brought her flowers. She accepted the bouquet and stepped back. "What a beautiful assortment. Will you come in while I put these in water?"

Chester entered, a musky scent following as he trailed her to the kitchen.

"Would you like anything to drink before we leave?"

Chester checked his watch, and then shook his head. "Our reservation is in fifteen minutes."

Sarah grabbed a Depression-era glass pitcher from a cabinet and filled it with water. She added a tablespoon of sugar, and then tucked the stems in the pitcher where they fell into a relaxed arrangement. "Let me grab a coat, and I'll be ready."

Chester escorted her to his silver BMW coupe, opened the door, and closed it once she'd slipped inside. His every action demonstrated that he was a consummate gentleman. She enjoyed the attention of a man who wasn't afraid to treat her like a lady. Quiet classical music served as a backdrop to the quick drive to the Clear Springs River and the Old Mill. Chester pulled into the Old Mill's parking lot. The mill wore its two-hundred-year history with the grace of an elder statesman.

Sarah loved the way the heavy wood beams intersected across the ceiling, turning it into a rich patchwork of squares. The dark wood gave the large space an intimate feeling, and the interior designer had played that up by constructing half walls to divide the space.

As soon as they approached the hostess stand, the woman serving as hostess picked up two menus. "Mr. Winslow. It's a pleasure to see you again. Follow me."

Sarah glanced at Chester. "I thought you'd never been here."

"I've enjoyed several meals here." He shoved his hands in his pockets and jingle-jangled coins. "That doesn't change the fact that a meal is more enjoyable with a beautiful companion."

The hostess seated them at a table next to a large paneled window. Chester sat down and then tugged at his jacket sleeves. "Here we are."

"Yes." Sarah picked up the napkin resting on her plate and placed it in her lap. Then she leaned forward, placing her elbows on top of the menu. "Chester, I appreciate the invitation to dinner. Really, I do. But are you ready to tell me the real reason behind the invitation?"

He cringed and looked away from her. "Am I that transparent?" Sarah nodded and Chester shrugged. "Well then. I'll get to the point."

"I'd like that."

"Our magazine is looking for someone to write an occasional column about quilts—their history, restoration, and value." He spread his hands out in front of him. "While I'm an expert on many things, quilts are far outside my area. You, on the other hand, come highly recommended."

Sarah pulled her shoulders back and cocked her head. "I'm not sure I've ever considered myself a writer."

The waitress wandered by their table. After placing their drink orders, Sarah shook her head. "A columnist?"

"Think about it. There's not much to it. Imagine yourself writing down a conversation with a client. The magazine editor would like to meet you, so if you wouldn't mind a drive over to Pittsfield, you and he can talk about the job."

Sarah leaned her cheek on her hand, intrigued by Chester's proposal. Chester picked up and opened his menu. "What do you recommend?"

"The crab cakes are wonderful. My friend Martha raves about the filet mignon, though I prefer mine a bit less rare than she does."

The waitress brought their drinks to the table. She set the glasses in front of them, then pulled a pen from her perky ponytail. "What can I get you folks tonight?"

"I'll have the crab cakes and house salad, ranch on the side." Sarah handed the college student the menu and waited while Chester ordered the filet mignon with a side of crab cakes.

"I thought I'd better try both." His grin held a hint of mischief that Sarah found very appealing. Somehow it gave Chester the air of a prep school brain who knew how handsome he was. Yet it didn't come across as vain. She shook her head, relieved when the waitress took his menu and moved to another table. Through it all Chester's focus never wavered from Sarah. "So you'll come in the morning?"

"That soon?" Sarah bit her lower lip then shrugged. "I suppose I can."

"Well then, we're set." Chester rubbed his hands together and leaned back in his chair.

Sarah scooted forward on her chair. "Tell me your impression of the estate sale."

He cocked his head and looked over her shoulder. "It was unusual."

"Yes."

"I've done a bit of checking, though. Comes with being a writer. If something catches my attention, I tend to chase it down." Chester picked up his knife and turned it over, examining it as if he'd never seen cutlery before. "I have my doubts."

"About what?"

"The Habers." He set the knife down and leaned over the table until his nose almost touched hers. "Something is off about them."

"Why would you say that?"

"The man claims to be the next of kin, but knows nothing about the sale? Strike you as odd?"

Sarah nodded. "It's bothered me since the sale."

"They're as likely Habers as I am the pope."

Sarah shifted away from him, shocked by the vehemence in his words. "Really?"

"If they were who they said, they wouldn't have barreled into the auction at the last moment." He shrugged, keeping his posture loose and relaxed. "There would have been no need because they could have called and arranged a delay."

"Louise seems convinced there's a family heirloom that's escaped. But she knows little about it."

"Of course, she knows next to nothing about it. There probably isn't one."

Sarah studied his face, noting the tight lines around his mouth and eyes. Annoyance ran in the lines of his body, erasing the relaxed stance of moments earlier. "What will you do?"

Chester deflated and leaned back against the chair. "I don't know that there's anything I can do." He took a deep breath and exhaled it slowly. "Sorry about that. Guess I run toward passionate."

"It's actually helpful. In a way it's nice to know I'm not the only one who feels something is off." But frauds? Sarah would have to think about that. Do a little investigating to see if Chester's instincts were correct.

He steered the conversation to the Patriots season, and Sarah nodded at appropriate times. Unfortunately, since her husband's death, she kept the game on in the background most Sunday afternoons, but rarely tuned in to the action. As Chester talked, she studied the patrons at the other tables. A group a few tables to her right celebrated a birthday, while at another table the couple shared the intimate look of young love. The flickering candlelight sent a soft glow across the woman's expectant face. Sarah wouldn't be surprised if the young man, clad in an oversize jacket and khakis, suddenly fell to one knee and slipped a ring on the girl's hand.

A soft mist clouded her vision at the thought, and she blinked quickly.

"You all right?" Chester's voice held the right tone of concern.

"Fine." Sarah cleared her throat and brought her focus back to him. "Just enjoying the evening."

He looked at her uncertainly as if knowing she really hadn't been paying attention to him.

The waitress approached with their salads. "House with ranch on the side." She slid that one in front of Sarah, and then placed a Caesar salad in front of Chester. "Enjoy." She sashayed from the table, and Sarah's gaze followed her in case she slipped something special on the couple's table.

"You're a romantic at heart, aren't you?"

Sarah glanced back at Chester and found him studying her with a curious look. "Silly for someone my age . . ."

"Not at all." Chester straightened up and shrugged. "Romantics are incredibly optimistic people. Nothing to be ashamed of."

"You're right." Sarah dipped her fork in the dressing and then stabbed it into her salad. She savored the bite, thinking about Chester's words.

She didn't usually get misty-eyed at the sight of young love. She'd have to ponder what it meant. Because it made her wonder what her heart wanted to tell her. *Was it time to consider whether her life had room for romance, too?*

Laughter bubbled inside her at the thought.

Surely she was too mature to entertain such thoughts. But as she studied the man seated across from her, she wondered if she shouldn't open her mind to the idea.

CHAPTER ELEVEN

ednesday morning, traffic had eased by the time Sarah merged onto the highway. The thought of visiting the *Country Cottage* offices had interested her, but seeing Chester again after their dinner last night made her hesitate—she'd had a wonderful time, but what were his intentions?

She'd keep the focus on the job. Over the last several months she'd had the privilege of helping several people with puzzles that plagued them. The first involved clearing her grandfather of suspicion in her grandmother's disappearance. Then there was the mystery that began with a visit to Mount Greylock with her granddaughters. After that she'd restored a quilt, finding a plea for help embroidered on its back.

Today, the key she'd found in the box of quilts sat in her pocket, heavy and a reminder of her new puzzle. Maybe Chester would be able to help her identify what the key went to.

She turned on her radio and sang along to a classic sixties tune. An hour later she turned off the road into Pittsfield. Following the directions Chester had given her the night before, she pulled into a parking spot behind the three-story brick office building. It wasn't the glitzy office she'd imagined for the magazine.

She unstrapped her seat belt and grabbed her purse. After climbing from the car, she straightened her skirt and walked to the door.

The lobby was empty, but a pulse of activity reached her from somewhere behind the receptionist's desk. Comfortable but worn vinyl chairs angled around the lobby, small side tables strewn with copies of the latest issue of the magazine sitting among the furniture.

A woman bustled to the desk. The headset that perched on her head made her gray curls stick out at crazy angles, but she wore a friendly smile. "Sorry to keep you waiting. Can I help you?"

"I'm here to see Chester Winslow."

The woman eyed Sarah. "That man is hopping this morning. You must be the fourth person who's come in without an appointment." She hit a button on her phone, and announced Sarah. "He'll be down momentarily."

While she waited, Sarah strolled to the far wall of the lobby, which held an assortment of antique advertisements and posters reminiscent of the decorations in a Cracker Barrel. Rustic farm and gardening tools hung between the ads.

"Interesting display, isn't it?"

Sarah turned to look at the receptionist. "Not what I expected."

"The editor's wife studied interior decorating, and she made this one of her projects." The phone rang and the receptionist picked it up. "*Country Cottage m*agazine."

Sarah wandered to a chair, plopped onto it, and then picked up a magazine from the neighboring table. She shifted until she found a comfortable position and flipped open the magazine. While she had a subscription to the magazine, she hadn't seen this issue yet. She glanced at the table of contents looking for Chester's column. In this edition, he talked about antique decoy ducks. Sarah smiled at his description of the battered wood forms as art worthy of collection.

"Sarah."

She looked up at Chester's voice, and heat flushed her cheeks. She closed the magazine before he could notice the article she'd been reading. "Good morning, Chester."

"Good morning. There's much to show you. Let's go."

He placed his hand at the small of her back as he guided her down a narrow hallway.

They passed several closed doors. Sarah's curiosity got the better of her as they walked by. "I expected this to be more like a newspaper."

"I like the closed nature. A newsroom can get so noisy it's hard to hear your thoughts. That always interfered with my writing. I like a little background noise, but not so much I can't string a sentence together."

They approached Chester's office, and he paused with his hand on the knob. "Prepare for the messy office of an award-winning columnist." He flicked his wrist and opened the door. His office was lined with floor to ceiling bookshelves and a large desk with a laptop and piles of paper sat near a window. Books piled along the floor and spilled over one of the two chairs sitting in front of his desk. As he walked to his desk, a pile of paper slid onto the floor.

Sarah couldn't fight laughter at the confounded look on his face. "This definitely isn't what I expected."

"Have a seat."

"After riding in your meticulous car, I thought your office would look the same."

"Nope. That's where I play. This is where I create—always a messy business."

"You should see my sewing room when I'm in the middle of a project."

Chester rummaged around his desk, bumping a box that looked familiar.

"What's that?"

"Hmm?" Chester looked at the box. "Oh, this is the letter box I purchased from your daughter-in-law last night. I noticed it at the sale, and saw she had it when I stopped by her shop on the way to get you. It took only a bit of polish and elbow grease to uncover its hidden beauty. You'll never believe what I received this morning related to it."

Sarah watched him, wondering what he would say.

Chester opened the top of the letter box and pulled out an envelope. He tapped the envelope on his hand. "Mr. Haber." The way he said the name left no doubt he still thought the man a fraud, "sent me a letter insisting that if I had purchased anything at the sale I must return it. Claims a family secret of some sort."

Sarah couldn't imagine anything hidden in the simple box. It wasn't tall and the sloping lid would prevent much from fitting inside it. "Does the box harbor a secret?"

"Not that I've found. Did you know the prior owner of the farm?"

"He was a passing acquaintance, like most people in a small town. Why?"

"Just wondering." Chester studied her a moment as if assessing the truth of her answer. Sarah decided she didn't like the scrutiny and crossed her arms.

Sarah pulled out the key from her pocket. "I found this in the box of quilts I purchased at the sale." She placed it on the desk in front of Chester. "Any ideas what it might go to?"

He picked up the black key and hefted it in his hand as if testing it. "What do you think?"

"Maybe a piece of furniture? I'm not sure. But you're the antiques expert."

"So you've brought me your own puzzle?" He chuckled as he examined the key. "It could go to many things. A chest or wardrobe. Maybe a door." He set the key on his desk. "Would you like me to do more research?"

"If you don't mind, as long as you don't lose it. It doesn't belong to anything I have." She settled back in the chair. "Can you tell me more about this column?"

Chester sat up straight. "As I mentioned, Mark is looking for someone to write an occasional column about quilts. One thousand words every other month or so. You're perfect. I knew it the moment I learned your reputation with quilts. Come, I'll introduce you to him now." Chester stood and moved to the door.

Sarah stared at him. "I've been thinking about it—I've never done anything like a column before."

"Talk to the man. It can't hurt to hear about it."

She shook her head. "What if—"

Chester held up a hand, stopping her words. He made a production of pulling back his sleeve and looking at his watch. "Oh, look at the time. We'll have to hurry if you're going to see Mark."

"I see you've got this all planned." Sarah stood and hitched her purse over her shoulder. He led her from his office, down the hall, and up a flight of stairs. He opened the door to the second floor and led her to the corner office. "Here we go. Mark's a good editor even if he is a tad young." Chester rapped on the door frame and then entered without waiting for an answer.

Sarah paused inside the door. A head poked above a tall executive-style chair. Mark held up a hand and kept talking on the phone, his back to them. Sounded like some type of advertising call. She couldn't imagine the kinds of tasks an editor had to handle.

"He's eager to meet you." Chester leaned close so his whispered words reached her.

"I can't imagine what you've told him then."

"Only that you're an intelligent woman with a talent for resurrecting antique quilts and solving mysteries. Your adventures have traveled far and wide." Chester shoved his hands in his pockets and grinned at her.

"Next you'll be telling me I need a press packet and a Web site."

"The Web site wouldn't be a bad idea."

Sarah slid her purse off her shoulder and held it in front of her like a weapon. "I enjoy keeping my business limited to word of mouth."

"Consider the column a way to spread that word."

Mark hung up and pivoted his chair until he faced them, then stood. Sarah tried to keep her surprise from showing. The man couldn't have been a day over thirty. His dark hair was longish, with waves across his forehead, and he wore a polo shirt shoved into baggy jeans. The complete antithesis to Chester's carefully groomed image.

"Mrs. Hart, it's a pleasure to meet you." He shook hands with Sarah with a firm motion. "Has Chester filled you in?"

"He mentioned a column."

"I bought this magazine a couple of years ago. It's doing well, but one thing our readers keep asking for is a column on quilts. Seems everyone has an antique quilt shoved in the back of their closets and they need to know how to care for it. Or they have quilts that need to be restored, or they want to know their value.

"While Chester's good at what he does, quilts are beyond his expertise. He suggested we bring you on board."

"I don't know ... "

"The column would start as an every other month deal. If you decide you like it, we could probably make it every month. Or if we don't have enough questions from readers, it wouldn't even have to be bimonthly. You could write it from home and e-mail it in."

Her own column? Could she really do something like that? True, quilts were her passion. But writing?

"Promise you'll consider it."

"When would you want the first column to appear?"

Mark leaned a hip on his desk and shrugged. "The next series of deadlines is the first of December. If that's not enough time, it could slide to the next issue. And it might take some tweaking to get the column right. Even after you submit it, we'll probably need to go back and forth a bit."

"Of course." Sarah nodded. "I'll pray about it and get back to you in a week or so."

A curious glint appeared in Mark's eyes. "All right. I'll look forward to your answer." He rubbed his hands together, and he winked at her. "A pleasure to meet you, and I look forward to working with you."

"Maybe." Sarah chuckled and stepped toward the door. "Thank you for the opportunity, Mark."

Chester ushered her to the front door. "You will think about it?"

"Of course. It's intriguing." She pushed the door open, then turned back around. "Thank you for dinner last night, Chester."

"I'd like to do it again."

"But you've already asked me to do the column. What will your excuse be next time?"

Sarah left her question hanging in the air between them as she smiled and walked to her car.

CHAPTER TWELVE

When Sarah finally returned to Maple Hill, she wasn't ready to go home. Her mind buzzed with the offer to write a column, along with other things. She pulled up in front of The Spotted Dog. Maybe a cup of coffee and one of Liam's pastries would help her settle down and focus.

Sarah hurried to the counter, but didn't see Liam back in the kitchen. Turning, she found him sitting at a booth with a dapper-looking man. Liam noticed her staring and waved her over.

"Ah, Sarah. Just the person I wanted to introduce to my new friend." Liam's smile was as full of blarney as his words. Liam gestured from Sarah to the man. "Mr. Vallard, this delightful woman is Sarah Hart. Sarah, Mr. Jacques Vallard is visiting from France."

"Bonjour."

The man's angular face lit up with her use of the simple French greeting. "Oui, bonjour, madam. It is a pleasure."

The man reached out to shake her hand, his grip firm but not overpowering. "What brings you to Maple Hill, Mr. Vallard."

"Let's say I am ... on sabbatical. Looking for a quiet place to relax."

"I've told him he's found the perfect place." Liam clapped his hands together. "What more could you ask for? Gorgeous mountains. Quiet town. And welcoming people. The big city is close, but you don't have to experience it every day. Perfection. Right here."

Sarah laughed at Liam's enthusiasm. "It *is* a wonderful place."

"If everyone is like you, then I must agree." Mr. Vallard settled back against the booth and pulled off his beret. Setting it on the seat next to him, he looked at Sarah. "Tell me about yourself. I think I already know everything there is to know about this crazy Irishman."

Liam shrugged. "I'm an open book."

Sarah enjoyed Vallard's soft accent, letting it settle over her. "There's not much to tell. I've lived in Maple Hill my whole life. So if you need anything, ask. I am curious though. Why Maple Hill? We're not that well known."

"True. I rented a car in Boston and drove. I didn't want the city and had heard the Berkshires are beautiful. For once the travel guides didn't lie."

"Where are you staying?"

The man shifted in his seat. "I have yet to decide. Suggestions?"

"There are several bed-and-breakfasts if you'd like some place more homey than a hotel." Liam stood and pulled a few handbills from a rack by the front door. "Here you go."

Sarah glanced over the ones he'd selected. "All of those are good. I bet they'd even give you an extended rate if you asked. That is, if you're staying more than a few days."

Mr. Vallard shrugged his thin shoulders. "Time will tell."

"The way of the French?"

"Maybe." His smile remained warm but his eyes reflected none of that warmth. Sarah wondered what had really brought him to the area. Few merely happened on Maple Hill. But she sensed he was a private man. One who wouldn't easily share.

She sat back and watched as Liam kept Jacques at ease with a steady line of stories about various Maple Hill residents. No surprise there, since Liam was one of the most outgoing people she knew. His Irish charm worked, and the Frenchman leaned back in the booth with a small smile.

After a few more minutes, Liam looked up and startled as if noticing something. "Sarah. You should have said something."

"What?"

"We've been so busy talking with our new friend, I haven't stopped to get your drink." He hurried toward the counter to prepare her chai latte.

Turning back to Vallard, she wondered if she'd be able to tease any details out of him. "What do you do in France?"

"A bit of this and more of that."

"Must be a nice position if it allows you the luxury of a sabbatical." Liam set a to-go cup in front of Sarah along with a lemon poppy seed muffin. "Thank you."

Jacques looked out the window over her shoulder. "I can't complain. But it was time to come to America. See this great country of yours."

Sarah took a sip, wondering why it felt like the Frenchman was avoiding giving out real information about himself even as he politely answered each question. The clock on the wall behind the counter showed that if she wanted to stop by the historical society before dropping by Maggie's, she'd need to hurry.

"Liam, thank you for the coffee and the treat. Mr. Vallard, it was a pleasure to meet you. I hope your stay is delightful." She slipped from her chair as Liam stood. "Good-bye."

Jacques Vallard reached for her hand, which she extended. He leaned down and brushed her hand with his lips. "Ma chérie." Heat climbed her cheeks at his unexpected gesture. "Good day, Mr. Vallard." She freed her hand and hurried from the store. She slid into her car and put her hands to her cheeks. What a silly reaction to an action that was second nature to the French. The man certainly meant nothing by it. But she could understand why women around the world found Frenchmen so charming.

With everything that had been going on, she'd been neglecting her quilt project at home. The *Country Cottage* editor would expect an answer from her soon, and the best way she knew to let her mind and heart evaluate his offer was to concentrate on something else. Working on the sampler quilt provided the perfect opportunity since she needed to finish her analysis of it anyway.

On her way home she stopped by the historical society, but found the door locked with a note that Irene would reopen in the morning. When she reached Jason and Maggie's house, as she'd promised Amy, there were no cars in the driveway. She knocked a couple of times, but no one answered, so she pulled a Post-it notepad from her purse and left a note. She'd have to catch up with her girls later.

She drove home and parked. She carried the latte offering into the sewing room and set it on the sewing machine, then settled on the chair in front of the quilt.

The left-hand column contained fairly easy to identify patterns. The top block had a small square in the center. Around that small square, triangles pivoted forming a pattern known as Flying Geese. The gray triangles were set against smaller blue triangles, provided a visual image of the flocks of geese that migrated south through the Massachusetts sky.

Beneath that block sat one that looked a lot like the sign to Vanessa's shop, the Wild Goose Chase. Again there was a small square in the center, this one a rich gold. Gold bands radiated out from it to form a cross. In each of the four squares that made up the corners of the block sat a large triangle with a smaller one behind it. The gold calico and brown fabrics didn't provoke an instant image like the Flying Geese block. Still it was a charming square.

The simple square beneath was a Windmill pattern. It must have taken no time at all to piece the large triangles in two fabrics into this easy design. The quilt maker had placed it in the same row as the intricately pieced Massachusetts square, a pattern that would have taken even a skilled quilter many long hours to complete.

The last block in the lower left-hand corner of the quilt had Sarah reaching for her pattern book again. Its construction was more complicated than the Windmill design. It was composed of nine squares—four corner squares pieced from pink and gray triangles, and alternating squares pieced from pink and gray rectangles. The center was a simple soft yellow square. Sarah was unsure what to call it, but after flipping through the section of her book that identified triangle-based patterns, she decided that it was actually an elaborate nine-patch block.

Sarah reviewed her notebook sketch and notes, then looked back at the quilt. She'd gleaned all the information she could from the quilt. But it couldn't be clearer that she was missing something.

Looking at the quilt, she couldn't imagine what.

The Split Rail pattern edged the right-hand side of the quilt. An interesting mix of green, brown, and cream calicoes, the rectangle held the familiar zigzag pattern. The rich brown paired well with the softer moss green, and it seemed very possible that the quilt's designer was trying to evoke an image of a fence against a green field.

Pulling her sewing basket from under the frame, she threaded stiff quilting thread through a needle. While she might not understand what overall design the quilt's creator had in mind, she could certainly reinforce and restore the quilt. Starting with the Split Rail section, she buttressed the loose stitches with her own. It was slow, painstaking work, but when she finished, the quilt would be restored to usefulness. And only someone who knew where she'd done her work would notice Sarah's contributions to the quilt.

When she had finished the Split Rail block, she turned to Cupid's Dart. Did the key to the puzzle lie in that pattern? Did it suggest that there were clues in the quilt to an old love story, one between a Haber boy and his sweetheart? Or between Kay and a beau? The Cupid's Dart block didn't really fit with the others with its mix of triangles shooting from left to right and back again. But if it was supposed to suggest a love story, shouldn't the pattern be in romantic shades of pinks and reds rather than fall colors?

After finishing her work on the square, Sarah dug through her sewing basket for thread that matched the colors of the Fox and Geese block. The minutes passed as she poked the needle in and out of the fabric. In the quiet she tried to decipher what she was missing.

Father, I'm here again. There's so much weighing me down. Jason, Maggie, the girls. Then there's the job with the magazine. And this silly quilt. Can you help me quiet my mind and turn over my cares to you?

She kept stitching as prayer continued to filter through her mind.

It is well... with my soul.

The words of the old hymn filled her mind. She sang the chorus over and over as she stitched, until she felt the burdens she'd placed before God lift. She continued singing as the words seeped into her heart and mind. "When peace like a river... attendeth my way..."

"You should sing more often."

Sarah poked her finger as she startled, then slipped the throbbing tip in her mouth before blood dripped on the quilt. Belle stood in the doorway, watching her. "You're home. I didn't expect you."

Belle grinned, her freckles seeming to dance on her face. "I didn't mean to interrupt your concert. I wanted you to know I'll be hiking tonight. The sky is clear, and it isn't too cold. Don't know how many more nights like this we'll have in the next few months."

"Are you sure you won't freeze?" A definite bite had filled the air outside.

"I'll be fine, though I'll take a tumbler of coffee along." She wrinkled her nose at Sarah, the same mischievous look crossing her face that colored Audrey's when she did the same.

"Have a good time and don't turn into a Popsicle. I'd hate to have to find you and thaw you out."

Belle laughed and then hurried back down the hall. The girl had to be the easiest boarder Sarah'd had in a long time. Having her around was certainly easier than unraveling the hidden secrets this quilt contained.

CHAPTER THIRTEEN

fter a couple of quiet days, Saturday morning dawned with a clear blue sky, one which hinted at a bright day perfect for an event like the one Maggie had planned. Sarah dressed with extra care. Instead of broken-in jeans, she paired her favorite khakis with a pretty evergreen sweater that had red, gold, and orange leaves sailing down the front. After putting makeup on her face and styling her graying blonde hair, Sarah left early for the store, planning to arrive at the village green long before Maggie opened the doors to customers. She slowed down when she saw Jacques Vallard entering Liam's.

When she pulled farther down the street toward Maggie's, she was surprised to find cars already lined the street. If they were any indication, Maggie had done a great job spreading the word on such short notice.

Sarah slipped from her car and dropped her keys in her purse before she noticed that a line of people waiting with items to be appraised extended outside the store.

"Excuse me." Sarah eased her way inside, sliding past a large oriental vase and then by a man holding a decoy duck. He must have read Chester's article and wanted to know if he owned a fifty thousand dollar piece of wood.

The sweet scent of cinnamon and spice tickled her nose as soon as she stepped inside the shop. Pumpkins and other harvest gourds stood in groupings in an attractive display in front of a mahogany dresser. By the cash register a plate of cookies and muffins greeted guests next to a silver urn of what looked like apple cider. How had Maggie found time to bake?

Maggie saw Sarah and flitted in her direction, stopping to say a word to most of the people wandering around on her way.

Sarah hugged the woman. "This looks and smells amazing. How did you pull it off?"

"The fruit of many sleepless nights this week." She looked around the store and smiled. "It's already worth every moment."

"I'm so proud of you. You weren't even supposed to open for another hour."

"Thank you." Maggie closed her eyes as if soaking in the words of praise. "I didn't think I could leave everybody standing in the cold. I just wish Chester would get here."

He shoved his way through the door. "Good morning, ladies." He took Maggie's hand in his. "It appears you've done a masterful job."

Maggie flushed, but stood an inch taller. "I'm honored you could come."

Chester eyed Sarah, something melancholy in his expression. "Sarah, a delight to see you again."

"Thank you. It looks like you'll be busy appraising at everyone's treasures."

Maggie looked from one to the other, then seemed to notice the buzz vibrating in the room. She slipped behind the counter and perched on the stool. "Good morning, everyone. Thank you for joining us. I'd like to introduce our special guest. Chester Winslow is an antiques expert and magazine columnist with *Country Cottage*. We're delighted to have him with us." Chester gave a half bow as a smattering of applause interrupted her. "He'll be in the far corner over there. Please form a line, and I'm sure he'll examine your treasures as soon as he can."

She stepped down and ushered Chester to the cozy corner she'd set up with two overstuffed chairs and a wrought-iron coffee table. She'd positioned several large lamps around the area so it was washed in light. A line of people followed them. After he was settled, she hurried back to Sarah, a sparkle of excitement in her eyes. "Can you believe this?"

"Amazing."

"Would you keep an eye on Chester while you mingle and welcome people? If he needs anything, can you make sure he gets it? Then I can stay close to the counter and ring up sales. Don't forget to encourage everyone to shop while they wait. I hope he has time to see everyone."

"I'm sure he'll be gracious." Sarah studied the antiques expert. As he examined a book Nina Forrester had handed him, he exuded the same kindness and intelligence she'd seen at dinner.

Sarah slipped closer to listen to Nina weave her story about her grandfather's journal. According to her, her grandfather had fought with Teddy Roosevelt in the Spanish-American War. The woman seemed to think her grandfather had single-handedly given the future president the strategy he used in battles. Sarah had her doubts.

She smiled when she saw Pastor John Peabody a few spots back in line. He carried a large vase she'd seen in his home on occasion. "John. How are you today?"

"Enjoying the excitement. Maggie's had some fun, hasn't she?"

"Ask her after today if it was worth it. Hoping this vase is worth a fortune?"

"No. It was a good excuse to join the fun." He stepped forward as Nina abandoned the chair, a pleased smile plastered on her face. "Wonder what he told her."

Sarah glanced at Chester. "I hope the truth mixed with kindness."

"Any reason to think otherwise?"

"No. Good to see you, John. I'd better get back to work."

She stopped several times to exclaim over the items people had brought. Irene stood in line holding a sword that must have weighed more than she did. Each time the line moved, she'd heft the thing and inch forward a couple of feet. People seemed content to give her a wide berth. Irene waved Sarah over.

"Can you believe this? I actually got Nathaniel's sword here."

"That must have taken a lot of effort."

"You have no idea." Irene winked at her. "But it's worth it to be able to learn if it has value and share one of Nathaniel's stories if I can. Here." The woman handed the sword to Sarah, then stretched her arms. "How do men carry them?" She reclaimed the sword and moved forward again. Behind Irene, a couple carried an armload of dusty books.

Sarah stifled a laugh as a man walked in wearing a Civil War uniform. And the woman behind him carried a small frame with a pastoral painting.

Maggie wandered by and bumped her shoulder into Sarah's. "I'll have you take him to lunch if we can squeeze in a break."

"Don't get any ideas, young woman."

"Who me?" Maggie might pretend innocence, but Sarah was only halfway kidding. She didn't need Maggie getting any crazy romantic notions.

Chester handled those who came in with a diplomacy and skill that gave each person the sense they'd brought a treasure even if it didn't have market value.

He'd worked his way through the first few when Curtis Haber strolled in, Louise a step behind him. She smiled at

Sarah, while Curtis ignored her. Instead, he walked slowly along the line of people. People began to shift from side to side as he scrutinized the items they'd brought.

"What is he doing?" Maggie hissed.

"I don't know, but maybe I can find out." Sarah hurried to Louise's side. "Louise, how good to see you. Did you bring something to be examined?"

The woman heaved a sigh. "No. We were walking by and saw all the excitement."

"It's something, isn't it? I don't think Maggie imagined this many people turning out."

"Did they all bring something?"

"Yes." Sarah smiled as Irene walked out, a big grin on her face. Whatever Chester had told her must have made her day. "It's been an interesting parade."

"Have you seen anything from the farm?"

"Heavens, I don't know." Sarah scanned the crowd. "There was so much at the sale, and I didn't see it all."

"I have a feeling Curtis will ask every person."

"Still looking for your heirloom?"

Louise nodded.

"Well, good luck with that." Sarah met Maggie at the counter. "He's still looking for that heirloom."

Maggie rolled her eyes. "I hope he has a better idea of what he's looking for then. I can't have him scaring everyone away. Not when they're actually shopping."

New people came through in a steady stream, keeping Curtis near the door, and making it fairly easy to keep track of him. Most people seemed mildly annoyed with his bumbling attention. For the most part he stared at what they held from a pace or two away, then he'd step to the next person or wait as the line moved past him.

Around one o'clock, the line eased though the Habers maintained their vigilant watch for the mysterious heirloom. Now they did it from a seat on one of the sofas.

Maggie handed some money to Sarah. "Why don't you grab sandwiches for you and Chester while you can? Bring them back here, and you can eat in the storeroom."

Sarah's stomach grumbled before she could protest. "All right. Seems you have a point." She hurried down the street to Liam's.

Liam stood behind the counter when she entered, and at the sight of her, laugh lines appeared around his green eyes. "I love it when the wind blows in a lovely lady. What can I get you this fine November day?"

"A club sandwich." What would Chester want? Sarah couldn't believe she'd forgotten to ask. "Better make that two and a roast beef with all the fixings."

"So how's the show going at the store?"

Sarah laughed. "Not exactly a show, though I guess everyone is showing off the things they value." She leaned against the counter, curling and uncurling her toes in her shoes, images of the outlandish and valuable treasures people had brought in parading through her mind. "You should have seen Irene Stuart hefting Nathaniel Bradford's sword. I'm so proud of Maggie. She did an amazing amount of work this week to make today a success. You would be amazed at the things people have brought."

"That girl has a touch." Liam added lettuce and tomato to the roast beef. "Does she want her sandwich toasted?"

"I don't know. Do whatever she usually orders." Sarah watched Liam pull the ingredients together for the club sandwiches.

The two chatted until Liam handed her a bag loaded with the sandwiches and chips. "Here you go. Don't be a stranger."

Sarah slipped from the counter and out the door. As soon as she reentered the store, Maggie shooed her to the back storeroom.

"Chester's waiting there."

"What about your sandwich? You could eat first."

"No, I have to stay up here, and I don't have the growling stomach. I'll wait." Maggie gave her a light push in the back. "Go on."

Sarah saluted her with the bag. "Yes, ma'am."

Chester sat at a dilapidated table in the back. Someday Maggie would transform it into a treasure, but right now it didn't look like much.

"I hope you like club sandwiches and chips."

"Sounds perfect."

Sarah studied him as she handed him a sandwich, a bag of chips, and a can of Coke. He'd done a great job today, but she imagined he had to be about talked out. "How has today gone so far? Find anything interesting?"

"Run-of-the-mill family treasures. A journal here, photograph there, a sword, and the occasional piece of truly beautiful art. Massachusetts is old enough that there are interesting finds. Did you bring anything for me to look at?" Chester picked up his sandwich and took a bite.

"No."

"Ah. I expected a lover of all things old to have something for me." Chester dabbed his mouth with a napkin. "History's mysteries can lie hidden in the simplest items. Take that letter box I bought from Maggie. The stories it could tell of letters. Challenges, joys, the cycles of life."

Sarah smiled, encouraged by the thought she'd met someone who understood her love for the stories. "Exactly. That's why I've always loved working on old quilts, as well as restoring them for the enjoyment of the family."

"The same thing attracted me to antiques. I've always liked finding the stories behind family treasures. I'll never understand how uninterested some people are." He took another bite and chewed, comfortable in the ensuing silence. "Take all those fine folks who wandered through this morning. How many will actually take my suggestions to unearth the rest of the story about their pieces?"

They ate in silence, then crumpled their sandwich papers, sticking all the trash back into the bag.

Sarah looked at her watch, then started. "We've left poor Maggie alone too long."

"If she needed us, I dare say she would have found us."

"True." Sarah stood and brushed the crumbs from her khakis. "I'll let you get back to the adoring hoards."

The bell that hung over the front door jangled. "I really should check on Maggie. See if she needs any help."

"Join me for tea?" Chester studied her, hope filling his eyes.

"We just had lunch together."

"True. But I'm in town, and it seems the perfect excuse to spend more time together." The force he put behind the words made her hope he really wanted to and wasn't being kind.

Sarah rubbed her collarbone as she considered him. What could a cup of tea and a scone hurt? "I'd like that."

"All right then. After the melee's over, we'll find a spot."

Sarah picked her way around the piles of furniture to the front room. What a wonderful day for Maggie. All the people in and out of the store had to have had a positive effect on sales. In fact, most seemed to have left with something more than they'd brought in based on the store's picked-over appearance.

Sarah pushed a strand of hair behind her ear and headed toward Maggie. She froze when she heard a raised voice.

CHAPTER FOURTEEN

B ut you've got to help me." Curtis stood at the counter, shoulders stooped forward as he stared at Maggie.

"Mr. Haber, there is nothing I can do to help you." Maggie had crossed her arms over her chest and didn't attempt to hide her annoyance. "I've already let you loiter here most of the day, harassing my customers, and making many feel uncomfortable with your staring. Talk to Bob Spencer. He ran the estate sale and would have the records of who bought what items."

Curtis snorted, then ran a hand over his hair. "You think I haven't tried that? If most people kept records like his firm, the IRS would have a field day. I can't piece together anything from entries like 'bought lot of household goods.'"

"What do you expect?" Maggie smiled as a customer approached. "If you'll excuse me, I have to help this person."

Curtis opened his mouth, and Sarah hurried forward, intent on coming to Maggie's defense before he could question her further. A restraining hand on her arm held her back. She turned to Chester. "What?"

"Be careful."

Shaking his hand off, Sarah marched toward the altercation. Louise Haber stood a few feet behind Curtis Haber and shot Sarah a small smile before turning her gaze to the floor. The woman looked as if she wanted nothing more than to be somewhere else.

"Curtis Haber." Sarah arrived at Maggie's side and tried to keep her voice pleasant. "You can trust Maggie's word. If she could help, she would."

"Why won't she show me what she purchased? I could at least see those items."

"You picked a busy day to come in asking for something like that. Maybe another day."

Maggie finished ringing up a customer and turned back to the Habers. "I don't mind showing Mr. Haber what I have left. But I can't do it right now." Maggie's voice had a conciliatory tone to it, smooth as any surface she'd refinished.

Louise said quietly. "Curtis, can't we go home?"

Curtis put a hand on her arm, and she stopped. "Not yet, honey." The word oozed from his mouth like he wasn't quite used to saying it. He glanced around the shop.

Maggie's brow crinkled as she eyed Curtis. "I've thoroughly inspected each piece and haven't seen anything special or valuable. I'm sorry."

Louise moved toward Curtis, and placed a hand on his shoulder. She whispered in his ear, and he nodded. He turned back to Maggie. "Maybe you could show me what you have and we could look the pieces over."

"I've already resold some of the items, but I'll show you what I have another time." Another customer approached the counter with a stack of antique lace tablecloths. "Right now I have to take care of my customers." She smiled at the woman and rang up her purchases.

Curtis glowered at her, but turned and marched toward the line that stretched to the door again. As Sarah watched, his posture relaxed and he pasted on a charming smile.

"Excuse me, Miss. Looks like you're quite the reader. Could you tell me where you got those books?"

The woman eyed him, then shifted the stack of books away from Curtis and frowned. She moved forward without a word, brushing him with her shoulder as she passed.

Undeterred, Curtis turned to the next person in line, another out of towner, and repeated the process. This woman at least told him the small painting had been in her family for generations. She launched into a story about how family lore said the painter was the Gilbert Stuart who painted the famous portraits of George Washington. Curtis stepped back and moved to the next person before she could go on.

Sarah's gaze followed him as he continued to work the line.

Sometime during their hushed conversation, Chester had moved back to his table in the corner, taking most of the attention with him. A few people milled in the store, looking at various items, while most lined up for appraisals.

Louise stepped closer to Sarah. "Could you show me what you remember Maggie buying? Then I can try to get Curtis to leave."

"I'll show you what I remember, but she bought so many things."

Sarah stepped toward the area filled with large pieces of furniture. "Maggie's already sold a few pieces. You should have seen this large dresser she bought. Looked like it would fill one of my small bedrooms."

She led Louise to the bed frame, pointing out the SOLD tag. "Could this be the heirloom?"

Louise shook her head, long earrings bouncing with each shake. "I can't see how."

"It would help if you could tell me anything about this heirloom." Sarah tried to keep the skepticism from her voice, but she'd begun to tire of their incessant search for something they couldn't describe. Maybe Chester was right, and they were frauds. But to what purpose? What could they gain from a piece of furniture that would be worth the elaborate charade?

"I wish I could. All I know is there's great sentimental value attachment to it. Curtis tells me family members always talked about it at reunions."

"You haven't heard the talk yourself?"

Color rushed into Louise's cheeks. "No. I've never attended."

"Maggie bought mainly large pieces of furniture. I bought the quilts, but Curtis checked them at the sale."

"It's not the quilts, we're confident of that." Louise wrinkled her nose and shuddered.

The bell rang as the door opened. Sarah glanced up and noticed the line for Chester was almost gone. Curtis sat slumped in a high-backed chair. "Looks like Curtis is ready to leave."

Louise startled and nodded. "Thanks for showing me what you could." She hurried to Curtis's side, and the two had a heated but hushed conversation. Sarah itched to hear what they were debating but hurried to the counter instead.

Maggie kept a wary eye on the couple as she smiled and handed Mrs. Webber a bag. "Thanks for coming in today."

"My pleasure. Be sure to let me know if you have Chester back. What a delightful man." Mrs. Webber zipped her purse closed, smiled at Maggie and Sarah, and then hurried toward the door.

"Any luck?" Maggie's shoulders tensed as if she weren't sure what answer she wanted to hear.

"No. It would certainly help if either of them could give some description of this mystery piece they want to find."

Maggie stifled a yawn and nodded. "It seems like an odd search."

The bell rang again as Curtis and Louise opened the door and left. Maggie's shoulders relaxed and she sighed. "What a relief to have him leave. Can you believe he eyed every item brought in?"

"No, I can't believe you didn't kick him out."

"I was tempted. Trust me." Maggie slipped her feet from her shoes and wiggled her toes. "I'm just glad they left without causing too much of a scene."

Chester's voice carried across the quiet store. "Let's see what treasure you've brought with you today." His voice held no trace of concern, and drew everyone toward him. "I see. What a beautiful example of a first edition."

Those who were shopping wandered toward him to see what he'd examine next. Sarah slipped an arm around Maggie's shoulders. "Why don't you go eat your sandwich?"

Maggie nodded and headed to the storeroom, her posture straight.

When the front door opened again, Sarah looked toward it, hoping it wasn't the Habers returning with more demands and questions. She smiled when she saw her handsome son enter, dressed in khakis and a shirt and tie.

"Where's my lovely bride? I wanted to see how her day's gone."

"It's been a crazy day."

"Crazy good?" Worry creased his brow. "I'd meant to get away at lunchtime, but couldn't."

"You can be very proud of the great job she did." Sarah gestured to the emptying store. "It's been full of people most of the day. The cash register should be very happy when she closes tonight."

Jason rubbed his hands together with a grin. "As long as she's happy."

"Go find out. She's in the back room eating a late lunch."

"Thanks."

"You're welcome. I'll stay here until she's ready to come back." Sarah turned to help a customer wanting to purchase a stack of weathered *Life* magazines.

When Maggie and Jason returned fifteen minutes later, Maggie had a relaxed and pleased expression on her face. Jason kissed her cheek before hurrying back out the door. He winked at Sarah on his way past.

Finally five o'clock arrived, bringing Chester's appraisals to an end. He approached Sarah, briefcase in hand. "Ready for our tea?"

Sarah glanced at Maggie.

"Go on. I've got everything under control." Maggie turned to Chester, taking his hand in hers. "Thank you for everything."

"A privilege. I'll look forward to a repeat event."

"Thank you." Maggie squeezed Sarah. "I couldn't have handled today without you. Thanks for everything."

"I enjoyed it. Call if you need anything else."

"Just enjoy your tea." Maggie winked, and Sarah felt warmth flush her cheeks. When was the last time she'd blushed like one of her granddaughters?

Sarah and Chester exited the store and strolled down the sidewalk. The day was still clear, a crisp blue with a few scattered clouds punctuating the sky. It was a perfect fall afternoon as a soft breeze blew, teasing more leaves from the large maples.

Chester looked at her. "Where would you suggest?"

"How about The Spotted Dog?"

"The Spotted Dog it is. Lead on."

Moments later they stood in front of the menu board. Liam exited the kitchen and stood in front of them. A friendly smile creased his face as he addressed Chester. "The man of the hour. Nice to have you here. What can I get you?" He noticed Sarah. "Sarah, nice to have you back, too."

"Liam, have you met Chester Winslow? He's been at Maggie's giving appraisals."

"I do believe I've seen you around, Mr. Winslow. Delighted to have you back. Tell me, was it my fresh scones?" Liam grinned at Chester, who squirmed a tad.

"The scone was good. Do you have any left this afternoon?"

Before Liam could respond, the click of tiny nails on the wood floor pulled Sarah's gaze down. "Oh, hello, Murphy. Shh, don't tell anyone, Chester, but he's a regular feature here."

Murphy sniffed each of Chester's legs, then sat down, short tail wagging. Chester looked askance at the dog.

"Don't worry. Murphy is harmless."

"I'm sure you're right, but I will be glad to see him focus his attention elsewhere."

Liam took their orders and within minutes Sarah and Chester settled at a front table in front of the windows with their tea and scones.

"Can I ask you a question?" Chester said.

Sarah pulled herself back to the moment. "Yes?"

"Why attend the Haber auction?"

"That's an interesting question." He shrugged with a smile, and Sarah considered her response. "I went to keep Maggie company. We enjoy old things...so estate sales are a fun outing. I didn't have my eye on anything but found the quilts."

Interest sparked in Chester's eyes, deepening their gray color. "Anything interesting about them? Maybe one could form the basis for your first column."

Sarah swirled the tea in her mug, watching it slosh up the sides of the cup. "I don't know. So far three of them are pretty battered, one is a nice patriotic pattern and the other is a crazy sampler quilt."

"Maybe pick that one. If it's 'crazy,' there's probably a reason." Chester shrugged, and picked up his mug.

"If there is, I haven't found it yet."

"Wouldn't it be a captivating piece? A quilt expert who can figure out any hidden meaning of mystery quilts with unusual designs. It makes a good column topic."

Sarah sipped her tea, not sure how much of Chester's words she could accept at face value. "I don't know that I can figure it out in time for Mark's deadline. If I accept."

"You will. Why wouldn't you? You have nothing to lose by trying."

"True." Sarah smiled. "It would be incredible to see my name in a magazine. Me, with a column."

The conversation drifted to other topics and Sarah found herself enjoying the time as much as she'd enjoyed their dinner at the Old Mill. Occasionally, Liam drifted toward them, but he always stopped at a table to chat with another customer. When they had finished, Chester walked her to her car near the store. "Thank you for a delightful break. I had a great time and would love to do this again."

"I would, too."

"Until the next time then."

Sarah climbed into her car and waved. Chester's words about Curtis Haber being an imposter came back to her. In light of Curtis's actions today, she didn't know what to think about the man. Maybe it was time to do some digging.

CHAPTER FIFTEEN

arah sat in her car a moment.

If she was going to write a column based on the sampler, Sarah needed something more than she'd found in her initial examinations of the quilt. Maybe Vanessa Sawyer, the owner of the Wild Goose Chase, could help her. If she hurried, she'd get there with a few minutes to spare before Vanessa locked up for the night. Ever since Vanessa and her husband had separated, she closed the store promptly each night so she could spend as much time as possible with her two kids.

Climbing out of her car, Sarah walked down the block and entered the shop on the green. Sleigh bells hanging from the doorknob announced her arrival. Vanessa Sawyer, the petite proprietor, turned from her perch on a ladder.

"What on earth are you doing, Vanessa?" Sarah stared at her on her precarious post.

"Trying to find a skein of yarn. Seems I've misplaced Martha's special order." The woman brushed her arm across her forehead. "Leave it to me to do that."

"With all the things you have tucked in here, I'm not surprised."

Vanessa laughed and hopped down from the ladder. "What brings you here tonight?"

"I bought a few quilts at the Haber sale and I'm working on one. It's a sampler quilt, but I can't shake the feeling I'm missing something obvious about it." Sarah pulled her quilt notebook from her purse and opened it to her sketch of the patterns. "Have you ever seen a quilt with so many mismatched blocks?"

Vanessa took the notebook and studied the drawing. After a minute, she shook her head. "Not this many. Have you studied the blocks?"

"I've spent a couple of nights working on the quilt, but this one is stumping me. I've identified the patterns, but have no idea how they relate to each other. Yet I'm convinced one person pieced and quilted all of them."

"The stitching is that uniform?"

"Yes." Sarah shrugged. "I hoped you might have an idea. Something to get me looking at it from a new perspective."

"I really like this one," Vanessa pointed at the block in the bottom row at the left side. "Puss in the Corner tucked next to a Shoo Fly variation and Windmill. That's an unusual arrangement."

"That's not Puss in the Corner. It's a modified nine-patch block."

Vanessa walked to the bookshelves lining the wall behind the counter and pulled out a volume that held glossy illustrations with captions, making it a perfect coffee-table book. She flipped until she reached a page midway through. Tapping a photo, she smiled triumphantly and tilted it toward Sarah. "Here you go. Puss in the Corner. I've loved that pattern ever since my grandma taught me how to make it."

Sarah studied the illustration and then her sketch. She had to admit they were close. "Maybe you're right."

"It could be either, but based on what I see of the quilt, I'd look at the squares again, this time looking for alternative names." Vanessa reclaimed the encyclopedia and flipped through the pages to the index. "You can look up the names here. In no time, you'll know if there are more names."

Of course. She couldn't believe she hadn't thought of that. The squares probably had more than one name. Maybe if she identified those, order would emerge from what looked like chaos.

"Why don't you borrow this book? It can help you identify alternative names for each pattern."

"Thanks, Vanessa." Sarah caught her friend glancing at her watch. "I'll get out of here so you can close and get home to those precious kids."

"My pleasure." Vanessa followed her to the door, and then locked it as Sarah left.

Could Vanessa be right? Might part of Sarah's frustration in trying to decipher the quilt's story come from the fact that some of the squares had different names? And if she was right, how would Sarah know which names were the right ones? There had to be an overarching theme. She'd just have to look at the quilt again with the intention of finding that theme.

With her car still sitting in front of The Spotted Dog, Sarah headed back that way. She tugged her coat collar higher, warding off the bite in the air.

Liam wiped down a table in front of a window as she passed. He rapped on the window, and she looked at him, a smile creasing her lips at the sight of him. The man gestured at the encyclopedia she was carrying. Sarah entered the store and waited for Liam to join her.

"What have you there?"

"A quilt encyclopedia."

Liam reached for the volume and pretended to stagger under its weight. "Where did you get this? It weighs too much for you to carry it far."

"It's fine. Vanessa's lending it to me for a project I'm working on."

He examined the spine and author information. "Maybe I should order one for the shop."

"I could use it."

"Consider it done. Let me borrow this a moment to capture the important information."

Sarah nodded and stood next to the counter as he went into the kitchen. Then she glanced around and spotted

Jacques Vallard seated across from her favorite overstuffed chair. He acknowledged her stare with a slight dip of his chin. "Ah, the charming seamstress graces me with her presence."

Liam stepped out of the kitchen and arched an eyebrow. "Someone other than me is laying the blarney on a wee bit thick."

"You could say that." Sarah kept her voice low but could tell by the smirk on Liam's face he'd heard. "A chai latte, please."

"One minute." Liam handed her the book then whipped a cup from the rack and went to work on his machine. While Sarah watched, Murphy walked over for his back scratch. She complied, then smiled as Liam handed her the steaming cup. "Watch yourself. It's extra hot this evening."

"Thanks." Sarah turned with the cup in her hand, heat seeping through the protective sleeve. Should she join Vallard?

The Frenchman stood and bowed toward the chair across from him. "Madam, please honor me by joining me."

Liam snorted, and Sarah barely stifled a snort of her own. Instead, she tipped her head in acknowledgment and walked to the chair.

"Bonjour, Monsieur Vallard."

His grin practically split his face. "You know French."

"Un peu. It's been too long since my high school classes."

"Understood. Here . . . sit . . . I have something to show you. Something Liam thought you might help with." Jacques settled into his chair and rubbed his hands together. "When he mentioned you, I hoped to run into you. I did not think you wanted me, a stranger, at your house."

Sarah blew on her tea, then took a sip. "I'm here now."

"So you are." He bent over and pulled a small attaché case onto his lap. He popped it open and rifled through its contents. "Ah. Here it is." He handed her a small black-and-white photo. "This is a photo of a family my grandfather knew. They may be from this area. Mais oui, there is no way to know for sure." He waved a hand, his gaze never leaving the photo she now held. "Perchance can you help me? Mr. Connolly said you like to help with riddles."

"That's true. Are you looking for the family?"

Vallard shrugged, the gesture mirroring a cat's languid stretch. "I am curious. My grandfather talked about the girl. My natural curiosity takes over. Do you recognize them?"

She pulled on reading glasses and examined the faces in the photo. An older couple, a young man, and a young woman stood in front of a worn white house. "This must have been taken during World War II. See the flag in the window? That looks like a Blue Star flag, a way for people to let others know they had a family member serving in the war. With two stars, it means two boys were fighting. And one of the stars appears covered in gold, so one had already died." Her throat closed at the thought of what it must have been like to receive a telegram with such terrible news.

"You are a compassionate woman."

"I hope so." She swallowed and pulled the photo close again. "Looks like they are on a farm. That's a barn in the background." A barn that looked a lot like the one on the Haber place. She tried to remember Willard's service photo. The young man might be him. "I can't be completely sure."

"Even a guess would help satisfy my curiosity."

Sarah glanced at the photo again, then handed it back to him. "It's possible this is the Haber farm. The home looks similar, but I don't see the current porch. Based on the star flags, it was taken during World War II after Kevin and Eric had enlisted. And after Eric died. That would make the young man Willard Haber, and the young woman next to him is Kay."

"Certainement." He held the photo a moment. "She was a beautiful woman. Do you know what happened to these two?"

"Both served in the war on the European front. I don't know much about Kay other than that she served in the Red Cross, but Willard died only a couple of months ago. As far as I know, he always lived on the family farm."

He shrugged. "Would you like to keep the photo for a while?"

"Yes. Yes, I would." Sarah accepted it, looking at the somber faces. How had Vallard gotten an old photo of the Habers? Could he somehow be connected to the mystery that continued to build around them? "I need to be going. Enjoy your time here."

"Merci for your help." He touched his forehead in a salute. "Until next time."

"You're welcome."

Mr. Vallard stayed seated as Sarah rose, some of his charm evaporating with the lack of courtesy.

When she reached home, Sarah sat down at her computer. She set Jacques's photo next to the monitor, wondering what his connection to the Habers could be. But for now, she wanted to investigate whether Chester might be right in his allegation that the Habers were frauds.

She'd considered the charge on her drive home and had come to the conclusion that the best way to test his theory was to identify whether another Curtis Haber remained in Florida. Opening her browser, she entered "Curtis Haber" and "Florida." Many things came up but none related to her search string.

Maybe the white pages would be a better help.

Sarah opened a new tab and clicked the bookmark to the online phone book. The site spit out one Curtis Haber in Florida with a phone number. One Curtis Haber in St. Petersburg, Florida. One number to call.

She took a deep breath, then stood and grabbed the phone. She dialed and waited as the number rang. And rang. And rang. When no one answered and an answering machine didn't pick up, Sarah hung up. Then she hit print to capture the number. No one might have answered this time, but it didn't mean she wouldn't try again. There was still too much she didn't know about the Habers.

CHAPTER SIXTEEN

S unday afternoon Sarah's thoughts spun in a dozen directions, none of them comfortable. Jason had taken Maggie and the girls out of town after church to celebrate the great success of the store's event.

Their absence made the silence in Sarah's home seem suffocating. She'd called Jenna and her family, but they weren't home either. She needed something to set her mind on. The door to her sewing room stood open and the colorful kaleidoscope of mismatched fabric caught her attention. Maybe reinforcing more squares on the quilt would quiet her mind as it kept her hands busy.

She filled a glass of water from the faucet and headed into the room. What was it about the quilt with its lack of an overall pattern that captivated her? Was it simply that she associated it with the crazy auction? And the Habers? Or was it the challenge of the quilt's puzzle? Usually she was attracted to quilts with harmonious patterns and colors.

This one wasn't like that at all. In fact, its patterns and fabrics ran more to cacophony than harmony. Yet as she ran a hand over it, she knew she couldn't sell this quilt.

The last rays of sunshine filtered through the lace curtains. She flipped on the light and pulled out her basket of quilt thread and needles. After threading a needle, she started reinforcing the quilting on the Star and Cross pattern.

She'd identified at least one name for each pattern. But after Vanessa's comments at the Wild Goose Chase, she wondered. *Had she found the right names? And did the names even matter?*

Steadily, she worked down the seams for the pattern, careful to match her stitches to the original quilter's tiny stitches. For someone who'd created such a haphazard mix of patterns, her stitches were the precise and ordered ones of a professional quilter. Someone who delighted in creating.

As soon as she finished that square, Sarah pulled out her notebook with the sketch of the quilt. She ran down the list again: Flying Geese, Weathervane, the diamond pattern, Flower Garden, Split Rail, Wild Goose Chase, Shoo Fly..., the list of patterns looked complete. Unless there were multiple names.

She opened to a clean two-page spread and wrote the pattern names in a grid across the pages and halfway down them. The only way she could think to identify whether she'd missed names was to go through Vanessa's encyclopedia looking up each block. She might not know the theme of the quilt yet, but she was fairly certain one existed. And maybe if she identified other names, she'd find it.

After she retrieved Vanessa's book, she sat in front of the quilt. The scent of the woman's floral perfume lingered on the volume. She said a prayer for her friend as she opened the book. Sarah randomly turned the pages looking for anything that matched what she saw on the quilt.

Finally she turned to the index, and she found the pattern Vanessa had identified. Puss in the Corner. The encyclopedia did not list multiple names for Puss in the Corner. She made a note of that on her grid, and moved to what she'd thought was a Shoo Fly variation pattern next to it. The index listed nine different Shoo Fly patterns. She looked each up until she found the one that matched her block. There were six possible names for the same pattern. She scanned the list. How would she know which one was right?

Hen and Chicks? Ducks and Ducklings? She'd have to write all the options down and keep looking. Maybe after she'd worked through all the patterns, the elusive theme would finally make itself clear.

The next pattern to the right was the one she'd identified as Bird's Eye View. Checking the index, she quickly flipped to the number listed for the pattern and found that Bird's Eye View was also known as Wheel of Chance.

The Fox and Geese pattern between Bird's Eye View and Split Rail also had multiple names. She entered each name in the grid, then studied the new list. It was another group of names without an obvious connection.

Sarah rubbed the back of her neck and her breathing quickened. Why was this such a maddening process?

She looked at the list. What was she missing? Or was she trying to force something that simply wasn't there? Maybe she wanted to believe there was a story to this quilt so much that she was imagining one where it didn't really exist.

She arched her back and closed her eyes. After a moment, she opened her eyes and studied the list again. Was there anything that might tie it to the Habers? She'd assumed Mrs. Haber or Kay had created the quilt. Was that a valid assumption?

Sarah had never imagined Willard hunched over pieces of fabric, especially considering the careful stitches. Men tended to be more utilitarian with their sewing, while women focused on precision and beauty. But she was no closer to knowing whether it was Mrs. Haber or Kay who had quilted the sampler. One thing that bothered Sarah was that she had absolutely no memories of Kay. Shouldn't she have a few, no matter how vague, after growing up in Maple Hill? Or had Kay moved at some point? Another research trail she should track down. And the historical society would be the place to find what she needed.

It wouldn't be open on a Sunday afternoon, so she'd have to wait until the next day. Might as well keep working on the patterns.

Sarah worked her way systematically across the next row from left to right. After weaving her way across the four patterns, she was ready to throw her hands up and walk away. The Windmill pattern had fifteen different names. Massachusetts joined Puss in the Corner as a pattern that had only one, beautiful, lovely, solitary name. She put a star next to that pattern in the grid. There was nothing left to research on at least that square. But the next pattern, Star and Cross, could have seven different names, and the last one before Split Rail, a Grandma's Garden pattern, could have any of ten names.

After adding all those names to the grid, the bottom half of it looked like a shopping list with a variety of options. Somewhere in that mix lay a cohesive pattern. An answer to whatever puzzle lay buried inside the random-seeming patterns.

She hated the fact that she knew with certainty only two patterns' names. But it was a start. A place to begin.

Why had Willard never married? Had Kay? If not, had they lived lonely lives? Willard's had seemed full, at least from her vantage point, but she really hadn't known the man well. The thought left her feeling vaguely empty now. She'd had a full life with Gerry, but she missed him. Missed being able to tell him what she was thinking. Missed gaining his perspective on the things that bothered her. And missed the hundred and one ways he could make her feel special and loved throughout the day.

The thought made her miss her kids. How she loved them and delighted in the fact that they'd found great spouses and wonderful careers.

Her only regret was that Jenna lived so far away. Her daughter loved living in Texas with her family, and that distance stretched between them. It had been so long since she'd seen Jenna and her family.

Glancing at the clock, she decided it certainly wouldn't hurt to try Jenna, just to say hi. Worst case scenario, she'd leave another message, and they'd play a few more rounds of phone tag before connecting. She dialed Jenna's number, then waited as the phone rang. She was braced for voice mail to come on when Jenna picked up.

"Mom? Is everything okay?"

The wonders of caller ID still startled Sarah on occasion. "Hey, sweetie. Everything's fine. I was missing you, that's all."

"You called at a great time. We just got back from Thomas's basketball game."

"He's old enough for that?"

"You wouldn't believe how young kids are when they start sports these days. He even made a basket and he's proud as he can be."

"How are things going with your job?"

"Great! They've offered me a promotion, one I didn't expect for a while yet. Looks like they think I'm ready to manage accounts."

"That's wonderful news, honey."

Jenna bubbled with enthusiasm about the new position with the marketing agency. The girl had found a way to harness her creativity, and from what she said, she was in high demand. Then she turned to stories about the boys' latest antics, almost frenetic in her recounting.

"That's great." Sarah felt her chest swell with pride.

"I love you, Mom, but you don't call that often just to chat. What's up?" Jenna's bell-like laugh filled an empty space in Sarah's heart.

"Is there any way you can come home for Thanksgiving? It's been such a long time since I've seen you."

"But you know we're planning to come in the summer."

Sarah sighed. "I know. The boys will have changed so much in the months between then and now. I guess I'd hoped we could all get together. Now that Jason and Maggie are here with the girls, it would be a perfect holiday if you were here to share it with us. It's been too long since we've all been together."

"Mom, I don't know. Things are so busy at work, it would be a real challenge to slip away even for a few days. And plane tickets could be crazy for all of us. Four's a lot to purchase."

Sarah sighed again, trying to keep it quiet, but Jenna must have heard.

"I'm sorry, Mom."

"No, that's all right. I'm glad things are going so well for you. That's what every mother wants. Her children succeeding in the world. Love you, kiddo."

"Love you, too, Mom."

After their call wrapped up, Sarah turned back to her notes and the quilt, but her mind kept straying. Maybe she should travel to Texas to see Jenna's family. It would be fun to have the whole family together, but going there might be her best option.

Until then, she needed to wrap up this mystery—if one even existed.

CHAPTER SEVENTEEN

Tuesday morning while Sarah did the necessary chores to keep the house livable, her mind kept turning to the Habers. Something about their search for a family heirloom pulled at her.

She formulated a list in her mind of the things she wanted to learn about Kay when she finally made her trip back to the historical society. After a quick lunch, she cleaned up and was ready to leave when the phone rang. She scrambled around the kitchen before finding the phone stashed next to her sewing machine. "Hello?"

"Sarah, this is Maggie. I'm so glad you're home." Her daughter-in-law's voice held a frazzled tone. "Can I ask a favor?"

The tinkle of the bell at the store sounded in the background. A conversation also ran somewhere behind Maggie. The store must be hopping.

"I'd be glad to help."

"I accepted an invitation to the Chamber event tonight but didn't realize it started before I'm supposed to pick the girls up from school. Audrey has play practice after school. Is there any way you can pick them up? They need to be collected around four o'clock."

Sarah smiled. A late afternoon with her granddaughters sounded wonderful. "I'd be glad to do that if Jason can't."

"He's working on something of his own. I can't believe I overscheduled us like this." Maggie's words crashed to a halt.

"Don't worry about it. I can easily get them."

"Thank you." Maggie already sounded less tense, and Sarah could almost see her shoulders relax.

"That's why I'm here. And don't worry . . . today's a good day to have them." There was no reason a trip to the historical society couldn't wait one more day. "When should I have them home?"

"Jason or I will swing by and get them, probably around seven." The bell tinkled again. "I've got to go. Thank you."

Sarah looked at the clock. She had a couple of hours before she needed to collect the girls. It would be fun to surprise them with an afternoon tea party. She'd loved tea parties with her grandmother when she'd been Amy and Audrey's age. She had enough time to throw together some cookies and scones before leaving. The perfect way to spend a cold fall afternoon.

She whipped together the ingredients for snicker-doodles and orange-cranberry scones. Soon her kitchen had the wonderful buttery aroma of her favorite sweets. Sarah left a pan of cookies cooling on the counter as she ran out the door.

The pickup line at the junior high took about fifteen minutes. She saw the girls before they spotted her, their heads swiveling side to side as they searched for their mother's SUV in the line of vehicles. The girls' confusion quickly disappeared when they saw Sarah.

"Grandma!" Audrey slid into the backseat with a smile. "We didn't know you were picking us up."

"It's a last minute pleasure."

"Let me guess. Mom's too busy to get us." Amy sat in the backseat, her arms crossed.

"Something came up, but I'm delighted for the extra time with you. I've got a surprise waiting for you at my house, but do you need anything from yours first?"

"Not really." Amy didn't sound enthusiastic, but at least she seemed willing to go along with the plan. Sarah would take that and pray the girl relaxed and loosened up as they had their tea party. Eventually Audrey filled the car with a running commentary on everything that had happened during the rehearsal. "There is no way we'll be ready. It'll be terrible."

Amy sank lower on the seat and looked like the poster child for insolence. Sarah studied her in the rearview mirror, taking in the stiff set to her jaw.

"How was your day, Amy?"

"Boring and I'm tired of waiting for Audrey at school all the time. She's always doing something. And I have to wait until she's done to be picked up."

"Is there something you can do then?"

"Now that the field hockey season has ended, no." The girl shuddered and slid further down in the seat.

"I'm sorry your day felt so awful. I always preferred outdoor sports. Why be inside when the wonderful mountains were outside?"

"That wouldn't be bad, but it's so cold here."

"It isn't that way all the time." Sarah caught Amy's gaze in the mirror and winked. "The warmth will return. And then we'll spend lots of time hiking. And I bet you'll find a team this spring."

When she pulled into the driveway, the girls raced from the car almost before she had it in park. Amy twisted the doorknob, then fell into the house, a look of surprise on her face as the door opened.

"Grandma, you really need to lock your front door." Audrey stared at her, hands on her hips and mouth open. With that stance, she was the spitting image of her mother.

Sarah smiled, and took Audrey's hand. "I lock it most of the time. I must have been too excited to get you girls."

Audrey followed her to the kitchen, and stopped to sniff inside the door. "What's that great smell?"

"Cookies." Amy looked up from the tray she studied at the counter. "I've been deciding which one I want."

Sarah nudged Amy to the side and turned on the burner under the teakettle. "I thought we'd have a tea party before you pulled out homework. Amy, you put the cookies on a plate, and Audrey, the scones need one, too."

"Scones?" Audrey wrinkled her nose and frowned.

"You'll like them, I promise." Sarah pulled a few tea bags from their boxes and placed them in a bowl. She set that on a tray along with three cups and saucers. The kettle began to whistle and she poured the boiling water into one of her pretty teapots. "Ready, girls? Let's sit at the dining room table."

The next fifteen minutes passed in a wonderful fashion as the girls told her all about their day. The cookies and tea disappeared. Most important, the girls smiled and giggled as they enjoyed the experience.

"Can we do this again, Grandma?" Amy set her empty teacup on the tray and then collected the others.

"Absolutely."

Audrey picked up the now empty plates. "You can even make those biscuit things again."

"How about I put chocolate chips in the next batch?"

"Perfect."

The girls headed to the kitchen with the dishes, while Sarah brushed the crumbs from the tablecloth.

"Come on, Grandma." Audrey bounced in the doorway. "Let's play a game."

"A game?" Amy grimaced.

Audrey grinned and started opening the china hutch cabinets. "I bet Grandma could teach us something fun to play. Maybe something fun you played when you were a kid?"

Amy rolled her eyes, but moved toward the dining room table where Audrey had placed several boxes.

"First, homework. And, no, you don't have to play a game if you don't want to. Get your homework done and then we'll see if there's a game you can agree on."

The girls groaned but pulled out their math books. While the girls were busy, Sarah tried to think of a game they would like. Something fun, but also something they might not play all the time at home. The mind of a modern twelve-year-old was still a bit beyond her. After about twenty minutes, Audrey slammed hers shut. "Done. Now can we play?"

"As soon as Amy's finished."

Audrey grabbed another cookie from the kitchen and waited somewhat patiently while Amy finished her math problems. As soon as she had finished, the girls jumped from the table and shoved their books into their book bags.

"How about I teach you a game I learned from my dad?"

"Okay."

The girls joined her back at the dining room table. "There are two games I thought you might like. The first is Scrabble." From the way Audrey's nose wrinkled, Sarah doubted that would be the choice. "Or Monopoly?"

"Scrabble feels too much like school."

Amy nodded. "I don't want to spend my time with you digging through letters for words."

"Fair enough. Then we'll play Monopoly. Have you played it before?"

The girls shook their heads.

"Mom always says it takes too long to play." Audrey pulled the box lid up. "But I'd love to try."

"Amy?"

The girl shrugged. "I'm game."

"Great." Sarah took a few minutes to set up the board, and then began to explain the rules. "You want to buy as much property as you can without going bankrupt—and you have to pay rent on everyone else's property."

Audrey scrunched her nose as she looked at the board, while Amy rubbed her neck.

"You girls still willing to try?"

"All right." Amy picked up the dice and rolled. "Just don't expect us to be any good."

Sarah laughed. "I don't expect you to get it all right away. We'll get as far as we can tonight and see how you like it."

Soon the girls were getting into the swing of the game. They groaned when someone landed on a property they hadn't purchased and squealed when someone had to pay rent. As the game progressed Audrey seemed to shift more as the game proceeded. Amy heaved a dramatic sigh. "Mom used to do things like this with us."

"Then we moved here." Audrey shrugged. "Guess that's part of the change."

"Doesn't mean I have to like it."

Sarah rolled and moved on to Boardwalk. With a flourish she purchased the key piece of real estate. "I know your mom does her best to be a good mother."

"I guess. I just miss the way things used to be."

Sarah winced at the bite in Audrey's tone. There had to be something she could do to lessen it. As she watched the girls, Sarah decided she needed to keep her schedule as clear as possible to help Jason and Maggie through this transition. And if that meant more time with her granddaughters, it was a commitment she would gladly keep.

"What time is it, Grandma?"

"I don't know." Sarah glanced at the clock on the wall. "Oh my goodness. We must have been having fun because it's after six thirty."

Audrey rubbed her stomach. "Good thing we had those biscuits and cookies."

Amy nodded. "I'm not even hungry for supper yet." She rubbed her arms. "When was Mom coming to get us?"

"She didn't really say. I'll heat some soup."

Sarah slipped into the kitchen and filled a pot with some homemade chicken noodle soup. The phone rang, and when she picked up, Jason didn't wait for her to say anything.

"Mom, have you seen my family?"

"The girls are here with me."

"I'll be there in a minute."

CHAPTER EIGHTEEN

The moment Jason came through her front door, Sarah knew something was wrong.

"Hi, Mom." He said with a halfhearted smile. "Sorry I was so frantic. Maggie didn't call or text or anything."

He took a deep breath and collapsed onto the living room couch. The overstuffed cushions wrapped around him as he sagged into them.

Jason rubbed his eyes, his five-o'clock-shadowed jaw tight. "I'm so glad they're here."

"It was my pleasure to have them. You know I would always help in a pinch."

"Mom, you shouldn't have to."

"That's what family is for. To pitch in when life gets crazy." She sat on the edge of her rocking chair, wishing Gerry was here to help Jason. Sometimes she felt unable to connect with him on the level that Gerry had reached so easily. Maybe all their camping trips when Jason was a teenager had forged their deep bond. Whatever led to it, she hadn't matched it.

Amy slid next to Jason, and he squeezed her. "How's my girl?"

"We had a great time with Grandma."

"Daddy, when did you get here?" Audrey hurried into the living room.

Jason sat forward as Audrey launched herself at him. He wrapped her in a bear hug that brought tears to Sarah's eyes. She blinked them away.

"We had a tea party. With fresh cookies and scones. We didn't save any for you."

Jason chuckled and ruffled Amy's pigtail and then tweaked her nose. "That's okay. What do you say we get you guys home? Have you started homework yet?"

Amy rolled her eyes. "Math. But that's it."

"Who'd want to waste time on homework when we can do fun things with Grandma?" Audrey said.

"Guess next time I'll make sure they complete all their homework first." She mouthed *sorry* to Jason. He shrugged.

"I'd better get you home, and get you cracking on the rest. Your teachers get grumpy if it's not turned in on time."

Audrey yawned and stretched her arms over her head. "And I get grumpy if I don't get my beauty sleep."

"Nice try." Jason ruffled her hair and then pushed her toward the door. "Get your coats and other stuff and meet me at the front door." Jason crawled off the couch and gave Sarah a one-armed hug. "Thanks for bailing us out."

"Any time, Jason. Any time." The sound of the girls quibbling caused Sarah to stand. "I'll get them squared away in a minute. Do you want to take some chicken noodle soup home for your dinner?"

Jason nodded. "Sure. That sounds better than anything waiting at home." He walked toward the front door. She wished he'd tell her more—but this was one of those areas where a mother could pry only so far. Guess she'd need to spend more time praying as she worked. But first she had to get the girls out the door with their father.

It took ten minutes, but after Jason herded the girls into his car with a Tupperware container filled with soup, Sarah settled down at the quilt frame. Tonight she moved to a new square, Cupid's Dart, a pattern that exploded in a riot of yellow and orange triangles. Looking at the bold colors, she realized she'd need different thread to work on this one.

Sarah stood and pulled her sewing basket full of quilting thread from the compartment in the closet where she stored it. She rummaged through the mishmash of threads until she found a yellow in just the right shade of goldenrod.

It still puzzled Sarah that Cupid's Dart pointed either to the tree pattern on its right side or Shoo Fly on its left, rather than to something romantic. Cupid's Dart always made her think of romance and love. But here, sandwiched between the tree and Shoo Fly, the pattern just didn't strike a romantic note.

Where could she find the romance?

A visit to the historical society had to be tomorrow's priority. Maybe there she'd find information about Kay Haber that would tell her whether or not Cupid's Dart had any significance.

Maybe she wanted to see romance behind every story.

She'd have to track down the details of Kay's life. Then she could determine if Kay had placed the squares the way she had to tell a story. One that involved love and romance.

A knock sounded at the door, and before Sarah could stand, the door opened.

"Hello?" Maggie's voice sounded tired and harried as the door shut.

Sarah leaned back in her chair and waved Maggie in. "Come on in. Your family's already headed home."

Maggie had her cell phone plastered to her ear. A small smile started to spread on her face before it died with a grimace. "Glad you found them." She shut the phone and looked at Sarah.

The cold had pinked Maggie's cheeks and her hair looked like she hadn't touched it since hours earlier that morning. From all angles the woman looked tired and a bit worn down. Sarah looked at the clock in the kitchen. Eight o'clock. Of course the girl was exhausted.

"Sorry to bother you, Sarah. Jason just told me he has the girls, so I'll head home."

"Thanks for letting me have them this evening."

Maggie nodded. "Thank you." The words barely sounded like a whisper as she kissed Sarah on the cheek and turned back down the hallway. "I'll see you later."

Sarah watched her until the door closed behind Maggie. She bit her lower lip as she wondered what she could do for her kids. They both looked like they were in pain, and it hurt her to see that. *Father, give me wisdom.*

Other than praying, she couldn't do anything for the kids tonight. She hated that, but she couldn't escape reality.

Wednesday Sarah picked up the *Encyclopedia of Quilt Patterns* that Vanessa had shoved into her hands. Then she grabbed her notebook and opened it to the grid she'd started. With two rows of the quilt filled in, she still had two to go.

Sarah flipped to the fat volume's index. Starting with the pattern she'd called Wild Goose Chase, she entered the eight possible names for it in the grid. Wild Goose Chase, that was certainly what nailing down the quilt had begun to feel like. Ducks, geese, and even flies seemed to be in many of the names. A farm-based set of names for the quilt. Sarah made a note to check whether the patterns had that as a common theme when she had all of the grid filled in. But as she looked at what she had, she couldn't imagine a farm-based meaning for Cupid's Dart. She flipped to the index and then to the one entry that was listed there. There was only one name for the pattern. She starred that pattern in the grid, relieved to know that another square had been accurately identified.

Examining the block above Wild Goose Chase, she flipped ahead a few pages in the index to see what listings there were for Flying Geese. There were six separate entries, and after looking at each one, she realized that one pattern matched the block she had. She marked it with a star on the grid when she saw it didn't have multiple names. Flying Geese. Nothing connected it to Cupid's Dart. She didn't know whether to be excited that there was only one name or disappointed because a second name might have provided a clue to the puzzle. Even if it fit a theme, it might simply be a filler square. Geese were common throughout the region. Especially as they migrated south for the winter and reversed their flight in the spring.

She stood and moved into the kitchen. Maybe a cup of tea would help soothe the tightness in her neck and shoulders that intensified with each new square she examined. She'd never expected the process of learning the sampler quilt's story to be so frustrating.

Should she give up?

There really wasn't anything compelling her to uncover the most accurate choice of name for each square. Especially if she intended to keep this quilt, nobody else would invest the time to track down every single name. And how would she know her guesses were right anyway? Kay had most likely created this quilt, and there was no way to ask the woman.

Maybe she needed to face the fact that she was wasting her time and energy on a task that would never lead to anything important.

The water finally boiled, and she threw a peppermint tea bag in a mug before filling it with hot water. She dunked the bag up and down, watching the herbs color the water and smelling the calming peppermint aroma. She inhaled deeply and then exhaled.

Could she walk away?

No. Even though it would never matter to anyone else, she wanted to know she'd chased down the answers to her questions about the quilt.

She carried her tea into the sewing room and went back to work. Thankfully, like Puss in the Corner, Massachusetts, and Cupid's Dart, Maine's Tree had no other possible names. She starred it with relief. That left three patterns to check against the encyclopedia. The top row contained four squares in addition to the Split Rail pattern. The block to the right of Flying Geese was made up of squares and triangles, a complicated pattern that Sarah had assumed was the Weathervane pattern. The encyclopedia showed no alternative names—another grid to star. Two squares to go. She refused to dwell on the long lists of possibilities as she moved to the next square, the one with the intricate pattern of diamonds. Since Sarah had never had a name for this pattern, the index wasn't going to be of any help. She turned to the front of the encyclopedia and ran down the table of contents. This encyclopedia, like Sarah's book of patterns, grouped quilt patterns by the shapes used in them—triangles, hexagons, squares. Since this block was composed of diamonds, perhaps she could find it by working through the diamond-based patterns. She worked slowly and carefully, and when she found it, she put her head down on the book and groaned. There were eighteen possible names for this block. *Eighteen.* How could she even begin to narrow that down?

One pattern.

She had to finish. Even if it killed her.

The flower in the pattern made it clear that it had something to do with gardens. And the encyclopedia confirmed her initial hunch that it was Flower Garden.

She picked up her notebook and half-empty mug and moved to the living room. Maybe a change of location would help her figure out what she'd missed.

She yawned as she walked down the hallway. She pulled a lap quilt on and settled against the cushions.

She was certain of Flying Geese, Weathervane, Flower Garden, Cupid's Dart, Maine's Tree, Massachusetts, and Puss in the Corner. Sarah scanned the rows of her grid again, stopping when she saw that the list for Fox and Geese included Crosses and Losses, and Old Maid's Puzzle. While geese were common in Massachusetts, would the quilt's creator have included so many patterns with the word *geese* in the title? Not if there was a story to be told. She ran down the list of names again. Old Maid's Puzzle? Since she'd assumed Mrs. Haber or Kay had created the quilt, did Old Maid's Puzzle eliminate Mrs. Haber? Could it indicate that Kay Haber was the quilter? Did Kay Haber ever marry? Her service record with the Red Cross hadn't indicated whether she had.

And if Kay had been an old maid, did this name also hint that there was some puzzle hidden in the blocks of the quilt? That her instincts had been right? Sarah had sensed that some hidden story existed, though she had yet to figure out what that story—that puzzle—was.

She scanned the grid again searching for an overall pattern.

Nothing jumped out from the blocks whose names she was sure of.

Suddenly she stopped. If she was right that this block's name was Old Maid's Puzzle, could Cupid's Dart indicate that Kay hadn't *intended* to be an old maid—and that the quilt truly did contain a puzzle waiting to be solved?

CHAPTER NINETEEN

Thursday morning Sarah launched out of bed and raced through her morning chores. She didn't want to let anything interrupt her plans to research Kay at the historical society. If she hurried, she'd arrive as the doors opened. And if she didn't find what she was looking for there, she'd try the library, another good place to explore the past. As soon as the clock in the kitchen read nine forty-five, she hurried to the hall and grabbed her coat from the tree and her purse from the hall table. Moments later she was on her way downtown.

A vacant parking spot waited in front of the white clapboard building. She pulled into the space, then climbed from the car. She tapped the sign announcing Maple Hill Incorporated 1786 as she walked by. The pine plank floor squeaked in its familiar way as she entered the building. Sarah looked for Irene Stuart at the front desk—if anyone would know about treasure, she would. She stopped short when she saw Tim Wexler sitting at Irene's desk. Tim looked up and grinned. The kid was probably thrilled to have someone in the building. Sarah answered his wave but bypassed him. He wasn't old enough to have heard anything about the old rumor.

Irene's special mix of cinnamon and apple potpourri couldn't quite cover the faintly musty smell of the old papers and books that lined the walls and bookshelves that popped out at all kinds of odd angles. While some might find the atmosphere odd or eclectic, Sarah loved everything it represented—knowledge of the area's past resided here.

She set her purse on a table and pulled her notebook and pen out of it. Time to collect any information she could about Kay Haber.

Tim strolled toward her, standing erect, unlike many of the teens who slouched around town—though it would be tough for someone as tall as Tim to hunch over. The kid was more than six feet tall and was still growing, according to his mom. The college basketball scouts certainly liked him.

"Anything I can help you with?"

"Hmm?" Sarah doodled across the top of a blank page. Truth be told, she wasn't sure where to begin with her search for details of Kay's life.

"Assist with finding books?" Sarah shook her head.

"I hate to bother you."

"Come on, Mrs. Hart. It's why I'm here."

"Which raises a good question. Why are you here during the morning on a school day?"

"I get released from classes. A work-study exchange Irene arranged with the principal. I sure don't mind the break from classes." He gave her a big grin.

Sarah studied him a moment. "I don't know if you can help me."

"Try me."

"I need to look up more information about Kay Haber. I was here a week ago, and Irene showed me her service record from World War II. But I left before learning anything about what she did after the war."

"Wow." Tim scratched his head then turned toward the desk. "Let's check the catalog."

"But the cards are over here."

"Those are fine for Irene, but I've been working on a new database. It helps me find information a lot faster than digging through that dusty thing. And I don't sneeze all the time anymore."

Sarah followed Tim and watched as his fingers clicked like lightning across the keyboard. He muttered to himself until he hit print and grinned at her. He pulled the sheet from the printer with a flourish and handed it to her.

"This should do it." He smiled sheepishly at her. "I should have thought of this without the search."

She scanned the sheet. Looked like it contained information on a book about local lore and a couple of yearbooks. "Okay. I don't see how this book on local history can help."

"It has some information on the Haber farm you might find interesting. You never know what's important. This way, madam." Tim led her to a row of bookcases next to the fireplace. Then he crouched down to pull a thin red volume from the bottom shelf. "If any book will give you a place to start, this is the one." He flipped to the table of contents and ran a finger down it. "It might not help at all, but I've found some great things in it."

Sarah pursed her lips and put her hands on her hips. "What exactly did you find?"

"I had to write a paper on a local legend. I found a cool ghost story in here." The sheepish look on his face left her wanting to pinch his cheek. "There might be other books and magazines that might help. Let me know after you've read through this. And while you're looking at that, I'll look for more information on Kay."

"Thank you. Sorry I didn't ask for your help sooner."

"Happens all the time. Who would think a high school basketball player is interested in local history?"

"Are we that bad?"

Tim shrugged, a motion that moved his body in a roll from the shoulders down. Sarah stifled a laugh at the languid movement her body could never replicate. "I'm used to it."

"Well, I for one am sorry. I'll take any help you can give."

"It's not that bad, Mrs. Hart. You just flow with Mrs. Stuart's slightly twisted organizational system."

"Not the way you'd do it?"

"Nah, but it works. Search this area and you'll find a few books on local lore. They're not the best written things, but they'll give you an idea of what local *historians* think." He rolled his eyes as he said *historians*.

"Let me guess—you're headed to a college history program."

"In another year. The best one I can get into. Someone has to care enough to get the local stories right." He pointed to a shelf a few feet to the right. "Over there are the books with obituaries. They aren't comprehensive— more like scrapbooks. I think Irene started them. But it's a place to begin."

Sarah eyed the book he'd handed her. "Thanks, Tim."

She grabbed a couple of neighboring books from the shelf, carried the stack to an overstuffed chair and eased into it. Balancing her notebook on the arm, she flipped through the red volume Tim had pulled. The table of contents didn't reveal anything so she flipped to the index. Maple Hill was listed twice and neither time referenced the Habers. A quick glance at those pages revealed the ghost story Tim had mentioned, but not anything relevant to her Kay Haber or her quilt. She put the book on the floor then picked up another one.

Scanning the table of contents she found one entry for the Maple Hill area. She flipped to the chapter, but as she skimmed it the lack of detail disappointed her. It read like a poorly written travelogue, like something she'd expect to see in a grocery store checkout-line rag, filled with innuendo and suggestion about many rumored happenings from witch hunts to ghost sightings, but nothing concrete. At the end of the chapter, the author even gave the barest mention to a possible treasure buried somewhere around Maple Hill.

Sarah sighed. Her notebook page remained conspicuously empty, that one citation barely worth writing down. She copied the information in case she needed it later.

After flipping through four more books, she stilled when she noticed the author of the final book in her pile.

Hidden Treasures in the Berkshires. Author Chester Winslow.

Chester Winslow. The man from the auction…the *Country Cottage* columnist and the man who had charmed her thoroughly.

Sarah fumbled with the book. He'd written an entire book on treasures in the area? Could they all be antiques? And did any of them have to do with the Habers? Her fingers shook as she flipped pages until she reached the table of contents. Surely, by *treasures* he meant things like hideaway spots and beautiful vistas. Anything else would make her wonder what his motives had been at the Haber auction.

Finally, she spotted an entry for Maple Hill and flipped to that chapter. After scanning the first couple of pages, her pace slowed.

Rumors have floated about that one of the children of Adam Haber returned from World War II with a secret treasure, but I

have been unable to establish the veracity of the rumor. There are
stories of Nazi paraphernalia stolen from the Eagle's Nest, other
stories of items coming from the bunker where Hitler committed
suicide. Yet none of the stories seems verifiable based on where
the Haber boys served during the war.

The rumors persist to this day, but have been largely unsub-
stantiated. However, the Habers remain tight-lipped about a trea-
sure, refusing to answer any questions when asked.

An outside source that tied the Habers to a treasure?
Surely if that was the case, she should have heard something growing up and living in Maple Hill. It was enough to
make her doubt the treasure was real. Sarah made a couple
of notes, then leaned back. Nazi loot...hadn't they stolen a
huge number of art objects? Could a painting or a sculpture
be the treasure? She just couldn't imagine something like
that buried somewhere in Massachusetts. Especially on the
Haber farm.

Maybe there was no treasure. Somebody had talked
things up at a local bar after returning from the war, spinning a tall tale or two. But could the treasure rumors have
lived long enough to travel to the Florida branch of the
family? And now Curtis and Louise had come here convinced they'd find something. Only there was nothing to
find. Surely, if there was any truth to the treasure, more people would know about it and talk. Sarah simply couldn't
imagine a secret that big remaining hidden for more than
sixty years. The Habers were chasing the wind and taking
her with them.

She shut the book, intrigued and disappointed. She wasn't ready to give any credence to the rumors. And she still needed information on Kay. She kept Chester's book—his account of the Habers and a possible treasure disconcerted her—so she could photocopy the pages on the Habers. With nothing else from the books, she approached the desk.

"Tim, is this the shelf with the obituaries?"

Tim looked up from the computer. "Yes, ma'am."

"Thanks." Sarah glanced at her watch, shocked to find it was already after eleven.

"Would you like me to copy something for you?"

"That would be great." She opened the book and showed him the pages she needed. He headed to the copier while she scanned the shelf, noting the dates on the spine. When she opened one, it became clear the dates related to the years the obituaries were printed. Without knowing the year Kay died, how could she find the right volume?

She opened a few randomly. But without an index of some sort, she was lost.

"Mrs. Hart, here are your copies. I'm sorry, but it's time for me to lock up for lunch." Tim stood in front of her, a hangdog expression on his face. "I'd stay but Mrs. Stuart has a way of knowing when I do things like that."

"No, that's all right." Sarah leaned over and collected the books. "I appreciate your help." Besides, her research might have given her questions, but it had also left her with a next step. "Quick question though. Do you have any type of index to these volumes?"

"Mrs. Stuart talks about building one, but we haven't started yet. It's kind of random finding anything."

"I can see that. Well, thanks for all your help."

Sarah left the historical society and walked down the street to the library, burning to answer her questions about Kay Haber. When she entered, Spencer Hewitt looked up from a book cart.

"Mrs. Hart. What a pleasure."

"Hi, Spencer. Can you help me find information about a town resident?"

"Sure. What do you need to know?"

"I'm doing some research on Kay Haber. I've been at the historical society, but without knowing when she died, I can't find her obituary."

Spencer thought a moment, then led Sarah to the circulation desk where he picked up the key to the special collections area. "I think we'll find what you need in the archives room."

Sarah followed him to the room and waited while he unlocked the door. The dusty smell tickled her nose before the motion controlled lights clicked on. "Where do I start?"

"The *Maple Hill Monitor* back issues are along that shelf in the green leather volumes."

Sarah looked at the wall and bit her lower lip. The volumes stood there. But they couldn't tell her where to look.

"Can you guess at the year?"

"No." Sarah picked a random volume and carefully opened it. "I don't have any idea when she died. The Red Cross service record only gave her birth date."

"Would you like me to Google her?"

"That would be great." At this point she didn't want to go home without some information about Kay. The woman felt like a ghost who had disappeared after the war.

"I'll be right back." Spencer hurried off and returned five minutes later with a sheet of paper. "Here you go."

Sarah took the sheet. It listed Kay's dates of birth and death. She hurried to the correct volume on the wall. When she pulled it out, she flipped to the clippings near the date on the sheet. "It's not here."

"Look at the few days following. It would have taken up to a week to get it in the newspaper."

"You're brilliant."

"Just the librarian." He smiled and moved to the door. "Feel free to photocopy the obituary once you find it."

"Thank you." Sarah kept flipping the pages and paused only when she finally saw Kay's name.

CHAPTER TWENTY

MAPLE HILL—Kay Louise Haber, 45, of Maple Hill, Mass., died Wednesday, July 24, 1967. She was born on June 25, 1922, at Maple Hill, Mass., to Adam and Norma (Fabrique) Haber. Her father was a local farmer. Kay was a graduate of Maple Hill (Mass.) High School and graduated from Boston University. During World War II Kay served in France and Germany with the American Red Cross supporting the troops. After the war she returned to Maple Hill where she spent her life dedicated to her family, friends, and community through her nursing position and many charitable activities. She was a member of Maple Hill Congregational Church where she led women's Bible studies and taught Sunday school.

Kay died alone in 1967. She'd been so young, only forty-five. Sarah read the obituary again, wondering what had caused Kay's premature death.

Her throat tightened at the thought that Kay had never found the kind of love she and Gerry had shared. While

Gerry had seemed too young when he'd died, they'd still had the pleasure of a long married life. Something Kay had never experienced.

Sarah swallowed, trying to clear the tears that clogged her throat. Then she opened her notebook and flipped to the sketch of the quilt. Did Cupid's Dart suggest that Kay had once loved? And did Old Maid's Puzzle suggest a life where that love remained unrequited or unfulfilled? Her heart felt heavy at the thought that a woman with as much zest for life as Kay's obituary suggested had never found love.

Spencer knocked on the door frame. "Can I get you anything?"

"I found," Sarah cleared her throat and continued. "I found what I came for. Thank you."

"Don't forget to make a copy." He turned as someone tapped him on the arm.

Sarah reread the obituary. So young to die. Yet what experiences Kay must have had as she bounced along war rutted roads in her role as a Red Cross worker. Had she found love while overseas, only to have her love killed or lost to her? A war romance sounded romantic until the realities of life invaded.

After collecting her purse and notebook, Sarah carried the volume to the copier and made a copy of the obituary.

"I'll reshelve that for you."

Sarah nodded at Spencer. "Thank you."

She stumbled from the library lost in a fog of what-ifs. Who could tell her more about Kay after the war? Maybe her dad or Mr. Frazier could help answer the questions the obituary raised.

She turned toward the nursing home, and after she'd pulled into the parking lot, she sat for a few minutes trying to quiet her thoughts and focus on what she hoped to learn. What if Kay's love had found her? What if she returned from Europe unwilling to open her heart to anyone else?

Before she could enter, Sarah stepped to the side of the double doors to let several people exit who were bundled up in coats, hats, and scarves on their way to a waiting van. She stopped at the information desk and asked where her dad might be. The nurse directed her to the lounge.

When Sarah entered, her dad was parked in his wheelchair in front of the TV. She scanned the room and saw Mr. Frazier back at the table working on a different puzzle. At the first commercial break, she approached her father and sank down in front of him.

"Good morning, Dad."

He slowly turned his head to look at her. The glazed look in his eyes had her praying he'd be able to tell her anything about Kay. "Hello."

"Can I push you over this way? I'd like to talk for a while."

"I suppose that would be all right. This show isn't very interesting today anyway."

She unhooked the brakes and pushed the wheelchair toward the tables. "Good morning, Mr. Frazier. Do you mind if we join you for a bit?"

The man looked up and smiled. "Why Sarah Hart. Didn't think I'd see you again so soon."

Dad leaned forward and fumbled through the puzzle pieces as soon as Sarah pushed him closer to the table. His gaze seemed to clear and focus as he sorted through the pieces.

"What brings you here today?"

"I wondered if you could fill in some blanks for me. I've researched Kay Haber some, but I'm not learning the details I'd hoped."

The welcome in Mr. Frazier's eyes died at the mention of Kay. "That was a hard woman."

William looked up and shook a puzzle piece in Mr. Frazier's face. "That's a harsh thing to say. You don't know what she saw in the war."

"What I do know is we dated a few times. But no matter how much I told her I really enjoyed her company and wanted to get to know her better, she simply erected a wall. I could get just so close and no closer."

"Maybe she found your mustache scratchy." Dad guffawed. "That was the scraggliest thing."

"The only way she would have known was if she'd let me get near enough to peck her on the cheek. No, the woman was colder than a polar bear in the Arctic."

"Is that right?" Her dad scratched his scalp, then shrugged. "That woman came back from the front changed. She was attractive before the war, but the glow that made her beautiful didn't come home. Your mother always wondered if she'd loved and lost in Europe."

Sarah took in the thought. "The obituary indicated Kay never married."

Mr. Frazier snorted. "She never let anyone get close enough to give her a ring."

"Maybe Mom was right. What did she do after the war?"

Dad scratched his chin and looked at Mr. Frazier with a shrug. "I don't remember. You, Charles?"

"This and that. I think she nursed at the hospital most of the years though."

"And never a serious relationship?"

Mr. Frazier shook his head. "That woman was walled off. Whatever she saw or experienced in Europe affected her deeply."

When Sarah arrived at home, she noticed the answering machine message light blinking when she set her keys on the counter. She hit the button.

"Good morning, Mrs. Hart. I don't want to pressure you, but I hope you've decided to join us here at *Country Cottage*. This is a great opportunity for you, and you'd be an asset to the magazine. We're eager to start with the trial column we discussed, but need to know if you'll have a piece in the next issue. Please let me know today if you'll accept the position."

Mark left his number, but Sarah didn't move to write it down. Instead, she stared at the phone. She wanted to say yes, but wasn't convinced she should.

"This is silly." She grabbed a pad of paper and a pen from her junk drawer, and sank into a chair at the kitchen table. She divided the paper in half and started listing pros and cons. The pros lined the page with only a few cons counterbalancing. The fact she felt good about the job combined with the fact that she could work from home on an as-needed basis sealed the deal for her.

She grabbed the phone, listened to the message, and then dialed Mark's number before she changed her mind. "Sarah Hart for Mark."

"Mrs. Hart, have you called to give me good news?"

"I accept your offer."

"That's great. We'll get you set up. When can you complete the paperwork?"

"I could try to squeeze it in tomorrow."

"Let's keep things easy for both of us. I'll e-mail it to you. You can scan and e-mail or fax it back. Did Chester give you everything you need for the first column?"

"We discussed ideas."

"Great. I'll include a copy of the writing guidelines. With a column you want to keep the tone conversational. Pretend you're talking to someone sitting across the table from you. Keep the language nontechnical because not everyone will know as much about quilting as you."

"All right." Sarah bit her lower lip, wondering if she had enough information to go on. "I think I've got a lead on a quilt already."

"Sounds like you're intrigued."

"I am. I guess I like a quilt with a story, no matter how hidden."

"Think you can write a thousand words on this one by the end of the month?"

Sarah glanced at her calendar. Other than Thanksgiving, there wasn't much of anything specific on her plate. "Will do."

"Get to work. I've learned that a curious and passionate writer is the best indicator of an interested public."

"I hope you're right." Sarah drummed her fingers on the table.

"Great." She heard voices in the background. "Gotta run. Welcome to the team."

Before she could say thanks, he hung up.

Well, she'd done it. And it didn't feel like a mistake. She almost laughed at the thought. Many things didn't feel like a mistake at the time—regret usually showed up much later.

The rest of that night and into the next day Sarah moved through her activities with her thoughts constantly returning to Kay and her short life. What did Chester know that he hadn't told her? And would she be able to unravel the quilt's puzzle in time to write her first column about it?

She startled when her phone rang, shattering the silence that had settled over the house.

"Hello?"

"Sarah, this is Chester."

Chester Winslow, author of *Hidden Treasures in the Berkshires*. The time she'd shared with Chester suddenly seemed cheapened by the realization he'd written a book that included information about the Habers and a treasure he'd never mentioned. Had he hoped she might lead him to it? Did he even care? She didn't know, but now she wondered. Her hopes that he'd enjoyed her company seemed silly and juvenile. Had she become one of those women who are so lonely they accept companionship without considering the motives of the person offering it?

She shook her head, trying to clear her thoughts. She realized she needed to Google this man and see what other surprises he had up his sleeve. See if he knew more than he'd written.

"Hi."

"Mark just gave me the good news. Welcome to the team."

"Thank you. I hope I can write what Mark expects."

"I have no doubt you'll do well."

His voice soothed her concerns but left her unsettled. Silence reigned for a moment as Sarah waited.

Chester cleared his throat. "I'd like to come to town. Take you to dinner tonight."

Should she say yes? Something about his voice made Sarah feel warm. While she'd enjoyed their times together, now that she'd found his book...he seemed different. Was that fair? She shook her head, wishing her confusion would disappear.

Chester sighed, a sound that conveyed disappointment. "I take it you're busy?"

"Actually, I'm not." She smiled, hoping he'd hear it in her voice. "In fact, I'd enjoy dinner." And she hoped she wouldn't regret spending more time with Chester. She wanted to believe it wouldn't hurt anything, but as Chester set a time to pick her up, Sarah wondered.

She wanted to focus on the witty man who had entertained her so thoroughly with story after story during their times together. Instead, as she hung up, she could think only of the book and whether he'd actually been at the auction to try to find the elusive treasure.

Could it really exist?

It seemed so incredibly far-fetched. Who buried treasure in the Berkshires? And the Habers had never lived liked they owned a hidden treasure. So where was it?

She didn't know what to think. But according to the clock, now wasn't the time to figure that out. Sarah ran upstairs and touched up her makeup with hurried strokes. Then she checked her shirt and slacks for stains. She'd barely run a brush through her hair when a knock sounded downstairs. She ran a toothbrush over her teeth and then added lipstick before hurrying downstairs.

When she opened the door, Chester had his hand raised as if ready to knock again.

"Sorry to keep you waiting." Her pulse pounded in her throat, whether from the race down the stairs or Chester's being on her front porch, Sarah wasn't sure. She tried to smile but felt her lips twitch at the corners. "Would you like to come in for a moment?"

His stomach growled and she laughed, the knots in her shoulders relaxing.

"I suppose we should hurry to dinner before I deafen you with more rumbles." He shrugged, color dusting the top of his ears. "Do you have any recommendations?"

"Well, you've been to the Old Mill and Liam's place. Have you tried the Miss Maple?"

He held her coat as she slipped into it. Then he ushered her down the steps and to his car. "The diner? I haven't been there."

"It's really nice on the inside."

"If you're sure. I'd begun to wonder if it was a front for some criminal organization."

"It's only open part of the year. It will be closing soon for deer hunting season when Ella cooks at the camp. But she is the sweetest thing you'll ever meet. Her heart is solid gold, and her meatloaf is amazing."

"Meatloaf?"

"Yes, you have to try it."

"I don't know."

"If you hate it, we can go somewhere else."

"As long as I'm with you, I won't hate it."

Words died in her throat, colliding with a boulder of uncertainty. Chester seemed so sincere. But...

Chester opened the passenger door for Sarah and waited. She swallowed and took a step back.

"I'm sorry. I thought I'd follow you since I have an errand to run after dinner." No matter how much she'd laughed with him, she didn't think she could trust riding in his car. Not yet. Not until she knew more.

Chester's mouth drooped and his shoulders slumped. "Are you sure?"

"Really. I'll meet you there. The nice thing about Maple Hill is how close everything is." Sarah bit her lower lip before she started babbling. She pulled her keys from her pocket. "See you in a minute."

Her concerns wouldn't leave her as she followed Chester to the diner. He parked in front of the restaurant and Sarah pulled in next to him. The neon glow of the diner's name reflected off his windshield.

Chester hurried from his car to open her door, and her heart squeezed. Was she being too hard on him?

He tucked her arm through his and led her to the diner. "Are you sure about this?"

"Trust me." She tried to smile, but her words echoed in her mind. Shouldn't she trust him, too?

He opened the door, and a cowbell announced their arrival. Gerry had always found the bell jarring, especially when the diner was busy and the door was constantly opened and closed. But Sarah loved it. It had hung from the doorknob as long as she could remember. And its jarring clang formed part of the backdrop of activity, one discordant note in a mix of them.

"Hello, Sarah," Ella called, her trademark apron around her waist. "Have a seat anywhere you like."

Sarah pasted on a smile "Thanks, Ella."

Chester waited for Sarah to slide into a seat on one side and then took the other. His simple courtesy touched her. And confused her.

Why hadn't he told her about the book?

CHAPTER TWENTY-ONE

I s everything all right, Sarah?" Chester's probing gaze seemed to bore into and through her. She resisted shifting against the cracked vinyl bench.

"Of course." She picked up a menu and used it as a shield, propping it against the red and white checked tablecloth. The menu rarely changed, and she doubted it had in the week or so since she'd last stopped at Ella's.

"I'm not certain I believe you."

She turned the menu over, as if examining the breakfast options. Chester couldn't have noticed they were only served until noon.

"You won't find anything on that side they're serving now."

Busted.

"You're making me want to ask my question again. Are you bothered by something? By me?"

She shook her head. "Of course not." She eased the menu down and met his gaze for a moment before studying the condiments. Whoever had bused the table hadn't put them back in their correct slots in the basket, so she rearranged them.

Chester's eyebrows shot up as he watched her. Then he leaned back against the bench and crossed his arms. "Why don't we get a slice of pie, and you can run your errand."

A wave of heat flooded Sarah. "No, please order whatever you'd like. I'm fine. Truly."

"Then where's the delightful woman I've engaged every other time we've been together. Something must be bothering you."

"Truly, it's nothing. Just the quilt I'm working on."

"So that's it. You're nervous about your column. Second-guessing your decision to write for the magazine."

Sarah started to say no, then realized his words held at least a kernel of truth. "Maybe."

"There's nothing to worry about. Once you get that first sentence on the computer, the rest flows."

"But how do you find that first sentence?"

"You type drivel and delete, over and over."

"That doesn't make me feel better."

"It gets easier."

Sarah scrunched her nose and considered him. "Really?"

"Well, no, but it sounds better than saying writing is extremely hard work. Can't have you quitting before your first column." He winked at her, a gesture that surprised her.

"I suppose you really *shouldn't* say that." She winked back. "Maybe I'll have you write my columns. Don't they call that ghosting?"

"Not going to happen, my dear."

She started to laugh at his serious expression, but the way he said "my dear" stopped her. She ran a fingernail over a spot on the red checked oilcloth.

Someone cleared her throat, and Sarah looked up to find Ella standing at the table, order pad poised. "What can I get you?"

Chester ordered the meatloaf and mashed potatoes. "My friend tells me they're the best."

Ella grinned at him. "I like to think so." She turned to Sarah. "And for you?"

"Just a bowl of potato bacon soup."

"Wait a minute. You tell me to order the meatloaf, but don't get it yourself?"

"Guess I'm not very hungry." She handed Ella her menu with a smile. "Thanks."

"I'll have it right out." She whisked off to the counter to deposit the order before hurrying to another table of customers.

Chester reached for Sarah's hands. His clasp felt warm and secure. "Talk to me?"

"About what?"

"Whatever you'd like."

"I think you were giving me column advice…"

"All right." He released her hands and settled back. "I'll give you my best advice. Always make sure you check facts. Don't assume that something is true because you've heard it from someone who should be reliable. The 'should be's' can kill a journalist."

"I'm just writing a column."

"But readers will read it only if they can rely on you to tell them the truth."

She crossed her arms and leaned on the table. "Sounds like good advice."

Ella hurried over, carrying a plate and a bowl. "Here you go, folks. Enjoy."

Sarah bowed her head and whispered grace over the food. She looked up to find Chester mirroring her posture. With the food in front of them, conversation slowed as they ate. The silence felt overpowering. She shifted in the seat, the squeak of the vinyl grating against her nerves.

Chester pushed his plate to the edge of the table and studied her with a serious expression. "I guess we won't order dessert."

"Probably best." Sarah swallowed the desire to take back the words. She couldn't encourage him, not right now. But the moment she walked in her front door, she'd sit down at her computer and learn what she could about him.

"I can't shake the sense that somehow I've done something wrong." He paused as if waiting for her to deny it. "I hope someday you'll tell me what that might be. I enjoy spending time with you, but if you don't feel the same, say so. I know how to slide into the sunset."

"Please don't do that. Not yet." Sarah grabbed her purse and slipped its strap over her shoulder. "I'm just distracted."

He arched an eyebrow.

"Okay, very distracted. Let me get this first column out of the way."

"Call me if and when you're ready to have dinner again." His lips climbed into a smile that didn't reach his eyes.

Ella slapped the check on the table between them, the vase with its single daisy pitching from side to side. "Have a great night."

Sarah reached out to steady the vase, then for the check, but Chester grabbed it first. "Can I at least leave the tip?"

"No. It's my treat."

He followed her to the door where she waited for him to pay. Could she be overreacting? Now all she wanted to do was get home as quickly as possible and Google him. Because if she was overreacting, she owed this good man an apology.

Once they were on the sidewalk, Chester brushed her cheek with a kiss and then tipped an imaginary hat in her direction. "Until next time." He climbed into his car and drove toward the highway.

Sarah hurried home, stopping only long enough to grab a gallon of milk at the grocery store. The kitchen light was on when she opened the back door, but Belle wasn't anywhere to be seen. Then Sarah heard footsteps overhead. The girl must have fixed some supper and forgotten to turn off the light on her way back upstairs. Sarah welcomed the light. She might be home now, but she couldn't shake the sense that she shouldn't have accepted dinner. Or she should have confronted Chester about the book. Ignoring it hadn't made for an enjoyable meal.

Sarah walked to the living room and flipped through her reading pile until she'd separated a stack of *Country Cottage* magazines. Pulling them toward her, she scanned each until she'd read Chester Winslow's columns. While she'd read them all before, this time she looked for some insight into his interests and hobbies. The man came across as having a passion for the stories behind pieces of furniture and other household objects. The older the better as far as he was concerned.

His columns revealed a man who'd accumulated a depth of knowledge about antiques, particularly those crafted in New England. But the columns revealed little of the man himself and never hinted at the idea he'd written a book on the treasures of Massachusetts.

All of his columns seemed grounded in discovering the stories of antiques. As she read them, she questioned how he'd even heard about the alleged treasure. She'd lived here her entire life and had never heard the faintest murmur of a rumor. The idea seemed carefully guarded, leaving no clues about how to validate that such a thing even existed. But Chester had included the information in his book. Did he have a connection to the Habers? If not, what interest did he have in the treasure?

She tossed the latest issue of the magazine aside and hurried to her computer. The computer sprang to life, and she opened a search engine. In Google, she entered Chester Winslow. In a moment, the screen was filled with possible hits.

Scanning through the first page, Sarah found that most of the information related to his columns or speaking engagements. She found nothing that connected Chester Winslow to the Habers. As she drilled deeper into the search results, the chance that he had any relationship to her mystery seemed to evaporate.

Could he be related to the Habers? She didn't know where else to go next, so she entered the address for her favorite genealogy Web site. She typed Chester Winslow in the right search fields and waited as the program searched its database.

A long list of names appeared. She glanced through it, looking for the Chester Winslow who lived in Massachusetts. Scanning the list, she didn't find him until she neared the bottom third. Chester Winslow. The age was about right. The location looked correct. She clicked on the record but no matter how she pecked through the program and searches, she couldn't find a link from the Habers to Chester. So he didn't know about the treasure from a family connection.

While the program was open, she entered Curtis Haber's information. A Curtis Haber popped up who lived in Florida, which was right. But if the program could be trusted, this Curtis Haber would be at least ten years older than the one she'd met. And he didn't seem to have a wife named Louise. In fact, it appeared that the man hadn't married.

She glanced at the clock. Seven thirty. It wasn't too late to try the number she had for Curtis Haber again. And as she printed off the new information she'd found, she knew she needed to find the man and ask him a few questions.

Grabbing the sheet of paper from the printer, she took it to the kitchen and set it on the island next to the phone. She opened her notebook and found the page with the number she'd located for Curtis. Dialing it, she prayed the man would answer this time.

Instead, after a moment she heard the tones that signaled a number had been disconnected or changed. Then the tinny voice came on with a different number to try. Sarah hung up and dialed the new number.

Her fingers tapped against the island as she waited for someone to answer. Just when she was about to give up, someone picked up.

"Hello?"

"Is this Mr. Curtis Haber?"

A moment of hesitation carried over the line. "Yes . . ."

Please don't hang up. "My name is Sarah Hart, and I'm calling from Maple Hill, Massachusetts."

"That's nice, but why would you call me?"

"I wondered if you might be related to the Maple Hill Habers."

"I am, but it's my understanding they've all passed on now." The man's voice picked up strength as he talked, as if he were ready to challenge the purpose of the call. "Do you mind telling me what this is about?"

"There's a couple who've moved to town in the last week or two. The man claims to be the Curtis Haber who's related to the Maple Hill Habers, but a few people have their doubts."

"Are you one of those?"

Sarah chuckled at his direct question. "Maybe. I'm not entirely sure. But I wondered if you would mind answering a few questions. The kinds of questions only a Haber could answer."

"Let's see what your questions are. Don't hold it against me if I can't answer them all. I've lived most of my life down here in Florida. Got as far away from Massachusetts's winters as I could. I bet about now you think that was a brilliant move."

"The weather's not too bad right now."

"Not yet. But it will be. Your winters are brutal. Now your questions. Almost feels like I'm on *Jeopardy*. Should I say, 'family history for two hundred,' Sarah?" The humor in his voice made her wish she was sitting across a table from him.

Sarah pulled her notebook closer and grabbed a pen. "Okay. First question. Where were you born and when?"

"I think you mean first two questions." He chuckled then wheezed to a stop. "Nothing like starting with the easy ones. Born in nineteen thirty right outside Maple Hill. My parents left as the Depression deepened, taking jobs in Florida picking fruit. No easy life, let me tell you."

After making a couple of notes, Sarah continued. "What did you do in your career?"

"I wouldn't exactly call it a career. I'd call it an exploration. A little of this and more of that. Service during Korea. Tried my hand at restaurants. Then worked in insurance. Once I even announced the professional baseball teams during spring training."

"Have you ever been married?"

"No, ma'am. Never saw the need to be tied down."

"The Haber family up here. Can you name the family on the farm?"

He snorted. "You really should come up with harder questions since we're on the thousand dollar question."

"We'll see after you answer."

"The kids were Kevin, Eric, Kay, and Willard. The parents were Adam and Norma. There. Satisfied?"

"Yes, sir." She certainly was. He'd answered her questions correctly and effortlessly. "I've heard rumors of a treasure related to the Habers. Have you ever heard anything about that?"

"I wondered. Sure. Willard came to a reunion. One night he had a few too many drinks and started talking about a treasure Kay had brought home. She shushed him up fast, and he never said another word until a couple of weeks before he died. Asked me to take over the job protecting it. Seems he could never find the rightful owners after Kay died. Don't know why he thought I could."

The treasure was real? And still at the farm? "Do you know where the treasure is?"

"Not really. Willard was going to call me back to tell me more, but he didn't. Don't know how I'm supposed to return something when I don't know its location. I can't exactly dig up a farm." His voice seemed to tire. "Anything else, young lady?"

"One last question. You know every round of *Jeopardy* ends with a bonus. Do you know a Louise?"

"The only Louise I've known is the woman who cared for me until I moved into this nursing home a few weeks ago."

"Why did you move?"

"Louise and her husband could no longer help around my house. Seems they were moving north."

CHAPTER TWENTY-TWO

In the morning, streams of sunlight slipped through the bedroom curtains. Sarah's dreams had been filled with her anxiety. She'd gotten up to get a drink and chase a dream away only to have it replaced by another. But this time, she'd missed her first deadline and been fired before her first column had even appeared in print. If she hoped to make her deadline, she needed to get cracking. In fact, she needed to unlock the puzzle of the sampler or the column would be an extremely boring one. It had seemed like a good idea to have that silly thing serve as the focus for the first column, but now ...

The back door opened, and Sarah hurried downstairs to meet whomever had entered.

"Belle."

"Good morning, Sarah."

"If I didn't know you better, I might wonder exactly what kept you out at all hours. Especially in cold weather like this."

Belle smiled, the infectious grin that caused her whole face to light up. "I like to keep people guessing."

Sarah pushed the button to get the coffee percolating. "You do have odd hobbies." Belle sighed and shuffled to the table. She collapsed in the first chair, pulling a crocheted hat from her curls. "I don't mean to make you worry. I'm really not doing anything exciting."

"No need to explain." Sarah joined her at the table. "Let's get you something to drink and up to bed."

"Can't rest. I've got to work an early shift today." Belle made a face. "And then study. Another full day."

"I don't know how you do it."

"I love my life—most days. I've got to shower, but I'll take you up on the coffee when I come back down."

"All right." Sarah watched the girl jog up the stairs, puzzled by her late night, early morning activities. The coffee stopped dripping into the pot, so Sarah stood, dug a travel mug from the cupboard, and filled it with the rich brew. She stirred in creamer and sugar before taking the mug to her sewing room.

Her mind continued to spin. Maybe it was time to visit the Habers again. Impulsively, she grabbed her travel mug, a muffin, and her notebook and then headed to her car. The drive passed and the farm appeared before she had prepared herself—what would she say if either Curtis or Louise was home? She didn't have a strategy, but she was already there.

She could see the Haber windmill before she noticed much else on the farm. Windmills were something of an oddity in Massachusetts. Some older farms had them, relics of the days when they pulled water to the surface. But most dotted the coast in the form of wide-blade wind turbines. Suddenly Sarah pulled her car to the side of the road and took in a wide view of the farm. Then she opened her notebook and studied the sketch of the quilt. She looked up at the windmill, and then she slowly pivoted to the right. There sat several garden beds surrounding stately trees, one very large maple dominating the landscape. And beyond the trees sat a splintered split rail fence.

Sarah got out of her car and walked slowly toward the gardens, trying to imagine what they looked like during the spring and summer. Were the beds a rainbow of colors? Or were they more uniform in their hues? It was easy to imagine Kay spending time over the years creating the elaborate beds. But Sarah struggled to picture Willard down on his hands and knees maintaining the beds. But even in their current dilapidated state, the outlines of well-maintained and tended beds remained.

She could see sunflowers towering over the other plants, their stalks bending under the weight of full heads of seeds. Birds would love the seeds, though chickadees would favor the blackberry brambles along the fence. Silvery asters formed a border around the sunflowers as the blue flowers reached toward the sky. In front of the asters, some trailing arbutus hid in a dormant state. And it looked like dahlias had stood between the sunflowers and and a patch of mums, though their once proud heads now bowed under the weight of dried petals and stems.

The fall bed could be turned into a beautiful quilt. Sarah could see the image in her mind. Rows of variegated squares forming a pattern—sunflower in the center, surrounded by the asters, dahlias, and other flowers.

It would take some effort to prepare the beds before the snow began to fly. Without that, they would turn into a mess by the time the spring sun melted the snow. Sarah shook her head. There was little she could do about that, especially when the lady of the house seemed reluctant to have her around the farm.

The farm looked abandoned as Sarah returned to her car and pulled up in front of the house.

No vehicles sat in the driveway. With the trees empty of leaves, they looked like skeletons scratching the sky. Sarah wished she'd brought her camera to capture the stark image.

She approached the house. Cheerful mums filled a garden with color on one side of the porch. Even in November they supplied an abundance of color among the leftover, dead plants that hadn't yet been cleared. She opened the screen door and rapped on the front door. Old newspapers collected in a corner of the porch.

Turning, she looked from the front porch to the farm's out buildings. The barn still stood with a couple of smaller buildings close by. A weathervane twisted in the breeze on its perch on top of the barn. And the hen house looked like it hadn't been used in years, its door hanging loosely on its hinges.

Sarah pulled her notebook from her purse and looked at the list of quilt patterns. Many of them had at least one farm-themed title on their list of options. Was the farm the unifying theme she was seeking?

Was the quilt a loose picture of the farm?

Her pulse picked up.

What were the chances?

As she scanned the list, her new theory seemed to take shape. Sarah flipped to a new page in the notebook and sketched the main landmarks of the farm. When she got home, she would review her lists of quilt pattern names and compare them to the farm's layout. Could she be holding a map to where the treasure had been hidden?

She felt she needed to look at the farm's out buildings more closely, so she set off for the barn and the windmill. The barn was an average-size structure with a rusted weathervane squeaking in a loose circle on top. As she walked around it, Sarah didn't see anything that indicated a spot where treasure might be buried. If it *was* out here, a lot of digging would be needed to find it. Of course, if the treasure was jewelry, a metal detector might help. She'd have to check on that.

She hurried to the windmill that stood in a small fenced pasture to the left of the barn. Again she didn't see anything obvious. Why had she ever thought she could find the treasure? If it really existed, it had been hidden at least sixty years earlier. She could only imagine how much debris and dirt had built up over that time.

She turned in a slow circle. Behind the pasture she could see plowed land waiting for the spring. She doubted anything of importance could have been buried out there—if it had been, it certainly would have been plowed up at some point in the last sixty years. Sarah had no idea what had been planted in the field, but it matched the quilt as much as something could sixty years later. She imagined migrating geese setting down in the field for a snack of corn before continuing their flight. A broken-down chicken coop sat across the yard from the barn. At one point chickens must have run within its dilapidated fence, but right now nothing would keep them in or the foxes out.

She walked to the coop and looked around it. It didn't take long since the structure was so small, but again she found nothing.

She might not have found the treasure's location yet, but perhaps, after all this time, the treasure could be uncovered and returned to its rightful owners. However she'd have to find them too. Some of her giddy feeling disappeared at the thought. This mystery just kept evolving, with a new question springing up each time she felt close to answering an old one.

A sound caused Sarah to turn. A shadow of movement through the window morphed into Curtis frowning at her. He moved toward the door and she started walking toward her car. Something in his gaze made her hesitant about staying and talking to him.

"What are you doing?" He stepped across the threshold and hurried over the porch.

Sarah picked up her speed, and then starting jogging to her car.

"Hey, I'm talking to you. What are you doing here?"

She slipped behind the wheel and backed out of the driveway, her tires scrabbling to move across the gravel. Curtis's scowl deepened and he stood there, hands on his hips, watching her.

Her breathing eased when he finally disappeared from her rearview mirror.

All weekend she tried to figure out what the treasure could be. What could Kay have found in Europe? Her Internet searches didn't give her much to work on that seemed believable. She simply couldn't imagine that priceless artwork had remained hidden for more than sixty years. But if the treasure existed, did the Old Maid's Puzzle suggest that a clue to where it was lay hidden in the quilt? A clue that had to be identified before the treasure—whatever it was—could be recovered?

Monday, while running errands, she thought she saw Curtis Haber at the grocery store and then again down the block when she came out of the post office. She told herself she was being ridiculous, but she couldn't imagine why he kept showing up. Was he following her? The thought rattled her. Maybe going to his house Saturday had been a foolish idea.

No matter what she'd learned, she didn't like the idea he might be following her now. Yet he didn't do anything other than lurk. As if he was intent only on keeping tabs on her.

As she pulled into the driveway after finishing her errands, Sarah's cell phone rang.

"Mom?"

Sarah smiled at the endearment. "Hey, Maggie."

"I hate to ask, but could you pick up the girls today?"

Sarah glanced at the dashboard clock. She had half an hour to get to the middle school to pick them up. "Be glad to."

"Are you sure?"

Sometimes Sarah wished Maggie would quit adding qualifiers like that and simply accept Sarah's help. "Of course."

"Thank you. I'll let Jason know where they are and I'll swing by to get them by six. They've been home alone after school a couple of afternoons this week already."

"How about I take them to your house? Then they can work on their homework until you get home."

"Perfect. Thank you." The bell tinkled in the background. "I've got to run." Maggie hung up as Sarah said good-bye.

Sarah pulled into her driveway and hurried to the kitchen. She'd grab a few things before collecting the girls. A few minutes later her phone rang again.

"It's Maggie. I just remembered that the girls have after-school meetings. So if you're there by four, they should be ready."

"No problem. Glad to get them."

Maggie sighed. "Thank you." The bell rang again, and Sarah heard a crackling noise, as if Maggie had pinched the phone between her shoulder and ear. "I'll be home as soon as I can."

Sarah hung up and held the phone a minute, waiting to see if it rang again. When it didn't, she pulled out some frozen cookie dough. She didn't have time to make cookies from scratch, but these tasted so good no one would know the difference. And there was nothing like a fresh snack after school to help kids decompress.

A while later she pulled the hot cookies from the oven and stacked them on a cooling rack. She walked into her sewing room and studied the quilt. Everything in her wanted to sit down and examine the quilt with her new farm theme, but she didn't have time.

After she put the cookies on a plate and covered them with foil, she grabbed her bag and headed back to the car. Fifteen minutes later, she looked in her rearview mirror wondering when two twelve-year-olds had become noisy enough to fill a car with their voices.

The girls chattered over each other, each eager to fill her in on their day. As soon as they got home, the girls raced out of the car and up the stairs. By the time Sarah followed them a minute later, Audrey already had her iPod in and a notebook in front of her. When Sarah looked over the girl's shoulder, she saw the beginnings of a sketch.

"What is this?"

Audrey kept drawing, so Sarah tapped her shoulder and repeated the question.

"I don't know yet." Audrey wrinkled her nose and smiled. "I sat down and..."

"She doesn't want to do homework yet." Amy dropped her book bag on the table and slumped into a chair. "Is it Christmas break yet?

Sarah laughed, and placed the plate of cookies in front of the girls. "You've got a few weeks to go."

Audrey grabbed a cookie and took a bite. "At least we have these."

"I'll get the milk, and then it's time to start your homework."

Their groans followed her to the kitchen, but she didn't let them sway her. Much as she loved to sit and play games with the girls, they needed to get their work done first.

The hours passed quietly as the girls settled into their schoolwork. With each girl wearing her iPod and intent on her assignments, Sarah pulled out her Bible and caught up on her devotions.

After a while, Sarah left the girls at the table and went to the kitchen to find something to make for supper. As busy as Maggie's day had sounded, getting this going for her would be a way to ease her burdens. She'd put some chicken in the oven to bake and set salad fixings on the granite countertop when she heard the backdoor open.

Maggie stepped inside and shrugged out of her coat. She looked at the countertop and frowned. "You didn't need to start supper."

"Nonsense. It's something simple. And now you don't have to worry about what to make." Sarah bit her tongue before she said something sharp that would undo the intent of her good deed.

A weary smile touched Maggie's lips. "Thank you. It *has* been a long day. Were the girls any trouble?"

"No, we had a good time. I can't say it looks like you had the same."

"To be honest, it was a long day. And then attending another Chamber of Commerce mixer was draining. I don't enjoy them. Everybody's drinking and yakking about people and places they assume I know. The only good part was that Jason joined me for a bit. He'll be home soon, but had to go back to the office for a while. At least he knows I'm not from here. I'm ready to make a button that reminds people I've only lived here a few months. Is that over the top?"

Sarah laughed and picked up a tomato to chop. "Not at all. Sometimes we need a reminder not everyone has lived here their whole lives."

The cloud didn't lift from Maggie's face. "I guess I should go check on the girls."

"Have a cup of tea first." Sarah turned to the stove, checked the teapot for water, and then turned on the burner. "They're still working on homework. Looks like you could use another minute to decompress."

Maggie folded her arms across her chest. "I look that bad?"

"That's not what I meant." Sarah studied Maggie. She didn't know many people more caring and service oriented than her daughter-in-law. In fact, she often led with an eye on everyone else's needs. Sarah pulled the kettle from the burner and grabbed a mug for her. As she filled the mug with hot water, she paused. Maybe that was the key to Maggie's challenges since the move. She was so focused on the demands others put on her she poured herself out in a way that left little for her family.

"Uh-oh. You've got that look again." Maggie sank into a chair at the table, her shoulders tense.

Sarah set the mug in front of Maggie. Then she grabbed the tin of tea bags and the basket of sweetener and put them next to the mug. "What do you mean?"

"The look that says you have some insight." Maggie crossed her arms and leaned against her chair. "Let me have it."

Sarah tried to laugh off Maggie's intensity as she softened her body language. "There's nothing to let you have."

"If you have insight, help me out. I'm tired of being exhausted and drained."

"Why don't you and Jason leave the girls with me this weekend? You could slip away, just the two of you. Make a reservation at one of the bed-and-breakfasts around here. What's the use of living near a grandmother if you don't do things like that?"

"But I did. This afternoon."

"That's not the same as slipping away for some time. You two have been so busy since you moved. I don't know how you manage everything."

Maggie turned away. "I don't know how I could leave the store, even for a day." She faced Sarah and swiped at her cheeks. "The store has so much potential. But right now I have to be there. All the time. And put in the time and effort it needs." Maggie yawned. "A couple of days away sounds nice. But from Thanksgiving to Christmas is the busiest time of the retail year. Maybe after a successful Christmas I'll be able to hire someone."

"Imagine if you had someone else in the store, and you could go to estate sales and work in the back during business hours."

"That's the goal. I just have to make it through the next few months."

"Can your family survive the next few months like this? Can you?"

Maggie didn't respond.

Sarah stood and poured water into another mug and settled on one of the stools. "Gerry and I—I can see now that so many times it would have been better if I had stepped back and given him more of my time. I tend to get a little focused. And at times that was at Gerry's expense."

Tears slipped down Maggie's cheeks. "I had no idea starting this store would be so hard. So complicated. And we moved here to make life less stressful. What was I thinking?"

Sarah covered Maggie's hands with hers. "You'll make it."

Maggie shook her head. "We've invested so much in the store." She bobbed the tea bag up and down, staring into the changing water.

Sarah took a sip of her tea, praying for the right words to challenge and encourage Maggie. "For both you and Jason, jobs are important, but being a loving spouse and attentive parent are your two primary tasks in life. Ultimately, your investment in your family will outlast any store or legal practice."

"So what do we do?"

The question hung in the air, its weight pressing against Sarah.

What should they do?

Her burdens looked overwhelming to Maggie, and Sarah could understand. She remembered the stresses of parenting, and she hadn't tried to start a business in the middle of that.

Cast your burden on the Lord, and he will sustain you; he will never allow the righteous to be shaken. The words of the psalm filtered through her heart.

"Maggie, I don't know. Only God can show you what's right for this season of life. He'll help you find practical ways you can show you care for each other." Sarah touched Maggie's hand, waiting for her to relax. "And I'm serious about taking the girls for a weekend so you two can get away for a bit."

Maggie studied her so intently Sarah could almost see the thoughts forming. How could she let her daughter-in-law know how special she was? How very grateful Sarah was she had married Jason?

"Maggie," Sarah squeezed the woman's hand, "You are a wonderful part of our family. I will help in any way I can. Whatever you need. Know I pray for you and Jason. God has plans for the two of you that you haven't even begun to glimpse."

Maggie wiped fresh tears from her face. "Thank you. I have a lot to think about."

"Mom!" Amy raced into the kitchen. "When did you get here?"

"A while ago." Maggie tugged on one of the earbuds hanging around Amy's neck. "I bet this kept you from hearing me."

Amy grinned sheepishly, then raced back into the dining room. "Audrey, guess who's home?"

"Let me pray with you before they come in here." Maggie nodded and Sarah took her hands.

"Heavenly Father, thank you for bringing my family back to me. All of my family, including this precious daughter Maggie. Father, you see all that is going on in their lives. I ask that you would give her wisdom on how to balance all the demands on her life. Help carry her burdens and fill her with strength to flourish during this time. May all that she says and does be to your glory. Amen."

Maggie squeezed her hand and then smiled as the girls launched at her.

Sarah stood and took her now empty mug to the kitchen sink. "Chicken is in the oven. Should be done in twenty minutes. The girls can wrap up the salad." She winked at Maggie over the girls' groans. "I'll let you guys have a quiet evening."

CHAPTER TWENTY-THREE

When Sarah got home, she went directly to her sewing room. After turning on some background music, she studied the quilt.

Her earlier excitement about a possible farm theme bubbled up again as she looked at the quilt blocks. She couldn't be a hundred percent sure until she spent some time with her grid, but she had a feeling she was on the right track. Finally.

Sarah pulled out her notebook. There was absolutely no doubt in her mind that the far-right column contained the Split Rail pattern. It formed the right-hand border of the quilt, just as the wooden split rail fence bordered the Haber property, separating it from the neighboring field. She placed a check above that column.

She felt equally confident about the patterns in the next row to the left. Flower Garden topping Maine Tree. Beneath that sat Grandma's Garden and then Fox and Geese or Old Maid's Puzzle. While the idea of a farm theme made Fox and

Geese a possibility, Sarah felt quite certain that Kay had created the sampler quilt and planted some riddle in its squares. Old Maid's Puzzle seemed the most apt name. Sarah starred that bottom square and then checked off the row. Those were the easy two.

No, she thought as she stared at the remaining three, *these are the rows that contain the key to the puzzle.*

The middle row should be easy. When Sarah had researched alternative names for Star and Cross, she'd been struck by one in particular—Farmer's Daughter. She crossed through Star and Cross and the other names in that piece of the grid. With Cupid's Dart and Farmer's Daughter, she knew two of the four patterns. But the top pattern still flummoxed her. All those diamonds intricately linked left her wondering what she was supposed to see. There had to be something. Kay had been so intentional about what she'd selected for the first two rows, Sarah knew this pattern meant something as well.

The final pattern in that row could be either Bird's Eye View or Wheel of Chance. Either fit. But at the moment she could let both names stay. She had a hunch that neither was likely to be the key to the quilt.

The grids for the two rows on the left-hand side of the quilt held long lists of possible pattern names, so many names that Sarah considering calling it quits for the night. Surely there was no urgency about finishing tonight. The quilt would still be there in the morning, all its secrets safely hidden for another day.

But she couldn't stop. She wanted to know she'd done everything she could to figure out the quilt.

She stood and stepped back from the quilt, stretching her lower back. She cocked her head to one side and then the other, trying to imagine what Kay had seen years earlier when she'd imagined what the quilt would look like.

She took another step back and changed her perspective.

It couldn't be that simple, could it?

She stepped into the hallway. Then back into the sewing room.

The quilt hadn't changed. If anything, it seemed to mock her for not noticing earlier.

If she'd been Kay and if she'd brought a treasure back from Europe, how would she leave a map to mark the treasure that wouldn't be obvious to everyone who saw it? *She'd make a quilt.* And as Sarah cocked her head again, she realized that might very well have been exactly what Kay had done. And that insight might help her unlock the secrets of the last two columns.

Her fingers itched to pick up the pen and get to work on those last two columns. To see if she was right.

She hurried back to the chair and plopped down. She might have found scores of options for the names of the blocks in the last two columns, but if the quilt was a map to the farm, she was sure she could identify the correct names.

At the top of the fourth column was Weathervane, one of the blocks with only one possible name. The weathervane on the barn? She made a quick note as she continued down the column. Next came the cross and triangle pattern that she'd assumed was Shoo Fly. Now she wondered.

Sarah grabbed the encyclopedia and flipped to the page she'd marked for that pattern. She stared at the page that showed the square, and then ran through the list of twenty names she'd written on the grid trying to find a name that fit the quilt. Double Wrench...Bear Paw Design...Honey Dish...None of them was right. Then she saw it. At the very bottom—Hole in the Barn Door. Perfectly placed for Weather Vane to perch on top of it. And perfectly placed for the actual location of the rundown Haber barn.

Her toes tapped in time to the music on the radio as she studied the quilt and the names she'd marked on the grid. She thought about the Haber farmhouse. It sat catty-corner from and near the barn. To the right of it were the gardens and the large maple tree. And the split rail fence bounded the farm just as the Split Rail bordered the quilt. So could the mystery diamond pattern at the top of the third column have something to do with the house? She made a note and kept looking.

The Farmer's Daughter sat near the gardens, but Cupid's Dart pointed away from her. And Puss in the Corner might be a great choice as the name for the lower left corner. Every farm had a barn cat or two or twenty. Maybe Kay had loved cats. Anything was possible. And in keeping with the farm theme, the last block in the next-to-last column was no longer a Shoo Fly variation. It had to be Hens and Chicks. Especially since the block was located roughly where the dilapidated chicken coop stood on the farm. But as Sarah stared at the quilt, she wondered if she had enough pieces of the puzzle to find whatever was hidden on the property.

She raced through the last column. She was sure the top pattern was Flying Geese and the bottom, Puss in the Corner, of course. The block just below Flying Geese could have any of eight names, most of them farm related. Ducklings...another Fox and Geese pattern...even Corn and Beans. But as she studied it in relation to the quilt and the farm, she decided it had to be Corn and Beans, since the plowed field she had seen lay in that general location. Below that was Windmill—clearly in its right place.

A minute later, Sarah leaned back and looked at the quilt, running down the new names for the patterns. She reconsidered the diamond pattern at the top of the third row. It had to relate to the farmhouse. But how? Most quilt makers would have appliquéd a house on a square or used a log cabin pattern to indicate a house. This pattern represented something more specific and thus was more difficult to identify.

Sarah examined the list of eighteen names she'd written on the grid for this block. Block Pattern, Variegated Diamonds, Golden Cubes, Tumbling Blocks, Stair Step...Stair

Step?...lots of houses had stairs. Could Stair Step be the name of the diamond square that had stumped her from the beginning? Looking at the square, Sarah thought an expert quilter would need at least five hours to piece it, never mind quilting it. A much different time commitment from what the quilter would have invested in some of the simple squares in the quilt. The thought of cutting all the diamonds out of the various fabrics made her cutting hand ache.

But why would someone include a Stair Step pattern in a quilt that focused on the outdoors? She couldn't imagine many barns or out buildings that would include a staircase rather than a ladder, and the pattern definitely wasn't formed like a ladder. It was filled with angles rather than straight lines.

So could the square represent stairs inside the house?

The house on the farm was small but neat. Could that be it? The house looked too low to have a second story. But that didn't mean there weren't stairs of some sort inside. And could the treasure be hidden near them? Or under them?

And could that skeleton key she'd found unlock a door in the house?

She yawned. It was after ten. She felt good about figuring out most of the quilt. It was a map. A smile creased her face at the realization that she held the key to finding the treasure that had been rumored for years. She might not be entirely sure how to find it yet, but she knew this quilt would mark the way.

The next morning Sarah hurried through her chores, then called Liam as soon as she thought his morning coffee rush should have ended. "Liam, I won't keep you, but do you know where I can find Jacques Vallard?"

"Why?"

Sarah paused, not willing to share the niggling idea she had. "I have a question for him."

"You don't have to go far. He's sitting in one of my chairs scanning a book on the area."

"Can you keep him there until I arrive? I'll be there in less than fifteen minutes."

"Sure, love. Anything for you."

Sarah paused at his term of endearment before she reminded herself he talked like that to everyone. "See you soon."

"I'll have a chai tea waiting."

When Sarah reached The Spotted Dog, Murphy greeted her at the door. She paused so he could sniff her shoes without being inadvertently kicked.

"Here you go, Sarah." Liam handed her a cup topped with a pyramid of whipped cream. "He's over in the bookstore."

"Thanks, Liam." She spotted Jacques, his beret perched on the arm of the overstuffed chair and an attaché case sitting at his feet. A stack of books had collected next to the chair and he held a travel guide, flipping through the pages so quickly Sarah wondered if he could actually see anything.

She cleared her throat, and he startled.

"Ma chérie." He jerked to his feet, the beret sliding from the chair. "Please, join me."

Sarah smiled and nodded. "Thank you. I hope you don't mind my interrupting your reading."

"Non. Traveling solo is lonely. I'd much rather spend my time with a beautiful woman than a dusty book." He waited for her to sit, then mirrored her action. "I see you have your café."

"Another chai tea today." She leaned forward, setting the cup on the table between them. "Do you mind if I ask you a question?"

He nodded, a closed look clouding his eyes. "I will be glad to listen."

"I've been on a journey the last couple weeks, and I believe our searches may overlap." She studied him, wondering how receptive he would be to her questions. Without some input from him, her theories might work, but she would be missing some key details. "Do you remember that picture you showed me?" She pulled it from her purse and handed it to him. "And your search to find the people in the photo?"

"Mais oui. One does not travel this far and forget the purpose of a journey . . . no matter how insane that search may appear."

"I may have found your search odd before, but not now."

He leaned forward, elbows planted on his knees.

"Will you trust me with your story? The reason for your search?"

Jacques looked over her shoulder, as if considering whether he could entrust her with that gift. After a minute he nodded. "Yes. I will tell you my story."

He leaned back and steepled his fingers in front of his chin.

"The story begins in 1944 ... "

CHAPTER TWENTY-FOUR

M y grandfather lived in Paris when the Allies liberated the city. The city might have been free, but it struggled to find itself after Nazi control. Somehow he'd hidden during the occupation, which considering the status of my family was a minor miracle."

Sarah leaned forward, trying to imagine what life had been like for the French. Her parents had survived rationing, a far cry from occupation.

"He often talked about those days. How it was still important to blend in, remain unseen. Those who collaborated with the Nazis now found themselves the targets, while those who had hidden needed to continue to stay out of sight. The Nazis could still be there. It was a highly unsettled time."

"I can imagine." Sarah took a breath. "But what does his story have to do with the treasure?"

"Patience." Jacques' lips tightened in a smile that did not reach his eyes. "My grandfather did his best to keep his life simple. Stops at cafés for simple things like café noire. All the while keeping his guard up. He'd spend his afternoons reading the paper, staying hidden in plain sight. Then one day everything changed."

Jacques looked down and patted the satchel, as if assuring himself it remained where he had set it.

"Yes?"

He looked up and met her gaze. "Kay Haber arrived at his café, sat at his table and stole his heart. He relaxed in her presence and soon spent every moment he could entice her to share with him." Jacques shrugged. "He called it true love. My grandmother called it temporary craziness."

"The Red Cross required her days, but my grandfather laid claim to her evenings. He wined and dined her in an effort to delight Kay with Paris's slowly reviving cultural life."

Sarah held up her hand to stop the flow of words. "How do you know all of this?"

Jacques shrugged. "I heard the stories from my grandfather as a small lad. Then my father delighted in telling the story of his father's folly, especially as women became appealing to me. He called this woman my grandfather's one true love—said the American stole my grandfather's heart and the family riches in one motion. Of course, he called her that only when my grandmother was not in the room."

"Of course." Sarah shook her head, trying to imagine what it would be like to live in the shadow of a love like that.

"You see, these two fell passionately in love as only happens in Paris during a war. But the fates were not kind to them." Jacques pulled his case onto his lap. "My grandfather had been entrusted with protecting something valuable. And the time came when he no longer felt able to do that. He looked for someone to entrust with his burden. Someone who would protect it for his sake and the sake of his family, whatever pieces had survived the Nazi war machine.

"He believed that someone was this woman. His trust was unfortunately misplaced."

"Why would you say that?" Sarah frowned at him. "Everyone I know speaks highly of Kay and her character."

"Because my grandfather entrusted her with the jewels and never saw her again."

"So he left her?"

"He had to. But he fully planned to find her again."

"How? Did they exchange addresses or other important information?"

Jacques shrugged, a languid movement that barely covered his irritation. "Supposedly she made a big show of tears and begging him not to leave, but then was so stunned that my grandfather decided he needed to escape while he could. He left, believing it would be easy to find one Kay Haber who worked for the American Red Cross. He could not comprehend the chaos that would cover Europe even after the war ended."

"Regardless, my grandfather never saw her again. No matter where he looked, it was as though the beautiful American had simply disappeared...become a ghost...taking my family's fortune with her. My father also tried to search for her, but grandfather died before he could get sufficient details to identify her. All we had was a name. And in those days...it was nearly impossible to find someone with such limited information."

Sarah considered his words. Could his story be the truth? She didn't want to think of Kay taking the jewels and disappearing. She certainly couldn't imagine Willard defending her treasure after her death if that were the case.

"I see by the doubt in your eyes that you require proof. A wise woman." Slowly he patted the case as if trying to decide whether to trust her further. Then he unlatched the locks on the case. He pulled out a file and slid it across the table to her. "See for yourself."

Sarah picked up the pages and gasped. Even though the photos were black-and-white, what they portrayed took her breath away.

"My family's fortune. Entrusted to your friend all those years ago. Foolishly entrusted, it would seem."

"But how do you have photos of them?" Even in black-and-white, the jewelry looked dazzling. A mix of diamonds, pearls, and precious stones. Sarah flipped through the photos, spellbound.

"Even in those days the wealthy insured their precious items. These photos are copies of those taken by my grandfather for insurance purposes. May I?" He reached for the photos and Sarah gave them back. Jacques flipped through them and handed one photo to Sarah. "Family lore has it that this tiara once belonged to Marie Antoinette. If it is true... well, you can imagine the value of that one piece.

"My father always said that this set," referring to a photo of a bracelet, choker, and earrings, "was crafted of pearls and diamonds for the coronation of another king. I forget now which."

"They're all beautiful."

Jacques slid the photos back in the folder and closed the case. "Why do you need to know my family's sordid tale?"

Sarah bit her lower lip as she considered how much to tell the man. She still wasn't certain that the quilt pointed to the treasure he sought. After hearing his story, the odds seemed likely, but she hated to raise his hopes. And what if he decided to take matters into his own hands after so long?

"Is there a reason you are here now? It seems a long time to wait."

"I've had a Web alert set on Kay Haber for years. I got a hit that looked like it might be the right person about a month ago. Once that happened, I couldn't stay away." He studied her as if wanting to see into her mind. "What do you think?"

"I need to pull a few more pieces of the puzzle together." She took a final sip from her mug and stood. "Thank you for your time and for sharing your story with me. I hope it has a happy ending."

"As do I." Jacques stood and gave her a small salute as she hurried to the counter.

Liam looked up with a grin. "Learn the man's life history over there?"

"Not quite. But he does have interesting stories to weave. Thank you for the tea."

His "my pleasure" chased her out the door.

When she reached her car, Sarah opened the door and sank behind the wheel. She pulled her notebook from her bag and captured as much as she could of Jacques's tale. Had Roberto really entrusted those magnificent jewels to Kay? And if he had, would she have held on to them and hidden them somewhere? If they had a love like the one Jacques described, Sarah couldn't imagine Kay not attempting to find Roberto. But certainly the sheer number of refugees must have made it difficult. Still, working for the Red Cross, wouldn't Kay have had an advantage?

The story captivated Sarah even as it broke her heart for the woman who had lived out her days after the war in Maple Hill. Alone.

Why had she come home? Why not stay in Paris and try to find Roberto?

There was still so much Sarah didn't know, but she couldn't imagine Kay abandoning her love willingly. And she certainly couldn't imagine that the Habers had ever benefitted from the treasure. They certainly had seemed to be merely scraping by—they had enough, but never an abundance.

Which led to one conclusion. If Kay had ever had the Vallard family treasure, and if that treasure had remained in her possession once she returned home, and if she had felt a need to protect it for the man who had left her, the treasure was somewhere in Maple Hill.

And if that was true, Sarah had the map. Now all she needed was the key to the map.

CHAPTER TWENTY-FIVE

As soon as she left Jacques, Sarah called the office of *Country Cottage*. "This is Sarah Hart. Can you tell me if Chester Winslow is in the office this afternoon?"

The receptionist paused a moment, then confirmed his calendar showed him in the office for the balance of the day.

"Thank you. Could you put me through to his voice mail?"

The receptionist complied and a minute later Sarah left a message for him. "Chester, this is Sarah. I'm headed your way. Please wait for me as I have something I need to discuss with you."

Her drive was filled with black-and-white images of Kay Haber and Roberto Vallard, and their ill-fated love during the days of World War II. Between the map and what she'd just learned from Jacques about the treasure, she knew enough to try to get Curtis and Louise Haber to tell her what they wanted. But first she needed to get the key back and confront Chester.

Driving to the *Country Cottage* offices seemed foolish. But now that she'd heard Vallard's story, she needed to figure out what role Chester played in this drama. The office seemed like a safe public place to confront him and get his story.

Why had he written about a treasure that so few knew about? She needed to know the answer to that question. And one more that bothered her deeply.

Had he only become interested in her after seeing her with the quilts at the auction?

She didn't want to believe their time together had been a lie, but she wanted to protect herself from believing it could be anything else.

An hour later she pulled into the parking lot behind the building. All she needed was the skeleton key and some answers. That was all. No reason to expect any problems from Chester. He'd always been a perfect gentleman in her presence.

Sarah took a deep breath and prayed that behavior continued. The receptionist smiled at her when she walked into the lobby.

"Mrs. Hart. Welcome to the team."

"Thank you. Could you ... "

"Let Chester know you're here. Certainly." The woman hit a button and spoke in a muffled tone. "Yes, she's here. ..."

Alright, I'll send her right back." She hit a button and looked up at Sarah. "Do you think you can find your way back to his office?"

Sarah nodded. How hard could it be to retrace her steps?

"Go on back." The phone rang, and the receptionist turned her attention to the call.

The door opened, and Sarah waited for a young lady to walk through and then slipped through behind her. There seemed to be more activity in the area today. As phones in several cubicles rang simultaneously, she thought Chester must be especially grateful to have an office with a door on days like this.

She headed down the hall to his office, and before she reached it, the door opened.

Chester strode toward her, a welcoming smile on his face. "Sarah!"

Her intentions of drilling him crumbled in the face of his warmth. She let him kiss her cheek before she stepped back. He wrinkled his brow, then motioned toward his door. "Come in, come in." He cleared a pile of paper off a chair and waved her to it. "I was surprised to get your message. Why drive all this way?"

"I need to retrieve the key I left here."

"But I would gladly have brought it to you."

But she couldn't risk that. No, she needed to see him in circumstances that put him slightly off balance. She fidgeted as the conversation fumbled to silence.

"Well, then," he reached into a desk drawer and pulled out an envelope. "Here's your key. I could find nothing remarkable about it. It appears to be quite old and the right size for a door or large piece of furniture."

"I don't think it goes to furniture." Sarah picked up the envelope, feeling the heft of the key. "Maggie bought most of it and the key was with the quilts. I think that was intentional."

"As a way to hide it?"

"Maybe ... but more likely because it goes with one of the quilts. Then again we don't know if it goes to anything." Though she had strong suspicions it did.

"Every key fits in some lock. We simply don't know which lock. Yet."

Sarah had to smile at his hope-filled last word. Then she remembered his book, and the tenseness in her shoulders returned. "Why didn't you tell me you wrote a book about the Habers and their treasure?"

"I didn't know it mattered."

"Yet you knew I was working on this puzzle."

"True. But don't we both want the same thing."

"If there's a treasure, I want to find it, make sure it goes to its rightful owners." Sarah bit her lip. She couldn't have asked for a better opening. "Why didn't you tell me about it when you first knew I was working on the quilt?"

"I didn't think you'd find anything helpful. No one else has."

"How did you hear about the treasure? I've lived in Maple Hill my whole life and hadn't."

Chester shrugged. "I don't remember the first place I heard about it, probably a party in college. I think a fraternity brother mentioned it."

"But how did he know?" Sarah crossed her arms, daring him to lie to her. *Really? A fraternity brother?*

"You know how people act. I didn't know if I could give credence to anything he said. He *was* talking about treasure after all. So I discounted it for a long time. When I did start poking around, nobody would even admit having heard of it.

"I decided to write that book and mentioned it to the editor as one option for a chapter. She loved it. And there you have it, I had to research it and write something. I didn't find much."

"Is that why you were at the sale?"

"Sure. After writing about the rumors, I had to see for myself what was at the sale. Too bad I couldn't imagine those quilts had any value." He leaned back in his chair and smiled at her. "That took a woman with your skill."

She shook her head and smiled. "Is there anything you learned about the treasure that didn't make it into the book?"

"I'm sure there is. That's the way writing is. Piles of research, much of which gets dumped."

"Do you think it exists?"

He shrugged. "Probably, but if it's been hidden this long, I don't expect to find it. And I highly doubt those Habers have a clue what they're looking for."

"I think you're right." Sarah quickly filled Chester in about the phone call she'd had with the real Curtis Haber in Florida. "So, if Louise overheard a call or the real Curtis told her about the treasure while she was providing home health care services to him, I'm certain she missed important details." Sarah stood. "Thank you for letting me stop by. Anything else I should know about the key?"

Chester shook his head, the furrow between his eyebrows deepening. "There's nothing distinctive about it. My guess is it goes to a door. Find the door, and you'll have a use for the key." He studied her a moment. "Do you know where the door is?"

"I'm not sure." Sarah picked up her purse and pushed to her feet.

"Wait." Chester rubbed his cheek. "Have I done something to offend you?" He stood and shoved his hands in his pockets. "I really thought we had the beginnings of a friendship. But something's happened. I don't know what or why, but it's changed."

Sarah swallowed, her gaze locked with his. She wanted to say, no, nothing had changed. But honestly, she couldn't. "I need to get something figured out."

"May I at least stay in contact?"

"Yes, that would be fine." Sarah turned to hurry from his office.

"And promise me one thing..." He waited until she turned back around, one hand anchored on the door frame. "Tell me when you find the treasure."

"I..." She didn't know how to respond. She didn't want to confirm his guess, but as she looked at him she realized he knew. He had all along, and that reinforced the impression he had been with her only to be there when the treasure was found. "Is that what this is all about? The treasure?"

"I'd love to see the treasure. But it if it's found, it's just a thing. You, on the other hand, are a true jewel."

The heat climbed her cheeks as she fled into the hallway.

Now that she had the key back, was she ready to go to the Haber farm and try to find the treasure? How could she do that with the Habers there? And as long as they were there, how could she get the treasure to Vallard if it truly belonged to his family?

She looked into her rearview mirror. Was that the Habers' beat up car behind her?

Maple Hill wasn't that big, so she ignored the car. The Habers could be going any number of places that would put them on the same streets. The car followed her onto Memorial Drive and she pulled to a stop in front of Jason's office. It continued by, so she pulled back out and headed home.

For the rest of the day it seemed as though wherever she went, she saw the Habers' car.

But the next morning Sarah wondered if she'd imagined the car in her rearview mirror. She hadn't gotten a clear view of the person driving, and it was entirely possible that it was a different car each time. Maybe she'd let the excitement of the hunt for the map and treasure make her hypersensitive to what was around her.

Her phone rang while she sat at the kitchen island with her breakfast and devotions. When she answered it, a harried-sounding Louise apologized for calling so early.

"I didn't know who else to call."

"I was already up so this is fine."

"Is there any way we could meet this morning? For tea or coffee. Maybe at The Spotted Dog."

Sarah glanced at her refrigerator calendar. The day was as clear as she'd thought. "I'd be happy to meet you there. I'm driving back into town, so can you give me an hour?"

There was an extended pause. "That's fine. Thank you."

Louise clicked off, and Sarah looked at her phone before turning it off. There had been something in Louise's voice that sounded more intense than she would expect of someone who had invited her to meet for coffee.

The more she thought about their short conversation, the less she could pinpoint what bothered her. She shook off the feeling as she hurried upstairs to get ready for the day.

Thirty minutes later Sarah was out the door. The smoky gray clouds hung heavy with snow. If it decided to break free, the area could be in for a heavy snowfall just in time for Thanksgiving, or it could blow over them with nary a flake hitting the ground. She imagined the trees lining the road bowed under the weight of the ice and snow. With a snowstorm, fall would abandon the area in the face of the icy breath of winter.

The Habers' older model Honda sat in front of The Spotted Dog when she arrived. Sarah climbed from the car wondering what Louise wanted to talk about. As long as she had one of Liam's chai teas, she'd be ready to listen to anything. Liam's waitress smiled at Sarah as she wiped down a table.

"Mrs. Hart. How are you today?"

"Good, Karen. Could you bring me a chai tea when you have a minute? No hurry."

"Sure." Karen Bancroft pointed toward the bookstore. "The lady you're meeting is already over there."

Louise stood pacing in front of a bookshelf. Her hand trailed along the spines of books, but at the rate she was moving, Sarah doubted she was actually seeing anything.

"Louise?"

The woman spun on her heel, a hand at her throat. "You're here."

Sarah smiled. "I promised I'd come. My friends know I do everything I can to keep my word. Curtis isn't with you?"

"No, he had other things to do."

She shouldn't feel this way, but Sarah relaxed in the knowledge he wouldn't suddenly show up. Maybe she'd learn something from Louise without Curtis there to serve as a filter.

But as she looked at Louise and the determined set to her shoulders, Sarah got the sense that Louise had an agenda for their get-together. They weren't meeting simply to spend time together.

CHAPTER TWENTY-SIX

Sarah tried to smile, but her cheeks felt stiff as she looked at Louise.

"Did you get anything to drink?"

"Not yet." Louise walked to a chair and perched on the edge. "I'm still not used to warm drinks. I like my tea iced."

"I'm sure they can do that for you."

"It's not the same."

Sarah nodded and then glanced back at the counter. Something felt odd about this whole arrangement. "I'm still not certain why you wanted to see me."

"Something has to be done and you're the only one I know well enough to ask for help." Louise's brow wrinkled as if etched in a permanent frown.

Sarah sank onto the chair opposite Louise, keeping her hand wrapped firmly around her purse. "Whatever it is, it can't be that bad."

"You've never lived with a man like Curtis. I can tell. He's so focused on this heirloom. He's had me look everywhere, but it's not in the house. And now that we haven't found it, he's extra unbearable. He's like a man obsessed, and I don't know what to do."

"I'm still not sure why you think I can help."

An intense look filled Louise's eyes. Sarah shifted in her seat and gripped her purse tighter. What could Louise be up to? She knew the Habers weren't looking for an heirloom, but for the treasure. No matter how Louise begged, Sarah couldn't lead them to it. Not when she was certain they had no claim to the treasure. But if she suddenly turned unhelpful wouldn't Louise wonder why?

"Curtis is convinced you can help us. You've lived here all your life and knew the Habers in their day-to-day lives. You surely know things we don't."

"How do you think I can help?"

"Come with me and look around the place."

"Help you unpack?"

"No, Curtis and I have been through the boxes. The only place those should go is Goodwill. Help us search."

Karen walked up with Sarah's chai tea. "Here you go, Mrs. Hart."

"She'll need that in a to-go cup," Louise said. Sarah was taken aback by her brazenness.

Sarah studied Louise a moment, weighing her options. She wasn't about to help them find the treasure. But she did have the map, as well as a key that she needed to find the lock for. She had to figure out how they went together. Maybe she could find the match while 'helping' the Habers. Yes, that's what she'd do. "Do you mind, Karen?"

"Not at all." Karen walked off with the mug, a happy-go-lucky swing to her step.

"When would you like me to come to the farm?" Sarah asked Louise.

"Can you come now? No sense wasting more time with Curtis in a funk. I am ready to get my man back." Something about the focused way Louise looked at the door told Sarah she'd already mentally left.

"Once Karen brings my drink, I'll follow you to the farm."

"Let me drive you."

"Don't be ridiculous. I'll be right behind you."

"The least I can do is drive you out there. I'd like the company. After all, you're the only friend I have here, Sarah."

Usually, Sarah would have been flattered that someone considered her a friend. But this time it left her with an uneasy sense. Louise seemed desperate. And that made Sarah wonder if going with Louise was a good decision. But she reminded herself that she needed access to the farm, to look around without raising suspicions. If she was there at Louise's request, she would have a legitimate reason for being there. She needed to ignore the butterflies taking flight in her stomach as she followed Louise to her car. This was part of the investigation. Nothing more. Louise might be a tad eccentric, but she'd always been nice. Offering Sarah a ride had to be more of the same.

Sarah climbed into the passenger seat, forming a plan as Louise pulled away. If the Habers pushed too hard, she'd simply give them bad information. Just because she'd agreed to travel to the farm didn't mean she had to share everything she'd learned. Especially since she was convinced the Habers weren't who they said. Sarah glanced out the window and saw Liam racing from his shop. She waved, glad at least one person knew she'd gotten into the car with Louise.

The drive passed in relative quiet, the only sound coming from a classical radio station. Once they entered the house, it took a moment for Sarah's eyes to adjust to the dim interior. Louise led her to the living room area and pointed to the couch. "Have a seat."

Sarah eased onto the edge of the couch. It seemed even lumpier than it had the first time she'd visited, its orange velvet faded and worn down to a nub in places. She shifted in an attempt to avoid the springs threatening to poke through the worn upholstery.

Nothing hung on the walls, not even the few odds and ends that had hung there earlier. Brighter blotches of cream paint showed where the art and photos had hung. What had the Habers done with the pieces? Even when people planned to move, most kept a couple of things on the walls to make the house feel homey.

Louise perched on the edge of a chair opposite Sarah. Her hands tapped on her knees as she looked toward the stairs and then back at Sarah with a forced smile.

Sarah glanced at all the boxes lined against the wall and piled in a pyramid by the stairs. Maybe the item the key went to rested in one of them. "Are you sure I can't help with these boxes?"

Louise's fingers stilled and she shook her head. "We aren't unpacking any of those. Just junk anyway."

The uneasy silence settled on the room. Why did she have such a driving passion to unravel the twisted webs of mysteries? She wasn't certain how to convince Louise to let her look...not without giving the definite impression she knew where the treasure lay. Maybe she should take what she knew to Chief Webber and leave the next steps to the professionals. The only problem came when she imagined his face if she plopped this one in his lap.

He wouldn't be amused.

Louise shivered, shaking her thin frame. "With the storm blowing in, I'm ready to go home to Florida." She shuddered the way Sarah would if someone mentioned a hurricane blowing into town. "How do you handle the cold?"

Sarah shrugged, and glanced beyond Louise. Was that a door partially hidden by the boxes? "You grow used to it. After a season or two you'll be acclimated."

Louise scanned the room. "Okay. So if you were Mr. Haber where would you hide an heirloom?"

Sarah studied the room. "I don't know that I'd hide an heirloom. Usually families are proud of the heirlooms, passing them from generation to generation with care."

"But if that were the case with this family, we'd have found it."

"Then why don't we recheck?" There was so much of the house that Sarah hadn't seen. She fingered the skeleton key in her jacket pocket. The lock it went to had to be somewhere around here.

"I suppose that would be okay." Louise glanced around the room. "Where do you want to start?"

Sarah stood and approached the tower of boxes. She wanted to see that door under the stairs. Heavy steps began clomping down the stairs, and Sarah froze, uncertain what to expect from Curtis this time.

Curtis paused on the landing and studied Sarah, his expression closed but not unfriendly. "So you're here. I'd begun to wonder if Louise got lost again. My wife has always had the internal compass of a goldfish."

Sarah felt a surge of tension with Curtis's presence. Not exactly comfortable before, she now felt like a clam that knew it was about to become the main ingredient in a chowder. She tried to smile but could sense it was a shaky effort at best.

Louise turned around. "We were just talking about how to proceed. Sarah wants to recheck the house and boxes."

"I think you can be more help by telling us what you know about the Habers then wasting your time going through those boxes again."

"I've already told Louise I didn't know Willard well. We really weren't more than passing acquaintances." Sarah leaned against a stack of boxes trying to position herself for a look at the door under the stairs.

"But surely you remember something about Willard. Anything at all."

Sarah sighed but complied since it was clear he wouldn't leave that alone until he knew what she did. "So, you see, my husband spent more time with Willard than I did. In fact, I've come inside the house more in the few days you've lived here than the whole time Willard did." She glanced back at the stairs. She needed to see that door. What did she have to lose by asking him? "Is there a door under here?"

Louise looked at the floor. "Where?

"Under the stairs." She pointed to the stack of boxes in front of it. "That door under there, Can I look inside?"

Curtis rubbed his chin. "Guess I don't know why not, except it's locked." He moved the boxes aside and rattled the doorknob as if to emphasize his point.

Sarah hesitated a moment, then reached into her pocket and pulled out the key. "I think I can help with that. Try this." Sarah held her breath as he poked the key around the lock. It took some maneuvering to get the key in the hole, but once it was in, Curtis gave it a quick twist and the clank of the lock turning sounded in the room. Curtis looked at her and his eyebrows hiked. He took a deep breath and turned the knob. Sarah inched forward, longing to know what he could see.

"It's pretty dark under here. If it's like the other closets, it'll be bare." He fumbled about, hitting against the wall and patting air. He grabbed a chain and tugged on it. Light flooded the small space. Sarah closed her eyes against the sudden brightness. Then she blinked.

Curtis growled. "It's empty. There's not a single thing in here. Why lock a door if there's nothing behind it?" Curtis pounded the wall with a fist, causing Sarah to jump back.

She bit her tongue to keep from laughing at his theatrics. If he only knew what the treasure really was. "There has to be something here. Let's check the floor."

"Have at it. I'm about done with this whole thing." Curtis leaned against the doorframe and watched as she tapped her boot heel along the planks on the closet floor. None sounded hollow until she reached the very back of the closet. Dust bunnies decorated the floor and she brushed them aside.

"Curtis?" Sarah said. "Did that sound like a loose board to you?"

"I'll be right back." She heard the front door open and close. A minute later, the door opened and closed again and then he joined her, a toolbox in his hand. "Let me get down there."

Sarah edged back and watched as Curtis tapped along the floor.

"You could be right." He opened the toolbox and pulled out a screwdriver. A moment later he used it to lever the board up.

"Is anything in there?" Sarah hunched forward but couldn't see anything in the shadows. Curtis reached into the hole and felt around. Sarah held her breath as she waited for his verdict.

"Yes, there is." He pulled out a thin volume and flipped it over. It looked small in his large hands. After a minute, he grunted and handed it to her. "You take a look."

The volume smelled musty and dust tickled her nose. She flipped over the leather-bound journal and opened it to the front page. *Kay Haber, March 1944-August 1945*. Sarah longed to read the volume page by page, certain its words were packed with a grand adventure. And maybe somewhere, tucked among the pages, lay the final clue.

He cleared his throat and she reached out to hand it back to him. "This is Kay Haber's journal."

Curtis grunted, but left the book in her hand. "That isn't what I'm looking for." He exited the closet. Sarah slid the journal into her bag as Curtis turned toward her. "You know a lot more than you're saying, I can tell, I'm tired of all the crazy games people play around here. That heirloom is ours."

CHAPTER TWENTY-SEVEN

Sarah slipped past him back into the living room. She avoided the tower of boxes and hurried to the couch. What could she tell Curtis to appease him without giving him enough information to actually find the treasure? One glance at his face told her he was getting desperate. She had to get out of there.

"Could one of you take me home now?" she asked, looking from one to the other.

"Not so fast. First I need the journal and the key," Curtis said. "You might be giving up, but I won't." Curtis towered over her.

Sarah tried to move away from Curtis.

"You're not going anywhere. Hand over that purse. I want to see what you've got in there." He tugged at the bag strapped over her shoulder. She pulled back.

"You won't find anything useful in here."

"Yu have to have something in there that will help us." Curtis's lips curved. "You know where the map is, don't you?"

Should she tell him the truth? That the map was actually a quilt? The way he was acting, she didn't think he'd believe her even though it was the truth.

"I don't have it." It was true that she didn't have it with her.

"You've seen it though." He loomed closer, and her thoughts raced. "You could draw it." He pulled on her purse strap, and it fell off her shoulder. He yanked it out of her hand.

"Okay," she said, grabbing for her purse. Would a sketch still satisfy him? She could switch a couple things around, and he'd be none the wiser. "I can try to sketch it."

"That's more like it." Curtis handed the purse back. His smile reached his eyes this time. "Give us a sketch, and then Louise can drive you home."

Sarah pulled her notebook from her bag and flipped to the back, hoping he wouldn't notice all the pages she was skipping. She quickly drew the four by five grid and sketched in the names for the patterns. "Here you go."

"What is this? A quilt?" Curtis stared at a moment, then thrust it back in her face. "You have to tell us what it means."

"See this one?" She pointed at Cupid's Dart. "If I were going to dig, I'd head for where the arrow points."

"And where's that?"

"The barn."

Curtis nodded and rubbed his hands together. "Great. Let's get to the barn."

Sarah shook her head. "Unfortunately, I really need to get back to town."

Louise smiled. "You rode with me, remember? You're stuck until we're ready to leave. And that won't be until after that pesky treasure is finally in our hands."

"Get your feet moving. Time to find that treasure." Curtis grabbed her elbow and propelled Sarah toward the door.

Her thoughts scrambled as she tried to construct a story the treasure-crazed man would buy. She was really and truly on her own here. And she needed to find a way to get away before he realized she'd drawn the map incorrectly.

His fingers tightened on her arm until she knew she'd bruise as he hauled her toward the barn. Louise followed close on their heels, and then pulled ahead of them and opened the door. A dank darkness wrapped around Sarah as they stepped inside. Curtis hurried to a small room to the left of the door and pulled out a couple of shovels. "Louise, you look along that wall, and I'll start here."

As soon as they were digging, Sarah began taking small steps back toward the door. As soon as she reached it, she slipped outside and then picked up her pace. She pulled her phone from her purse. She dialed nine-one-one, and then called Jason and Chester. Without her car, all she could do was make herself scarce and pray the Habers remained distracted by their search for the treasure until help arrived.

Minutes later tires spun on gravel as a couple of cars turned from the highway into the driveway. The lights flashed, but the sirens were silent as they pulled into the farmyard. Sarah glanced up from where she waited on the porch, relieved to see Chief Webber arrive with reinforcements.

Chief Webber approached with a hand on his gun. "Sarah. You called this in?"

"Yes. The couple who's been living here is in the barn searching for the Haber treasure."

"Is that where it is?"

Sarah shook her head. "They can dig there all day and not find anything of value. The man is impersonating the real Curtis Haber who lives in a nursing home in Florida."

"Do you know if they have any weapons?"

"I didn't see any. And I seriously doubt Louise would carry any kind of gun. Curtis might own one, but if he does, I don't think it's in the barn with him."

"All right. You stay here."

Sarah willingly made her way back to the porch and sank onto a step.

"Let's go." Chief Webber motioned with his hand and Officer Hopkins and another officer Sarah didn't recognize followed him toward the barn. The new officer stayed immediately outside the door while Chief Webber and Officer Hopkins went in. "Hi, folks. I'd like to have a conversation with you..." Chief Webber's voice trailed off as the sound of running feet echoed from the barn.

A minute later Officer Hopkins brought Curtis out, the man's arms handcuffed behind him. Once he'd been shoved into the police car, Chief Webber came out with Louise. He handed her off to the new officer, and then paused in front of Sarah. "Wait here a bit longer."

"Are you sure you need to handcuff her?"

"She fled from an officer."

"I think Louise just got caught up in Curtis's plan." Sarah winced as she watched the officer shove Louise into the car. "I don't even know if Louise is her real name."

More tires crunched against the gravel. Sarah smiled as she saw Jason and Chester approaching in their cars. Her smile broadened when she noticed the Frenchman seated next to Jason.

Chief Webber turned toward the new cars and frowned. "When did this turn into a circus?"

"I asked them to come."

"When?"

"Right after I called nine-one-one."

He studied her, his feet set wide as he crossed his arms. "Why?"

"I need a way to get home."

"And that takes two cars?" He shook his head. "You know I would have given you a ride."

"Yes, but we also have a treasure to find. And that requires all the right players."

"And I suppose you think these are the right ones."

"Well, I think we need the rightful owners' heir. And it doesn't hurt to have one of the men who wrote about the treasure here."

Jason walked up and studied her as if he were examining her for a wound. "And I'm here..."

"Because you're my son. And one of the smartest men I know. You can help me make sure I've got this thing figured out."

"Wait here a minute while I touch base with my men."

She nodded and leaned into Chester's arms, her muscles collapsing in a trembling mess.

Jason watched them, hands shoved into his pockets. "I can tell you're glad I came today."

Sarah tried to laugh, but the sound almost turned into a sob.

Chief Webber stopped in front of her. "Ready to tell me what you've been up to?"

"I think I finally have most of the pieces put together."

"Then let's step inside, and I can take your statement."

Jason led the way and sat on the couch. Sarah joined him, grateful again he was there. She explained about the events that had happened since the estate sale, Chief Webber nodding, making the occasional note in a thin steno pad he pulled from his inside jacket pocket. Then she explained how she'd worked on one of the quilts she'd purchased at the sale and had begun to believe it was the map to the treasure. "My research seems to back up the fact that everyone's assumed incorrectly that one of the boys brought back the treasure. I'm certain Kay was actually the one."

"So where is it?" Sarah startled and turned to Chester, having forgotten he'd followed them inside.

"I'm not a hundred percent sure. But I have a good idea where to start."

CHAPTER TWENTY-EIGHT

W hat now?" Jason glanced at his watch, then removed it and tucked it in his pocket.

Chester cocked his head. "Why did you do that?"

"Because it doesn't matter what time it is. I'm here as long as Mom needs."

"Thanks, Jason." Sarah looked around the room until her gaze rested on Jacques Vallard. "I believe I've found something that will be the key to locating the treasure."

"Isn't the quilt the map?" Chester looked at her like there was only one answer.

"Yes, but I've never quite figured out where the map points us." She reached into her bag and pulled out her notebook and Kay's journal. "But the quilt made it clear Kay was the one who was entrusted with the treasure. And after hearing Mr. Vallard's family story and seeing his photos, I'm convinced I know what the treasure is."

Jacques expression brightened as if hope bloomed inside his chest. "Really?" Sarah turned to Chief Webber. "Nate, can you stay with us while we search?"

"My officers can book the Habers or whoever they are."

Chester rubbed his hands together and began pacing. "So you think the treasure is here somewhere?"

"Yes. I'd hoped we'd find it under the staircase, but Curtis and I have already looked there. What we found was this journal." She stroked the cover eager to read what Kay had written. "I haven't had time to look at it yet."

"Why don't we look through the house, while you scan the journal. Make sure the Habers didn't miss anything." Chester looked like he was itching to get his hands on the journal, but he started backing toward the stairs. "I can look upstairs with Vallard, while the Chief and Jason look around down here."

"I don't expect you'll find anything, but we should look to be sure."

"Does the quilt give any clues on what to look for, Mom?"

Sarah considered Jason's question and thought about the grid she'd created with all the pattern names. She flipped to it and scanned it quickly. Then she shrugged. "Double-check under the stairs. That's my best guess."

The men dispersed. Jason headed for the closet, while Chief Webber went into the kitchen. In a minute she heard Chester and Vallard clomping around overhead.

Sarah sank onto the couch and held Kay's journal. The volume smelled musty and the dust tickled her nose. She flipped the leather-bound journal over and opened it to the front page.

Kay Haber, March 1944-August 1945. Sarah longed to read the volume from cover to cover, but she flipped through the pages, looking for a date that would match the beginning of the story Jacques had told her about his grandfather.

September 19, 1944
Paris, France

I'm here, and I can barely believe I've finally arrived. Then I walk through the streets and stumble around piles of rubble. At times I want to pinch myself. Am I truly standing in the city of love?

Everywhere I go, I wear my Red Cross uniform as ordered. Even though the Germans abandoned the city on August 25th, pushed back by the Allied forces, for safety's sake my superiors insist I be clearly identified.

Earlier today I was able to travel the city on my own. I had three glorious hours before I needed to report in. So I took a bit of money and some stationery and planned to find a café where I could soak in the city's battered elegance and write letters home.

G.I.s and Tommies passed, many with wolf whistles I ignored. These lucky blokes had made it through the push from Normandy and had earned the right to enjoy life a bit. They can look ... from a distance.

The last thing I need is someone to entangle me during my taste of adventure. No, I plan to enjoy every moment. Every last one. And between this journal and my letters home, I'll capture it all to fill my dreams for years to come.

The sidewalks were crowded, and I allowed myself to be jostled by the crowd. Let it carry me where it would.

Every café I passed was crowded. Tables overflowing with customers relishing their newfound freedom. While I enjoyed the sight, my feet had begun to ache in the ridiculous heels required with my uniform. At the next café, I saw an empty chair, and I eased into it with an apologetic smile. The man didn't even seem to notice, hiding behind his newspaper.

A harried waiter rushed to the small table. "Mademoiselle, may I get you anything?"

The newspaper lowered a fraction until I looked into the deepest chocolate brown eyes I've ever seen. I felt frozen, locked in this gaze, wondering what he saw and if he liked it.

"She will have a café au lait."

While I tried to decide whether to be offended or flattered by his assumptions, the man folded the paper before resting his elbows on it. "To what do I owe this pleasure?"

His accent tickled my ears in a pleasing way, yet sounded different from the Parisian accents I've grown used to.

"You had a vacant chair at your table."

"Then I thank fate for smiling on me."

Later he told me his name. Roberto Vallard.

November 20, 1944

My days have been a whirlwind. Roberto insists on seeing me in my spare time and introducing me to the slowly reviving culture. I love Paris, but I'm not sure if it's because of the city or the man.

I am about to find out which it is.

Tonight he left me.

I could not stop crying as I begged him not to leave. I clung to Roberto trying to force him to stay. Yet he still stepped away. Farther and farther away even though mere inches separated us. I felt the wall he had erected in his heart.

"I cannot, ma chérie." He held my cheeks, the gentleness of his touch breaking my heart. "I promise we will reunite. After the war." He wiped a tear away with his thumb and I sank into his touch, memorizing the feel of him, the scent of him. Begging God to help us actually find each other again. "I must do this. And I need you to watch these treasures for me. My family will need them after the war to rebuild. So much rebuilding."

"But how will I find you?" He's told me so little of himself. Is a name enough? In the postwar chaos will I somehow find him or he find me? I bit back the sobs that threatened to overwhelm me. "Please don't leave me. Please . . ."

Roberto stepped back, slowly pulling his fingers from my cheeks. The slightly rough calluses on his fingertips felt like they left trails along my skin.

Then he did what yesterday I thought was impossible. He walked through the door, his eyes on me until the door closed between us. Yet I know he will not be back. Not soon.

Sarah was overwhelmed by Kay's emotional account. She had loved deeply and lost. How she must have longed for Roberto to come back. It sounded like she valued him far more than the jewels he'd entrusted to her. And now Sarah knew that Kay had indeed had the treasure. It had to be here. Somewhere. Sarah flipped to the end of the written entries.

October 15, 1948

I've been home for hours. My brothers have urged me to accept the reality that Roberto will not come for me. I hold his family's heirloom jewels and have no way to return them. Because they are not truly mine, I have decided to bury them for safekeeping. Rumors are already circulating around Maple Hill that one of the Haber boys brought home a treasure. Not true, but not far enough from the truth either. After having them appraised, I do not feel safe keeping the jewels in my bedroom. So I will bury them in a safe place and leave a map that will reveal the location in plain sight for those with eyes to see.

If I am able to someday locate his family, I will return the jewels. Otherwise, at some point they will become my family's. But not now. It is too soon.

Chester cleared his throat, and Sarah looked up with a start. "Jacques and I didn't find anything upstairs."

"I didn't find anything either." Chief Webber came and stood next to the couch. "Did you, Jason?"

Her son shook his head.

"Jason, were you able to go home and get the quilt?"

"Yes. I felt like quite the errand boy."

Sarah slugged him in the shoulder and then pointed a finger at him. "Then go get it." A few minutes later Jason brought it to her, and she spread it out on the couch. "So we haven't found it under the staircase or in the house.

Of course, it's still possible the treasure is in the house somewhere. But," she traced Cupid's Dart with a finger, "I wonder if it might be buried near the maple tree."

Chester stroked his chin. "That makes a bit of sense."

"If you want to dig, that's where I would begin."

Jason raked a hand through his hair. "Wouldn't the tree have grown over the treasure in the sixty years since it was buried?"

"If it's even the right tree." Vallard's voice was quiet, the accent heavy.

"There's one way to find out." Jason headed toward the door, then turned back to Chief Webber. "If it's all right with you, I'll start digging."

Nate nodded, and everyone followed Jason outside. The maple's spreading branches stood bare of any leaves, and Sarah prayed the ground at its base wasn't frozen yet. If it was, they'd be forced to wait for spring, which seemed like an eternity now that she was convinced the treasure was buried there.

Digging was slow going. Chester took the shovel from Jason and dug until he could barely breathe.

"Here, let me try again." Jason stepped up and took the shovel back. He dug in a fresh place. Sarah walked around the tree, studying it and wondering if it hid any clues. But in sixty years so much could have changed as the tree grew that she couldn't imagine finding a clue. Jason handed the shovel to Jacques, who started to dig with vigorous stabs.

"I think I've hit something." Jacques stopped and leaned against the shovel, sucking in a couple of deep breaths. The others hurried to his side, but Sarah couldn't see anything but dirt when she looked into the hole. Jason shooed them back, claimed the shovel from Vallard, and then went back to work. A couple of minutes later he stepped to the side. "Here you go."

This time when Sarah looked in she could make out the outline of a box. Chester bent down and began to dig the dirt away from the box with his bare hands. A few minutes later he pulled it out and set it on the ground.

He pointed at the padlock. "Do you have the key, Sarah?"

"Yes, but it worked on the closet door. Do you really think it will work on this too?" Sarah smiled, unable to contain her excitement at seeing the treasure box. "I'm certain one of you burly guys can take care of it without a key." Sarah handed Vallard the key. "Sir."

Vallard accepted the key with trembling hands, then carried the box inside. He sat on the couch, setting the box on his lap and holding the key in one hand. A look of mixed dread and anticipation crossed his face.

Sarah sat next to him. "Aren't you excited to see what's inside?"

"I don't know. What if it's nothing? What if this journey was a waste?"

"Impossible. Even if there's no treasure, we had a grand adventure we'll talk about for years."

The man swallowed, his eyes never straying from the box. "All right. Let's see what secrets are inside."

Vallard inserted the key in the lock and wiggled until a loud click echoed in the still room. Sarah released a breath she didn't know she'd held. He lifted the lid.

As she joined the others in staring over Vallard's shoulders into the box at the twinkling collection of diamond and pearl jewelry, Sarah knew she had the perfect ending for her column.

CHAPTER TWENTY-NINE

I ce had coated the bedroom windows when Sarah's alarm buzzed early Thanksgiving morning. She hit the button to turn it off, then threw the covers back and pulled on her robe. In order to have the turkey cooked in time for dinner with Jason's family, she needed to get the big bird in the oven pronto. She smiled at the memory of Maggie, insisting she could host Thanksgiving, just without the bird. She refused to tackle one, insisting you could be just as thankful over a ham or roast as over a turkey.

A bit of sleet tapped the window and she looked outside. A couple of inches of snow had fallen overnight, enough to ice the trees with a beautiful layer of frosting. The sleet must be recent since there didn't seem to be ice on the asphalt yet. The family would still be able to gather. Belle and Martha and her husband Ernie were joining them as well.

A full table filled with bounty, family, and friends. Sarah couldn't imagine a more perfect day to thank God for her many blessings—including unlocking the story of the quilt.

She hurried down the stairs and into the kitchen. In moments, coffee was brewing and she gave the turkey a quick bath. Then she dressed it with her grandmother's sausage stuffing.

After popping the turkey into the oven, she pulled a refrigerator package of sweet rolls out and arranged them in a pan. No reason Belle and she couldn't have a treat as they waited for the big meal. She examined them and regretted they weren't homemade, but she'd been busy these past few days.

Sarah hurried upstairs to get dressed and came back down in time to pull the rolls out. Once they were slathered with cream cheese frosting, she could almost pretend they were her usual treats. At least Belle wouldn't know the difference this morning, and she could *really* surprise the girls on Christmas.

She checked on the turkey and then went in search of her baster.

The morning passed in a blur, yet time didn't move as quickly as Sarah wanted. She kept glancing at the clock and then at the front door, waiting for her granddaughters to race down the hallway and throw themselves in her arms. She checked the cranberry relish. Then she cooked the potatoes and mixed the green bean casserole. When the potatoes were soft, she pulled out her stand mixer and whipped them with a generous helping of sour cream, chives, and some cottage cheese. Pouring the mixture into a pan, she set it on a counter to wait.

Wait.

She pulled her Bible off the shelf and tried to quiet her thoughts to read while she waited. She had so much to be thankful for. *Thank you, Father, for everything.*

Her prayers continued for a long time as she praised him for so many things. Her family. Her friends. Her home. Her work. His work in the world. The beauty of his creation. So much filled her heart when she slowed to think about all he'd done and the way he moved.

The front door banged open, and Sarah raised her head.

"Grandma! We're finally here. It was like an ice-skating rink out there. But we got our errand done anyway. Wait till you see what…"

"Audrey, be quiet." Amy pulled Audrey up short a few feet from the kitchen.

Audrey bit her lower lip and tugged her arm free. "I know. I wasn't going to say anything."

Audrey hugged her, a wonderful two-armed squeeze that caused her thankfulness to bubble over again. How could Thanksgiving be better?

"So where are your parents?"

Amy rolled her eyes as Audrey gave her an intense stare. "Don't worry. They're coming. They just had one thing to take care of."

"Okay." She'd saved pie making until the girls arrived. "Here's a paring knife for each of you." The girls looked at the knives with wrinkled brows. "The bag of apples is on the island. We have to peel and slice them so we can make pies. And then we'll mix the pumpkin pie."

Audrey looked from the knife to the apples. "This is why people buy pies in the freezer section."

Amy elbowed her. "I'm sure this will be better."

Sarah laughed at the girls' skeptical expressions. "Yes, it will be ... wait and see."

She glanced at the door but didn't see Jason and Maggie yet. Maybe they really had dropped the girls off before running an errand. "Is everything okay at the store?"

"Yep. Keeping Mom busy, but it's okay." Amy's shoulders bobbed in a minishrug as she tried to peel an apple. It seemed an awful lot of the sweet fruit's flesh ended up on the counter with the peel, but that was okay. Everyone had to learn, and there were plenty of apples.

"Yeah, she has us helping her in the afternoons and on Saturdays some. She even says she'll pay us if we keep helping clean the shop." Audrey set down her first apple and picked up a second.

"Guess we're cheaper than hiring an employee." Amy rolled her eyes. "But it is somehow better than cleaning at home."

"I know what you mean." Sarah could remember times she'd helped others and it removed the drudgery of everyday chores. "That sounds like a great idea ... your mom gets help and you get some spending money."

"We'll see if Mom actually pays us, but it's nice to help her out some."

The girls kept up a steady round of chatter as they worked their way through the pile of apples. Sarah rolled out the crusts, then sliced the apples and put them in a gallon-size baggie. When the apples were all sliced, she squirted some lemon juice in the bag, then had the girls add the spices and sugar. The girls took turns shaking the bag until the apples were coated with the mixture.

Each girl arranged the fruit in a pie.

They were following the recipe for the pumpkin pie filling when Jason opened the door.

"Hey, Mom." He hollered down the hall but didn't leave the doorway. "I've got something to show you if you can leave the miniature chefs for a minute."

"I'll be right there." Sarah gave the girls a couple of instructions, then wiped her flour-covered hands on an apron and hurried to the porch. "What have you got?" The words died in her throat as she looked past Jason. "Jenna!"

"Mom." Her daughter ran up the steps and threw herself into Sarah's arms. "Are you surprised?"

Sarah held her close, smelling the light floral fragrance of her shampoo and conditioner. "Very. When did you decide to come?"

"Jason and I were already scheming when you called. I couldn't spoil the surprise but wanted to come home so badly. It was hard to pretend I wouldn't make it home."

From behind Jenna, her boys tore up the stairs, Thomas's arms flailing like a windmill as he slipped. Jonathan skidded to a stop, his eyes big as saucers. He tiptoed up the remaining stairs then stopped in front of Sarah.

Sarah knelt in front of him. "Can I have a hug?"

A grin split the four-year-old's face and he threw himself into her arms. Thomas quickly followed, wrapping his arms around Sarah's neck.

Sarah kissed each boy, then looked at Jenna. "How long can you stay?"

"Not long enough, but we're here through Sunday."

Jenna's husband David smiled from the foot of the steps, gripping a suitcase in each hand. "Where can I stash these, Sarah?"

"Top of the stairs. Thank you so much for bringing your family. This is the nicest surprise I've had in a long time."

Everyone hurried into the house, stomping snow off shoes on the rug inside the door. The boys raced through the rooms as if determined to see every last thing in as short a time as possible.

Sarah locked arms with Jenna and then squeezed Maggie. "Both my families here. All my grandchildren. This is such an amazing blessing."

Minutes later the front door opened, and Sarah stuck her head into the hallway to see who it was. Martha shook a few snowflakes off her coat. "Yoo-hoo." The woman's graying brown curls bounced around her face as she pulled off her winter boots and slipped on pink fuzzy slippers.

Sarah hurried out to greet Martha and Ernie, biting back a laugh at the slippers. "What are you doing with those?"

"Preparing for an afternoon on these cold plank floors."

"Your house has the same thing."

Ernie walked in behind her, stomping his feet on the rug. "Heating coils under the floor. You really should try it, Sarah."

Sarah hugged Martha, then Ernie.

"You have the salad, Ernie?" Martha groaned when he shook it in the bowl.

"Where do you want this, Sarah?"

"The dining room table will be fine."

"Martha and Ernie, you'll never believe what a wonderful surprise I got today."

Martha linked arms with Sarah as they headed to the kitchen. "Surprises are good."

"Jenna's family is here for the weekend. She kept telling me they couldn't come. Jason and Maggie just brought them in here a few minutes ago."

Ernie, Jenna, and Jason settled in front of the TV to watch the first football game, while David, the other women, and the girls congregated in the kitchen. The remaining preparations went quickly.

"Martha, can you pull the potatoes and green bean casserole out of the oven?" Sarah turned and caught Audrey snitching a piece of the Dutch crumble from the pie. "Jenna, slide the pies into the empty spots."

"Mom, you should get the turkey out first. The button popped."

"All right." Sarah said. "David, can you haul the turkey from the oven?"

The room seemed small with so many bodies bustling about. Sarah looked around for the twins. They'd just disappeared. "Where did the girls go?"

Maggie stopped pulling silverware from the drawer for the extra places. "I think you'll find them rolling in the snow with the boys. Guess you don't get much more of it in Texas than we did in L.A."

David laughed and shook his head. "It's a new experience for them."

The good-natured conversation continued until Maggie called the kids inside. After some grumbling, the kids stomped in and shucked coats and shoes at the back door.

"Can we go back out after lunch?" Amy put her hands in front of her and batted her eyelashes. "The boys really like the snow."

Jason tweaked her nose. "And you don't?"

"Well, maybe a little bit."

Everyone laughed as Sarah shooed them to the dining room. The table groaned under the weight of so many dishes. The crystal and china shimmered in the candlelight.

Belle slipped downstairs in time to join them for the meal. People sat shoulder to shoulder and it was a good thing nobody was left-handed. But as Sarah glanced around the table she loved that at each place sat someone meaningful to her.

"Grandma, can we eat our candy corn please?" Thomas grinned at her.

"Not before you eat some turkey and salad, young man." Jenna wagged a finger in his face, then turned to Sarah. "What's with the candy corn? I don't remember you giving us candy with dinner."

"Yeah, Mom." Jason picked up a small piece then moved it to his mouth.

"Wait just a moment, Jason." He froze, eyes wide and a sheepish grin on his face. Sarah picked her three pieces up. "The three kernels should remind us of how hungry the Pilgrims were the first year at Plymouth. And also to be thankful for all we have. So, yes, Thomas, you can eat the candy corn, but only after you tell us three things you are thankful for."

The boy studied the corn, his nose wrinkled. "My toys, my mom, and my dad." Then he popped the corn in his mouth and chewed.

"What about me?" Jonathan placed his little fists on the table and frowned.

"All right. I'm thankful for you, too."

The adults laughed, and then everyone took turns sharing.

The conversation continued at a low roar as everyone filled their plates from the bounty. Jonathan and Thomas teased Amy and Audrey as only younger cousins can. Maggie and Martha had their heads together, while Ernie and Jason talked football. David and Jenna talked with Sarah over the boys' heads, and Sarah felt as if her cheeks would crack from her smile.

The food disappeared in a flash. Together they cleared the table and agreed to wait for dessert. The men headed back to the living room, taking the boys with them.

"Grandma, can you show us your quilt again?" Amy batted her long lashes at Sarah, as if Sarah needed the encouragement to do anything her granddaughter asked.

"Sure. Come with me." Belle, Maggie, and Jenna followed them into the sewing room. "Sorry this room wasn't designed for a crowd. Here's the quilt." She patted the soft fabric. Only a few squares still needed work, and then she'd be finished with the restoration. Maybe the real Curtis Haber would like the finished quilt. She'd offer, but part of her hoped he'd say no. The squares felt like old friends now that she'd unlocked their mystery.

"Jason told us a bit about the quilt on the drive here." Jenna turned to Sarah. "Did you really confront the Habers?"

"I did. This quilt has certainly led me on quite a journey." Sarah stroked the surface. "Three more squares and I'll be done restoring it."

"Did you find the treasure, Mom?" Jenna studied the fabric like it was an odd specimen.

"Jason didn't tell you? I've never seen so many diamonds, precious gems, and pearls in one place. Breathtaking."

"What will Vallard do with the jewels?" Maggie stepped back to let Martha squeeze into the room.

"I don't know. He said something about taking them home to France." Sarah shrugged. "My part was to unravel this quilt's story. And what a story it was."

A knock pounded on the door. Sarah looked around the room. "Do you suppose the boys snuck outside and need help getting back in?"

"I hope not since their coats are still at the backdoor." Jenna hurried down the hall and opened the door. "Hello."

Sarah stopped a few feet from the door when she saw Chester standing there, a container of chrysanthemums clutched in his hands.

"I didn't stop to think you'd have a house full of guests." He shoved the flowers toward her. "Maybe I should leave."

Sarah accepted the planter. "The gold and red are such a beautiful combination. Please come in. You've missed the meal, but we can reheat something for you."

"Coffee would be fine."

Sarah set the flowers on the side table, and then took Chester's hand, trying to ignore the strong connection she felt to him after everything they'd experienced.

"Everyone, I'd like to introduce you to my friend, Chester Winslow."

 EPILOGUE

T he house was quiet for the first time in hours. Chester had been the last to leave, and now David and Jenna were in the free bedroom upstairs, while the boys had crashed in the living room on the floor. Sarah's heart felt full after the wonderful Thanksgiving filled with friends and family. She couldn't sleep. Not yet. First she had to capture the thoughts buzzing around her mind. The beginnings of the column.

Sarah slipped into her sewing room, a steaming mug of peppermint tea in her hand. She sat at the computer and waited while a new document file opened up. When it did, a blank screen stared back at her.

How exactly did one start a column?

She didn't know. And the white screen whispered that she'd never be able to do it. She shook the thought, knowing it wasn't true. Yesterday, she'd confronted a crook, something she'd never imagined doing. But she had. Writing the column had to be easier.

The cursor blinked.

Suddenly, the thought that she was supposed to turn in a finished article on Monday froze her fingers as they hovered over the keyboard. Why had she ever agreed to write the column? This might be a trial run, but she wanted it to be good and to turn into a permanent opportunity. Every quilt had a story. Sometimes you just had to dig deep to uncover it.

Just start.

Every new journey begins with a single step. Each new investigation begins with one question. A column begins with one word. She placed her fingers over the keyboard and started typing. *Some quilts have a magnetic draw. The kind of quilt that from the moment you see it you want to know its story. This quilt's story begins at an estate sale I never planned to attend.*

Isn't life like that?

In a happenstance decision, a new chapter is written in our lives.

My new chapter began when I saw my friend standing next to a box of quilts ... rags she called them as she shooed others away. She might not know much about quilts, but she knows me, so Martha defended the quilts until I arrived.

Most people would have looked in the box and seen piles of faded calicoes, scraps of long-ago created quilts, better put in a rag pile than displayed in a home. I saw pieces of art, in need of restoration but beautiful in their own way. Little did I know that when I took that box home, I took with it the key to a mystery. A mystery rumored about a farm in Maple Hill. A mystery extending back to World War II. A mystery that involved beautiful jewels.

Most stories worth learning begin that way. With a sentence here. A chapter there. And in the end it all comes together into a complete adventure. This one involved a local girl sent overseas with the American Red Cross. A French nobleman afraid his family's jewels would disappear in the chaos of the war. And a trust that hasn't been violated in the intervening years.

Examine your home. Look at your treasures. Where others see junk destined for a ragbag, what do you see? Capture the stories and share them with others.

It's in the knowing of these snippets and rumors that our stories become complete, filled with the timeless treasures of the past.

About the Author

Timeless Treasures is Cara Putman's tenth novel and twelfth book. A sometimes lecturer at Purdue University, attorney, and active member of her home church, Cara lives in Indiana with her husband and three (almost four) children. You can learn more about Cara and her books at http://www.caraputman.com.

CHAPTER ONE

Sarah Hart scooped more golden brown cookies onto the waiting cooling racks. The granite countertops in her daughter-in-law's kitchen were laden with pinwheels, pecan tarts, gingersnaps, and oatmeal spice cookies. The afternoon baking session with her twin granddaughters Amy and Audrey had been more than productive.

Sarah glanced out the window. An icy wind gently rattled the windowpane as it whipped down Bristol Street, swirling the few remaining leaves off the ground. Temperatures were supposed to drop into the teens, but the twins and Sarah had been snug indoors baking all afternoon. After a break for a quick soup supper, they were finishing up the sugar cookies while Sarah's son Jason strung up Christmas lights outside on the 120-year-old Victorian, and his wife Maggie worked on bookkeeping for her antiques store in the dining room.

Sarah's cell phone rang, tearing Sarah's gaze from the window.

"Hello?"

"Oh, I'm so relieved you answered." It was Martha Maplethorpe, Sarah's best friend. "Something's happened, and I need to talk. Where are you? You didn't pick up your house phone."

Sarah paused, spatula poised over the cookie sheet. The stress in her usually cheerful friend's voice tripped her heart into overdrive. "What's wrong? Did something happen with Ernie?"

"No, no, everyone's fine, although I may be developing an ulcer. Where are you?"

"I'm over at Jason and Maggie's."

"Perfect! I need to talk to Maggie too. I'll be there in fifteen minutes."

"Okay, but—" the line went dead, and Sarah stared at the phone with dismay. What could be so urgent to make Martha venture out on such a cold winter evening?

"Who was that?" Amy asked. Sarah's granddaughter sat at the kitchen table surrounded by small bowls of colored frosting. Lime green stained the tip of one of her blonde braids, and the blue frosting smudged on her cheek matched her eyes.

"Mrs. Maplethorpe. She'll be coming over in a few minutes."

Sarah surveyed the kitchen. Despite the growing disaster area around what the girls had designated the decorating station, the scene warmed Sarah's heart. No amount of dirty dishes could deter her from cherishing this evening with her granddaughters. If only her daughter Jenna and her boys were here.

"One more batch to go. You girls are doing great," Sarah said, then turned at a loud sound behind her.

"I hate Christmas!" Audrey said, staring at the yellow mass oozing from the overturned egg carton on the pine flooring.

"Are you upset just because you broke a few eggs?" Sarah asked. "Don't worry about it. We'll get it cleaned up."

"You don't hate Christmas," Amy said with a roll of her eyes.

"I can hate Christmas if I want to." Audrey snatched a wad of paper towels. Angry tears glazed her eyes before she turned away.

"Can I have your presents then?" Amy flashed a big grin.

"Amy," Sarah cautioned with a slight shake of her head. What had gotten into everyone tonight? Maggie and Jason had seemed tense during supper. Martha, who was perpetually sunny, had sounded ominous on the phone. And now, the twins were getting at each other.

"Can you check to see if that batch on the counter is cool enough to frost?" Sarah asked Amy.

"Okay." Amy set her paintbrush down and skirted around the mess Audrey was trying to clean up.

Sarah grabbed a mixing bowl and squatted down by Audrey. The twelve-year-old's miserable expression tugged at her heart. She wanted to pull the girl in for a close hug, but she wasn't sure Audrey would welcome it right now.

"What's the matter, dear?" she asked in a gentle tone.

Audrey shrugged, her focus on picking up the broken egg shells.

"It might help to talk about it."

Audrey shook her head. She tossed the shells in the bin under the sink, and after a few moments blurted out, "It's so boring here!"

Sarah paused in her cleanup efforts. Boring? The last two weeks had been frantic with activities as the twins finished up their school semester, attended practices and the school Christmas program, caroled with the youth group, shopped for their family, decorated the Christmas tree, and now baked dozens of cookies.

"Okay, I think it's time for a break and to sample some of your hard work. Why don't you girls sit at the table, and I'll get the milk." Sarah straightened and dumped the paper towels into the garbage can. She grabbed a milk carton from the refrigerator and poured two glasses.

Amy bit the top off a Christmas tree. "Yum. These sugar cookies are the best."

Sarah sat next to Audrey after the girl devoured a couple of cookies and asked, "Is there anything I can do to make things better?"

Audrey took a long swallow of milk and grimaced. "Nobody can. Everything's changed. Christmas doesn't feel like Christmas anymore. We used to have so much fun. We'd go down to Grandma and Grandpa's house near Newport and watch the boat parade with all the lights and sing Christmas songs. And I miss shopping at the Galleria with my friends and visiting the reindeer at the zoo—"

"Every time Audrey gets a text from Madison, she gets grumpy," Amy said.

"I do not!" Audrey narrowed her eyes at her sister. "Were you looking at my phone again?"

Amy shrugged and licked a drop of orange frosting off her fingertip. "I thought it was mine."

Sarah slid her arm around Audrey's shoulder before the quarrel escalated. "I'm sorry you're feeling bad, honey. I've lived in Maple Hill all my life, so I don't know exactly how you feel, but I imagine missing your friends and grandparents is really hard, especially at Christmas."

"Like you miss Grandpa Gerry?" Amy asked.

"Yes, something like that," Sarah answered, surprised at Amy's perceptiveness. Although Sarah still carried the ache of her husband's passing, she didn't discuss her pain with the twins. She only wanted to share happy memories of Gerry.

She gave Audrey's shoulders a squeeze. "I just want you to have a wonderful Christmas. We're going to have fun. You'll see."

Audrey nodded but didn't appear convinced.

Amy picked up a knife and spread soft yellow frosting on a star. "I just wish it'd snow so I can build a snowman and learn to ski. Our first Christmas in New England and no snow. How lame is that?"

Sarah playfully tugged Amy's braid. "Be careful what you wish for. There are some huge storms heading our way. After a month, you'll be so tired of having cold toes, frozen ears, and a red nose, you might be wishing for spring."

"No, I won't." Amy giggled. "I'll wear a hat and scarf. I got new boots too. Did you play in the snow a lot when you were a kid?"

Sarah nodded. "When I was your age, I used to spend hours playing outside. We made snow angels in the park and giant snowmen. But the most fun was sledding. Mrs. Maplethorpe's parents lived at the top of this big hill, and all the neighborhood children used to race down it on our sleds."

"That sounds so cool."

"It was," Sarah said, grinning at the memory of Martha hollering with glee as her sled bounced over the ruts, her long braids flying out behind her. Which reminded her, Martha was on her way over.

"You girls keep frosting. I'm going to tell your mother that Mrs. Maplethorpe is coming for a visit." Sarah pushed open the swinging door to the dining room where Maggie sat at an antique mahogany table. Piles of invoices and receipts surrounded her laptop. She leaned toward the screen, her head propped on one hand as she studied a spreadsheet.

Sarah cleared her throat. "How's it going?"

Maggie straightened in the spindle-backed chair and rubbed her lower back. "Six more days, and the Christmas craziness will be over. I can hardly wait."

"Have sales been going well?"

"Yes. Much better than expected. And I know I shouldn't be complaining. The holidays are terrific for business, but I feel so behind in *everything*, including the bookkeeping. Maybe next year I'll be able to afford a part-time accountant." She glanced toward the kitchen. "How's the baking marathon progressing?"

"Pretty good. We're almost done. I don't think the girls will want to bake another cookie for months."

"Was that Audrey I heard complaining?"

"Yes, but not about the baking. She said she hated Christmas. Everything is boring."

"Boring?" Maggie let out a short laugh. Her green eyes twinkled. "How can she be bored? They've only been on Christmas break for three days. I thought they'd enjoy some quiet time at home after the big rush of finishing tests and all that work with the Christmas play."

"Apparently not," Sarah said with a small smile. "I think Audrey's missing her friends and the fun you had in California."

"Well, that's understandable. We used to do a lot of things at Christmas. Running here and there. Fun, but it got pretty hectic. Personally, *I'm* looking forward to an old-fashioned, small town Christmas. Jason has some great memories of the holidays here."

Sarah's smile widened. "And I'm so glad you're here to make new memories with me. I just hope the girls will enjoy the change."

"They will," Maggie said confidently. "And if they're bored, they can put their energy to good use and help me down at the store. There are people popping in all the time. Besides, I'd like to spend more time with them during the break..."

Sarah chuckled. Over the years, she'd watched Martha interacting with her nine grandchildren who all lived in town, and wished her own lived closer. Now that her wish had come true, she planned on enjoying every rambunctious second of their time together, especially their first Christmas in Maple Hill.

"I was going to tell you Martha called a minute ago and said she needed to talk to us about something. I'm sorry. I should've mentioned it right away. She's on her way over," Sarah said as the doorbell rang. "Sounds like she's here. If you're not up to seeing visitors tonight, I can invite her into the kitchen and see what it's all about."

"Oh, no, that's fine. I'm finished working for tonight. Jason should be done with the lights soon too."

Audrey charged past them to the foyer and looked through the peephole. "It's Mrs. Maplethorpe." She flung the door open, letting in a blast of frigid air.

"Hello, hello. Merry almost-Christmas! I hope I'm not intruding," Martha said, clouds puffing out of her mouth with every word.

"Of course not." Maggie smiled. "We're always glad to see you. Come in by the fire. You look frozen." She shut the door behind Martha. "How's your husband doing?"

"Ernie's doing as well as can be expected. Thank you for asking." Martha unwound her orange scarf and unbuttoned her heavy wool overcoat.

"Would you like some cookies? I decorated a whole bunch of them," Amy asked.

"I can see that." Martha laughed. "You have frosting on your ear. It must've been fun."

Amy nodded and grinned as she rubbed her ear.

"There's also hot cocoa if you'd like some." Maggie took Martha's coat and scarf and hooked them on the stand by the door. "Or I can make fresh coffee."

"Grandma put her secret ingredient in the cocoa," Audrey said. "It's good."

"Well in that case, I'd love to try the cocoa and the cookies." Martha smiled as the girls headed back to the kitchen and then raised her eyebrows at Sarah. "Secret ingredient?"

"If I told people, it wouldn't be a secret, now would it?" Sarah replied as they headed into the parlor.

Martha paused by the heat of the fire before settling on the pale blue camelback sofa by Maggie. "It feels good to sit down. I'm getting plum worn out. I should've been suspicious when Marlene Hobber said organizing the Old Town Holiday Home Tour would be as easy as baking a cake. Have you ever seen Marlene's cakes? They look like those elaborate creations you see on the Food Network." She took a deep breath. "I have a problem."

"Oh?" Sarah raised an eyebrow. "I thought everything was going well with the tour." Martha was this year's tour director for Maple Hill's annual Old Town Holiday Home Tour. She had convinced Sarah to open her snug, three-bedroom Queen Anne for the occasion, and already had most of the details of the tour planned.

"It was until today, which brings me to why I'm here." Martha leaned forward, rubbing her hands on her navy slacks. "The pipes in the Nelsons' laundry room burst while they were at church this morning, and flooded the entire downstairs. They're going to have to rip up all the carpets and move the furniture into storage."

"How awful. Is there anything we can do to help them?" Sarah asked.

Martha waved a dismissive hand. "I'm sure the offer will be appreciated, but they've already hired a company to do the work. Meanwhile, they've decided to visit relatives in Florida for Christmas, which is why I need to ask a huge favor, Maggie."

Sarah sensed what was coming. She tried to catch her friend's attention, but Martha's gaze was focused on Maggie.

"We have five homes participating in the tour already, and the Nelson house was going to be number six. I know this is short notice, but would you and Jason consider taking the Nelsons' place and opening your home for the tour?"

"Cool!" Amy said, coming into the room carrying a plate of cookies. Audrey trailed with a steaming mug. "Our house will be famous."

"Whoa, wait just a moment." Maggie clasped her hands together. She blew out a deep breath. "Mrs. Maplethorpe, I'm so flattered you asked to include us, and I'd love to help, but as you can see my house isn't ready for any-thing...extravagant."

"But you have such a lovely home. Great lines and struc-ture. A classic Victorian. And your house is in the perfect lo-cation so I won't have to fiddle with the order of the homes on the tour."

"But we're in the process of remodeling." Maggie ges-tured toward the hall where paint cans and drop cloths par-tially covered the scratched hardwood floors. "And the mess is worse in other parts of the house. We're still replacing tile in the downstairs bathroom."

Sarah said quietly to Martha, "Maybe we should let Maggie think about it for a while."

"Nobody will mind a work in progress," Martha went on, oblivious to Sarah's hint. "People will just be thrilled to get a glimpse inside this lovely home. Besides, you can limit the tour to only the rooms you want to be seen. I've been in your kitchen before, and it's delightful. You have wonderful taste. With some minor decorations through the rest of the down-stairs, it'll be fine."

Maggie paused. "Well...I suppose that's possible. But people will still need to come in here, and there isn't any-thing I can do about this wall." Maggie pointed behind her to the wall above the couch. A dark, rusty water stain ran down the plaster, which was riddled with holes and deep scratches. "We're waiting for the contractor to come give us an estimate on replastering before we decide how to fix it."

The front door swung open, and Jason walked in with several strands of Christmas lights wound over one arm. "These aren't any good. I think one of the sockets is broken. Luckily the previous owner left behind a box of lights in the attic, but they still only covered two-thirds of the house. I didn't realize how much bigger this house is compared to the one in California."

Audrey wrinkled her freckled nose at the old-fashioned colored bulbs. "We had white twinkly lights in California. They looked like icicles. I liked them better."

"Well, it doesn't hurt to try something different, Audrey. These are nice too." Jason said in a merry tone. He looked up from examining a bulb and noticed Martha on the couch. He pulled the wool cap off his dark hair. "Hello, Mrs. Maplethorpe. I'm sorry, I didn't mean to be rude. How are you?"

"I'm fine, thank you, and you're not being rude, just a busy husband and father." She smiled at him. "I'm afraid I've been badgering your wife into helping us with the home tour." Martha repeated her sales pitch to Jason. "It's really a lot of fun and a great way to widen your social circle. The exposure will be good for both your businesses."

Jason's face settled into what Maggie called his "court face." Over the last couple of months, Sarah had worried about the couple, with Maggie's heavy workload and Jason's law practice's slow growth, but things had been going well lately. She hoped Martha hadn't tweaked a nerve with her request.

"And remember, it's for a worthy cause," Martha added. "Half the profits from the tour and all of the other little fund-raisers we're having will go to the Children's Home. I know this is an imposition, but I'm in a bind. Sarah and I already have our homes in the tour, otherwise I'd use one of us."

Jason grinned. "If you were arguing a case in a court-room, I'd sure hate to be on the opposing side."

"So, you'll do it?" Martha asked.

Jason shrugged. "It's up to Maggie. Whatever she wants is fine by me."

"We'll help, Mom. We can do this as a family," Amy said, elbowing Audrey who nodded. "You'll see, it'll be so much fun."

"Well I suppose we could clean up most of the remodel-ing mess," Maggie said, her resistance obviously weakening. "But what about this wall? We won't be able to fix that, will we, Jason?"

"Not before the tour," he answered. "And we really shouldn't spend any more money on decorations."

Since Maggie seemed okay with the direction they were moving, Sarah piped in. "I still have lots of old decorations in my cellar. You're welcome to them. This morning I lent our manger to the church for their nativity scene, since theirs broke, but there's still the old Santa's sleigh you and your father built. There might be extra lights too."

She turned to her daughter-in-law, giving her a supportive smile. "And Maggie, don't worry about the wall. I have an idea."

A NOTE FROM THE EDITORS

Guideposts, a nonprofit organization, touches millions of lives every day through products and services that inspire, encourage and uplift. Our magazines, books, prayer network and outreach programs help people connect their faith-filled values to their daily lives. To learn more, visit www.guideposts. com or www.guidepostsfoundation.org.